The woman's bright laughter was an almost ordinary sound . . .

Jack PenMartyn saw exactly who he expected to see when she turned their way, a tall, slender girl—no, not a girl, a woman.

Her golden hair did not tumble wantonly around her lovely face, but it was the same wheat-honey amber color he remembered.

She was not wearing a clinging silk robe with nothing on underneath, but an elaborate evening gown of stiff, shimmering black.

The dark material served to outline every lush curve just the same, and to accent the flawless paleness of her skin. She was perfect.

She was still—Scheherazade.

Other **AVON ROMANCES**

THE FORBIDDEN LORD *by Sabrina Jeffries*
HIGHLAND BRIDES: HIGHLAND ENCHANTMENT
by Lois Greiman
MY LORD STRANGER *by Eve Byron*
THE RENEGADES: COLE *by Genell Dellin*
A SCOUNDREL'S KISS *by Margaret Moore*
TAMING RAFE *by Suzanne Enoch*
UNTAMED HEART *by Maureen McKade*

Coming Soon

LOVING LINSEY *by Rachelle Morgan*
THE MEN OF PRIDE COUNTY: THE PRETENDER
by Rosalyn West

And Don't Miss These
ROMANTIC TREASURES
from Avon Books

HOW TO MARRY A MARQUIS *by Julia Quinn*
SCANDAL'S BRIDE *by Stephanie Laurens*
THE WEDDING NIGHT *by Linda Needham*

Author's Note

Sir Richard Burtan's translations of *The Arabian Nights* first appeared in 1885. This book takes place in 1887. However, there was an abridged version of the tales told by Scheherazade translated by Edward William Love in 1840—which is how Sherrie Hamilton came by her name.

For Ethan Ellenberg and Lucia Macro.
Thank you. Thank you very much.

SUSAN SIZEMORE

THE PRICE OF INNOCENCE

AVON BOOKS  NEW YORK

AVON BOOKS, INC.
1350 Avenue of the Americas
New York, New York 10019

Copyright © 1999 by Susan Sizemore
Inside cover author photo by Glamour Shots
Published by arrangement with the author
Library of Congress Catalog Card Number: 98-94810
ISBN: 0-380-80418-2
www.avonbooks.com/romance

First Avon Books Printing: April 1999

AVON TRADEMARK REG. U.S. PAT. OFF. AND IN OTHER COUNTRIES, MARCA REGIS-
TRADA, HECHO EN U.S.A.

Printed in the U.S.A.

WCD 10 9 8 7 6 5 4 3 2 1

Chapter 1

"The price of innocence," he said, "is what someone is willing to pay to destroy it."

He took a step closer, forcing her back against the cage he'd pulled her out of a few moments before. Her hand curled tightly around a rusted iron bar behind her and her body tensed as he reached out. Instead of a blow, his fingers sifted ever so slowly through her hair, as though weighing each strand as if it were precious gold.

"Price." She wasn't questioning him, but all hope died when she voiced the word.

His fingers moved to her cheek, her throat, lingered, traced, leaving invisible brands on her cold skin. He nodded. "In your case, that would be quite a lot. White women bring a high price out here."

She shuddered, responding to his shocking words with a new, nameless emotion, though she told herself it was just a different form of fear. She'd had a great deal of experience with the nuances of fear in the last two days. The hungry inflection in her latest captor's low-pitched voice struck deeper than anything she'd felt so far, making her knees go weak and heat flood her despite the raging wind that pushed at her torn clothing. She couldn't be cold with him touching her like that.

When his hand moved to her shoulder, she gasped. His touch was intimate against her bare flesh; she could feel the strength waiting in the hard, flat pads of his fingers. When he touched her breast, she neither moved nor made a sound. Every muscle in her body stiffened, and her insides twisted in very real terror.

She felt as though he was daring her to look at him. She accepted the dare. She made herself look into blue eyes, rather than at the storm clouds rearing up on the horizon beyond his shoulder. His face was bronzed from too much sun, wind, and hard living. His features were obscured by a heavy growth of black beard and shoulder-length black hair. He was dressed in black silk trousers, his chest bare. She was all too aware of his sharply defined smiling mouth and the cold, crystal blueness of his eyes.

This man was touching her in a way she'd never experienced before, never expected, and never in a place like this. How could she possibly have planned to be in a place like this? They were surrounded by at least a dozen other men, but she knew it would do no good to call for help, in Chinese or Malay or English. Especially English. She refused to look away. She took a deep breath. She made her voice work. "What do you want?"

His laugh was soft, but it cut through her. It cut to the core of her, to a level where she was a stranger to herself, to a part of her that understood exactly what the man meant. It set her to trembling again. She hated that she was so weak. She hated even more *that he was so intimately aware of her weakness when she had no definitions for her own responses.*

"You're worth a fortune to me," he told her. "A fortune I'll forgo to make a bargain with you."

She said nothing. How could she respond when she had no idea what his words meant? His hand was still on her breast, radiating white-hot fire. "You're burning me."

"Burning?" Something flared in his cool eyes. "Not hurting?"

"Will you be wearing the pearls this evening, Mrs. Hamilton?"

Sherrie opened her eyes. She did not recognize the voice. For a moment her surroundings were utterly unfamiliar. She was wet, and naked, and—

Sherrie Hamilton threw back her head and laughed. The bright sound that filled the room was from relief, and at her own foolishness. She'd merely fallen asleep in the bathtub. Of course, her surroundings were unfamiliar, but not utterly so. Certainly not forcefully so. She and her family had moved into the rented London house only hours before.

The screen that shielded the bath from the rest of her quarters was plain, not decorated with a pattern of peacocks and willows. The ceiling over her head was painted, but not a bright lacquer red. The dressing gown she'd tossed over the top of the screen was silk, but without embroidered dragons. There wasn't a hint of the Orient about the place, which was just how she wanted it. She had come to Britain to experience this land for itself as the English celebrated their queen's Golden Jubilee. China was for another time.

As for the unknown voice, Sherrie smiled reassuringly at the startled-looking English maid, part of the live-in staff that came with the rental of Primrose House. The large staff, beautiful furnishings, and Mayfair location constituted about the only amenities offered by Primrose House. The mansion was still lit by gaslight, and the plumbing was old-fashioned, to say the least. Still, she'd had worse, and the gardens were lovely. It would do as a residence for the time her family spent in London.

Sherrie rubbed the back of her hand across her cheek, swiping at water she'd splashed up at her sudden waking. "I'm sorry, Todd. I seemed to have been dreaming." She'd been sleeping long enough for the water to get cold, which was adequate explanation for the tight tingling sensations that suffused her and made her nipples hard and tender.

Todd nodded, obviously trained to accept any action of an employer without comment. Sherrie's personal maid had chosen to remain at home in America. Meanwhile, her constant traveling companion was still recovering from an uncharacteristic voyage-long bout of seasickness. This left Sherrie alone with a stranger—a perfectly acceptable, no-doubt discreet Englishwoman who was hovering over Sherrie's bath, asking about her pearls.

Todd's bland expression did alter a bit as Sherrie stepped out of the deep copper tub, naked as the day she was born. Sherrie stretched and shook out her hair before accepting the bath sheet. "Modesty stopped being a strong point with me some years ago," Sherrie told the blushing Todd. "In fact, you'll find that my whole family's a bit eccentric. Though we don't generally walk around buck naked in front of company," Sherrie went on as she dried off, then slipped into the white silk dressing gown. "You'll have to warn the rest of the staff to expect some rather peculiar behavior from the crazy Americans you'll be taking care of."

Todd looked thoughtful for a moment, then said, "You're attempting to be humorous, aren't you, Mrs. Hamilton?"

Sherrie smiled. "Not in the least. Well, not much."

Todd diplomatically chose to stick to business rather than engage in conversation. "Will you be wearing the pearls, Mrs. Hamilton?"

"Yes." Sherrie surveyed the large array of feminine underthings neatly folded on the bed. She sighed, and glanced at an ornate clock on the fireplace mantel. Her unexpected nap had cost her an hour, an hour she could have been spending with Minnie. She sighed. "We better get started."

Todd answered Sherrie while helping with hooks and eyes, buttons, and lacings. "The butler instructed me to remind you that the case containing your pearl necklace was not with the inventory of other valuables placed in the safe this afternoon. I did notice the case on the bed table."

"Tell the butler not to worry," Sherrie told

the maid. "No thief is ever going to make off with that necklace."

Sherrie was convinced nothing was ever going to separate her from the necklace. Once, long ago, in a childish, extravagant gesture, she'd thrown the pearls back into the ocean— and half-drowned before she'd fished them out of the tidal pool they'd landed in. For a long while she'd kept the necklace locked up in a bank vault with written instructions on their disposal in the event of her death. A year ago she'd taken the pearls out of the vault, burned the instructions, and started wearing the necklace every chance she got. Pearls went well with everything, after all.

Sherrie took a deep breath and held it while Todd tightened the heavily ribbed corset that pushed up her bosom, flared out her hips, and dramatically nipped in her already slender waist. Had she not been about to attend one of the most select entertainments of the Season, Sherrie wouldn't have bothered with all the armor. Since she believed in dressing appropriately for the occasion, whether it was a visit to a Tibetan lamasery or a London ballroom, Sherrie was prepared to fit in no matter how uncomfortable it made her. Even as she got dressed, she was eagerly anticipating taking her clothes off once more. A dream-laden nap in the bathtub had been anything but restful. A decent night's sleep was what she wanted.

She wasn't going to get it yet. She wasn't going to have any peace and quiet, either, she realized, as the bedroom door unceremoniously banged open. "I knew you'd only be half dressed." Dora Comstock waved a finger at Sherrie as she marched into the room. "You'll be late for your own funeral, child."

Sherrie laughed at her aunt's words. "I certainly hope so."

Aunt Dora sat down on the edge of the bed. She was dressed in a great deal of deep purple taffeta and lace that rustled with every movement. "Well, I don't want us to be late this evening."

"It's fashionable to be late, isn't it? We want to be fashionable, don't we?"

"What I want," Dora replied bluntly, "is to see my girls married to men with titles."

"That's about as fashionable as you can get, Auntie." Sherrie shook her head. "I don't understand this attraction rich American women have for impoverished English noblemen. Aren't cattle barons and captains of industry good enough?"

"No. No jumped-up cowboy or miner is good enough for my girls."

"But Aunt Dora, we're—"

"I want *civilized* men for my girls," Dora interrupted. "Englishmen are civilized."

I knew an Englishman once, Sherrie thought. *He was anything but civilized. Of course, he was half Irish.* A shudder went through her, a stab of cold followed by a lance of heat, but she kept her voice light as she said, "Didn't we fight a revolution to get rid of English influence?"

"Nonsense, dear," Dora dismissed her objections. "The menfolk fought to get rid of English taxes. We womenfolk have always found dashing red uniforms and fancy accents attractive."

"I don't."

"You just haven't met the right man with an accent, and I don't know why, what with all the traveling you've done."

"I don't travel to meet men." *Just the opposite, actually*, Sherrie added to herself.

"Well, you should. I think Daisy and Faith deserve dukes at least, don't you?"

"I don't think there are that many dukes to go around," Sherrie answered, as Todd approached with the dress she'd chosen to wear to the ball.

As Sherrie put on the many yards of embroidered and beaded satin, Dora eyed her critically. "Honey," she said. "Sometimes I swear you wear black more because you know you look good in it than because you're a widow. I mean, Jeremiah Hamilton's been dead eight years, and it's not like he was anything worth weeping over."

Sherrie didn't argue with her aunt's opinions. She laughed indulgently as she fastened the heavy strands of pearls around her throat. "Well, Jerry left me with Minerva. I'll always be grateful for his help with that." She sat down before the mirrored dressing table. While Todd worked on her hair, Sherrie watched in the mirror as the door behind her opened. A little girl and a large dog came into the room.

Sherrie grinned. "Speak of the devil and there she is."

"I'm no devil, Mama," Minnie declared, as

she came forward to give her mother a hug. "You said I was your little angel just this morning."

Sherrie pretended to be puzzled. "Did I? Maybe it was Lhasi I said was a devil," she added, as the big dog settled down beside the little girl.

"She's a Tibetan mastiff."

"Oh, that's right. Just don't let her near me right now, honey. I'm not going to my first party in London wearing a coating of dog fur on my fancy dress." Sherrie laughed as she flicked her skirt away from the dog's large paws.

"It's mostly black fur, Mama. It won't show." Minnie was already in her nightgown, her thick black hair securely braided. She leaned against the dressing table and gave her mother a forlorn look out of bright blue eyes. "Do you have to go tonight, Mama?"

"She most certainly does," Aunt Dora answered, before Sherrie could suffer more than a faint pang of maternal guilt at leaving her eight-year-old daughter alone for the evening.

Minnie turned to her great aunt. "I'll be lonely."

"You'll be asleep," Aunt Dora assured her.

"I won't."

Sherrie knew from the stubborn look on Minnie's face that the girl would certainly do her best *not* to be asleep. "There's a potion that'll help you sleep, you know." When Minnie tilted her head curiously to one side, Sherrie explained, "Some warm cocoa, and Ira reading you a story. Perfect prescription to have you asleep in no time."

"I like it when *you* read me to sleep."

"I like that, too, honey, but I can't tonight. Tomorrow night, I promise." Minnie still looked stubborn, but she didn't argue anymore. She knew her mother never broke a promise. Sherrie gave a quick glance in the mirror as the maid finished her hair. "Thank you, Todd," she said and stood up.

"You look pretty, Mama. What if I have bad dreams?"

"And here I thought you were done arguing."

"I'm not arguing. I'm questioning."

"She's spoiled," Aunt Dora contributed. "You have noticed that about your daughter, haven't you?"

Sherrie laughed. "Aren't you the one bent on marrying her little girls off to dukes?"

Dora was completely unrepentant. "I didn't say there was anything wrong with spoiling 'em. I just think parents ought to be aware of when they're doing it. Now, will you get a move on, Sherrie Hamilton? I have no intention of being late to my first party in London. Fashion be—" She gave a swift look at Minnie. "Darned."

Minnie paid no attention to this exchange. She concentrated her very intense stare on her mother. "What if I have bad dreams?"

Sherrie put her hand on her daughter's shoulders. "You don't usually have bad dreams."

"What if I do?"

Well aware of what Minnie was really worried about, Sherrie turned her daughter toward the large French windows on the other side of the room. "You know what I noticed earlier? That the balcony of my bedroom is exactly across from the nursery. So you can look out your window and see my window anytime. If *you* have a bad dream tonight, you can look out the window and see if I'm home yet. I promise to keep a lamp lit so you'll know that I'm here."

"Then can I come to bed with you?"

"If you have a bad dream, yes."

"Are you coming, Sherrie?"

"Just a moment, Aunt Dora." She bent and kissed Minnie's forehead, and spared a pat on the head for the big dog as well. "Now, you let Ira put you to bed, and Mama will go pretend to be Cinderella at the ball."

Chapter 2

❝A—person—to see you, my lord.❞
Jack's regular butler would never have come so close to being rude about one of his guests, but his regular butler was not minding the door this evening. Rather, it was the under butler who had been taken on a month ago. Despite his annoyance and the inconvenience, Jack PenMartyn believed in even the best of butlers being given a night off. Hawton was indeed the best of butlers, discreet, discerning, deft, devoted. The only "D" word the Earl of Pen-Martyn could summon to describe Hawton's apprentice was "damned." As in "damned officious fool."

"Thank you, Moss," he said, rather than voice his thoughts. "If the visitor in question is Inspector MacQuarrie, show him to the library, and bring him some brandy."

"The—person—has already retired to the library, my lord." Jack pulled off his gloves. He handed them and his hat to the butler. The objects were damp and soiled. The butler reluctantly accepted them. "And Moss, I'll have some tea in the library," Jack called after the man's stiff retreating form. Jack smoothed his hair after a glance in the hall mirror, then went to the library.

David MacQuarrie rose out of one of the deep leather chairs by the roaring fireplace as Jack entered. MacQuarrie was a big, raw-boned red-haired Scotsman, at least two inches taller than Jack's six foot two. At first glance one was impressed by the man's size. It took a second look to see the intelligence. It took longer acquaintance to discover the man's tenacity and integrity. He was perfectly suited for what he was, a divisional inspector at Scotland Yard.

MacQuarrie looked Jack over critically as he came forward. "Been in a bit of a dust-up, your lordship?"

"A bit," Jack conceded, as he waved the big man back into his seat. He took the chair opposite MacQuarrie. "I spent the last several hours in Limehouse. It was not a pleasant excursion."

MacQuarrie feigned concern. "What was a delicate toff like yourself doing in a place like that? Not slumming, like some of your lot, I hope?"

"Has anyone ever mentioned that your attempt at a Cockney accent is dreadful? Comes from your being from Glasgow, I imagine. I wasn't slumming," he explained. "But a friend's son has been."

MacQuarrie's eyes narrowed. "Opium?"

Jack nodded. He could smell the reek of

sweet smoke permeating his clothes, still taste it on the back of his throat, familiar and seductive. It was a good thing MacQuarrie was here, or he might be tempted to drift off into memories that were better left alone. He sighed. "My friend asked me to find a son who's gotten a bit too fond of frequenting the drug dens." People often asked favors of him. What choice did he have but to do what he could to help?

"You found the lad. He didn't want to come home?" MacQuarrie guessed.

"And that's when the dust-up occurred. The lad is now safely home." Jack flicked at a trace of mud on his jacket collar. "But my valet is not going to forgive me for what I had to do to get him there." He focused his full attention on his visitor. "To what do I owe the pleasure of your company?"

Before MacQuarrie could answer, the butler brought in a laden tray.

The men remained silent while Moss handed MacQuarrie a snifter of brandy, then turned to serve Jack tea in a handleless white porcelain cup. He left the matching pot on the table beside Jack's chair and withdrew. Moss managed his duties flawlessly, but with such an overt air of disapproval that both men broke out laughing once the butler had shut the door behind him.

"Think he was a bit put out over something?" MacQuarrie asked.

"I'm not sure if he's more annoyed at having a policeman in the house, or at the fact that all I drink is tea. Not even proper British tea, but 'nasty green Chinee stuff,' " Jack added, as he took a sip of the jasmine mixture he preferred. He put the cup down after that one sip, finding the flavor, as much as spending a day speaking Cantonese and breathing in opium smoke, dangerously evocative. He concentrated on the present, focused his attention on his guest.

MacQuarrie took an approving sniff of his brandy before downing a small sip. "You might not drink, but you know what to serve."

"Thank you. You didn't just come to annoy Moss and drink my brandy, though, did you?"

MacQuarrie cradled the glass in his hands. "I was hoping to ask you for a bit of help 'unofficially.' "

Jack had once worked for the Foreign Office. He was retired, but took the occasional assignment. MacQuarrie was a city policeman. Their paths should never have crossed, but in the last several years they'd pooled their resources on more than one occasion. Friendship had grown out of dealing not only with dangerous situations, but with shared frustrations with the bureaucracies of the British Empire. Neither coped particularly well with officious fools, which was why they occasionally worked with each other in an unofficial capacity.

MacQuarrie swirled the brandy around in his glass, just a hint of the aroma from the warming liquid scented the air. Jack watched as the Scotsman breathed it in with more appreciation than a lad who'd crawled out of the Glasgow slums should be able to summon. One of the many reasons Jack liked MacQuarrie was that the

Scotsman wore as many masks as he did.

They were as likely to encounter each other quietly reading in the British Museum as brawling in a back alley. Though perhaps the upper-class Earl of PenMartyn belonged in the back alleys more than the law-abiding copper did.

Jack shook off the cynical thought, and leaned forward, happy to have a distraction. "What can I do for you?"

"Nothing that will ruin your tailoring this time, your lordship."

Jack chuckled. "My valet will be grateful."

"This should be right down your street, with your knowledge of the Orient and all."

He'd had more of the Orient than he wanted already today. Jack's voice was hard-edged when he responded, "Really?"

MacQuarrie lifted an eyebrow. "If you haven't the time—"

"No, no," Jack waved away his curt response. "You know I'll be glad to help you in any way I can."

"Good." MacQuarrie drained the brandy, set the snifter down, and got to business. "Ever heard of Lord Gordon Summers?"

Jack nodded. "Vaguely. Scholar, isn't he? Something of a specialist in Asian folklore?"

"That's the lad. Was traveling around the Orient about the same time you were."

"Our paths never crossed. Asia's a rather large place," Jack reminded his guest.

"Well, you know more about this Lord Summers than I did until a few days ago. You and he cross paths now? London, and the lot you run with, isn't so big," MacQuarrie reminded Jack. "And knowledge about Asia's your particular patch."

Jack shook his head. "I'm more likely to show up at a boxing match than dull Royal Society meetings. And the hostesses of London are more interested in wearing silk than discussing where it comes from."

"Now, that's where you're wrong, laddie. You *haven't* been out much lately, have you?"

The Earl of PenMartyn was not used to being referred to as "laddie," even by his good Scottish friend. He cocked an eyebrow with faint annoyance, even as he noticed the gleam of amusement in MacQuarrie's eyes. Jack decided that he must be sounding like a cat with its back up, and not hiding his tenseness at all well from the discerning copper. "Am I coming on as a bit of an arrogant toff, *laddie?*"

"That you are, governor."

"Don't pay my tone any mind. I'm tired. And no, I haven't been going out much lately. My evenings have been quite full."

MacQuarrie's amusement sparked into a full smile. "What's her name?"

"You couldn't pronounce it."

"One of them foreign opera singers, eh?"

Jack sipped his tea. "I believe Jhou Xa actually has done a bit of training with the Peking Opera, but he isn't much of a singer."

MacQuarrie's eyes lit. "You talked that martial arts master into coming to England?"

Jack nodded. "He's teaching me the Eagle technique." Jack returned the conversation to its original topic. "I take it Lord Summers is making the rounds of society dinner parties."

"That he is. That and much more. Quite the persuasive conversationalist, apparently."

"And just what does his conversation have to do with Scotland Yard?"

"It doesn't. The man hasn't broken any laws. Not yet."

Like all good policemen, MacQuarrie didn't believe *anyone* was pure, innocent, or incapable of committing a crime. Jack was hardly in a position to disagree. "Go on."

"Last week Sir Matthew Knightley came to my office demanding I do something about Summers." MacQuarrie's eyes glinted with humor at the memory. "He said Summers had seduced his wife and daughter with his 'damn fool notions' and now his son was involved and that it oughtn't to be allowed. Went on at great length about how all that chanting and living in harmony with nature was disrupting his household, and the worst of it was his wife wouldn't allow Cook to serve good British beef at table anymore. How was a man supposed to live on roots and greens in a house full of mad, chanting, incense-burning women, by God? The police had better stop it or he'd know the reason why!"

Jack smiled at his friend. He took a sip of tea. "That does sound dangerous. I take it that there's a vicious plot headed by Lord Summers to spread a bit of Eastern philosophy to the English upper classes?"

"Looks that way."

"You had better run him in."

"Sir Matthew certainly thought so. Only way I could get him to leave was to promise to look into it. Which is where you come in."

"Is it? I'm to make good on your promise to an outraged country squire?"

"Not exactly. Don't know why, but hearing about Lord Summers gave me a feeling. Something seemed dicey. Kightley suspected his family was giving Summers money. I did do a bit of investigating. Lots of people are giving him money."

"I don't distrust your instincts, but is that illegal?"

"Depends on how he's getting it from them, I reckon. Summers calls his teachings the Golden Light Mission. Got himself set up in a house in Mayfair where he teaches all this chanting and nonsense. The following he's building includes some of the wealthiest people in the country, and some of the poorest. Pulling in the duchesses and their housemaids. And skinning them all out of their lifesavings, I suspect."

"But you haven't been able to find any evidence."

"Not a whisper. There is one other thing, something more on your Foreign Office lot's patch, which is another reason you might be interested in looking into Summers. Seems he has been renewing an old friendship with the Prince of Wales lately."

"And Her Majesty's government might be a bit concerned if the heir to the throne were to start chanting and burning incense?"

MacQuarrie stood. "I suspect so. Will you find out what's going on with this Lord Summers for me?"

Jack stood as well, and rang for the butler. "As long as I'm not asked to do any chanting. I have an invitation to Lady Anne Beaumont's ball tonight. Chances are Summers will be attending. I'll start there." When the butler came in, Jack said, "Moss, have my valet lay out my evening clothes and have a bath drawn. It seems I have to go off and play Prince Charming this evening."

Chapter 3

Intelligence gathering is an art form. Jack was not feeling like an artist this evening, but here he was at the Beaumonts' ornate door. He nodded pleasantly as the maid opened it.

"Good evening, Margaret."

She smiled shyly as he called her by name. Jack smiled back as he came into the overheated front hall of Beaumont House. Behind him he heard the clattering on the cobblestones of another arriving guest's carriage as his own was driven slowly away.

Jack would much rather have spent the evening at home. His duties took him out far more than he liked. In fact, if not for those duties, he might happily have turned into a recluse. Smuggler, assassin, reprobate—recluse. He smiled as he listed the various phases of his life, thinking that he preferred the last to all the others. Still, he'd promised MacQuarrie that he'd look into the Summers matter. He was a man who kept his promises. He always had been, though he made a point to stand by his

word much more promptly these days than he
had in the past.

A past that was stalking him more than usual
today. Try as he might to block it out, it always
padded relentlessly behind, a tiger that tore unexpectedly into his flesh even at moments when
he thought he was on the safest ground. He
knew very well that even if MacQuarrie hadn't
sought out his help, he probably would have
come to Lady Beaumont's party. Even though
his mission was to seek out Buddhists lurking
in the ballroom, he needed a reminder that he
was the Earl of PenMartyn. He was no longer
a penniless fourth son who'd been shipped off
to the Orient. After a day spent in the dark alleys of London's Chinese slum, he *needed* to be
that privileged nobleman for a while.

He walked up the long, sweeping steps of
Beaumont House toward the formal rooms with
an outward calm that belied the awareness of
the tiger at his heels. He smiled at people he
passed, not betraying a flicker of unease or the
feeling of being an impostor among all this
wealth and luxury.

He'd come back rich and found himself with
a title he'd never expected and wasn't quite
sure what to do with. For some reason, London's hostesses delighted in luring him to their
dinners and dances. London's hostesses and all
their friends had daughters. He might not know
what to do with a title, but all those eager mamas knew exactly what it was worth. It amazed
him that he'd become one of the most sought-

after bachelors in England, since he was hardly a fit mate for a decent woman.

Fortunately, Lady Anne Beaumont was the one woman who liked him for himself. Her tastes were broad, her kindness boundless, and she made him feel comfortable inside the skin of an English lord. He gave her a grateful smile as she greeted him in the reception line in her mansion's upstairs hall.

"Jack! Well met, Jack. Just the man I want to see."

Lady Anne was a large woman in her late forties, unashamed of her matronly figure and the gray streaks in her auburn hair. She was a friend of just about everyone in the small world of the aristocracy. That she also had no qualms about stepping outside that little world, or drawing others into it, endeared her to Jack.

He smiled warmly as she held her hands out to him. He kissed first one, then the other, and received a girlish giggle in response. "Run away with me, Annie," he said, "and I'll show you the world."

"I've seen the world, or as much of it as I want," she said, as she stepped out of the receiving line, leaving her amiably smiling husband to continue greeting their guests alone. "It's taken me years to train Robert in to just the way I like. I'd hardly start over even for a mad, passionate affair with the handsomest man I know." She slipped her arm through his and headed them through the crowd toward the ballroom. "Besides, I've something altogether more interesting in mind for you. Come along, young man, and meet your fate."

Jack stopped at the entrance to the ballroom, surprise catching him like a blow. He eyed his friend suspiciously. "Annie, do you have matchmaking in mind?"

"Yes."

"Oh, lord, woman, not you too!"

She was thoroughly unashamed. "I know you thought you were safe with me, but I'm afraid I've just been saving you for the right woman." She wagged a finger under his nose. "You'll have to do your duty by the PenMartyn line and sire an heir eventually."

Jack was known for his ability to remain cool and calculating even in the most life-threatening of situations. This turn of events was enough to make him forget his training altogether. Lady Anne's words left him nonplussed as he stared speechlessly across the room from the edge of the dance floor.

People moved by before them in a bright swirl. The women were dressed in a hundred vivid colors, their partners in black like himself, with stiff white shirtfronts, or in dashing red uniform coats gleaming with braid and medals. The crystal chandeliers overhead caught and sparked on the rich array. The polished floor vibrated beneath the practiced rhythm of the flying feet. Many women smiled at him as they danced by. Jack wondered helplessly just which one Anne Beaumont was preparing to throw his way.

Lady Anne drew back his attention as she said, "There are so few good-looking men in this world. I hate it when one of the best-looking ones lives like a monk."

Jack put aside his shock at this betrayal on his friend's part and tried to face the situation with some grace. "Hardly among the best looking. Definitely not a monk."

"You need a wife."

"I've heard that too often before."

"I know," she sympathized. "But you haven't heard it from the right woman."

"From you."

She nodded emphatically. "I've watched those silly women throw their girls at your head, and I don't blame you for running the other way as fast as you could every time it's happened. You know I wouldn't throw a foolish girl at you, and I'm certainly not going to try to subtly put you together with the one I have in mind and hope for the best. I'm telling you flat out what I'm up to, and that it's right for both of you."

Jack couldn't stop the laugh, nor could he help that the sound was a dark and dangerous one. "Woman, you have no idea what you're getting into."

"You need a wife," she said. "You could make a woman very happy, Jack PenMartyn, if you set your mind to it."

"Lady Anne, you surprise me."

"I do no such thing."

"How about shock, then? Terrify?"

She gave a strident laugh. "Terrified of love? Romance? The perfect woman?"

"I've had the perfect woman, Annie," he said

without thinking. "Believe me, the experience nearly killed us both."

Her eyes lit with curiosity even as he damned himself for blurting out the words. "And here I thought you'd told me all your stories."

"Not a tenth of them," he whispered, before he could get himself under control.

"This sounds like one I simply must know."

To avoid Lady Anne's interrogation, Jack flung himself back into the original unpleasant conversation. "Just who is this paragon you have in mind for me? Or is it me you have in mind for her? Who's doing the catching and who the being caught, my dear?"

Lady Anne happily returned to the initial subject. "She's an American. A lovely, wealthy, charming young widow."

He quirked an eyebrow at her, deciding that seeing the humor in it was the only way to deal with the situation gracefully. "An American? And wealthy? Hmm. Husband hunting, is she? I'm told it's the favorite sport among American females just now. Lady Anne, are you willing to sacrifice me for the sake of international relations?"

"It's no sacrifice. Besides, it's Mrs. Hamilton's cousins that are husband hunting—and being quite cheerfully blatant about it. At least, their mother is. They've taken Primrose House for the Season—a mistake on their part, I think, since it's just next door to the silly man who's gotten everyone chanting—but I'm sure they'll make the best of it; Americans are so adaptable. I've promised to sponsor the family and am looking forward to helping them get the girls betrothed. American women are so charming, don't you think?"

I knew an American woman once, he thought, and heat speared through him at the memory. *She wasn't charming. She was—addicting.* He forced the memories aside and concentrated on his redoubtable hostess. "I suppose Americans have a certain robust character that can be enjoyable."

"You make the entire population sound like a wine you're planning on serving with cheese and fruit."

"Madam," he replied dryly. "I am not from Borneo, I am from Cornwall. I do not practice cannibalism—at least, I haven't recently."

"Then London society has done you some good, my rustic friend." She urged him forward. "Time for you to meet Sherrie. I met her on my trip to the American West last year. Quite a remarkable woman. Ah, good, the music's stopped. And I see her by the windows. Looks like she's finally shaken off that ridiculous Lord Summers. The man's been pestering her since he found out she's traveled extensively in the East. That's something else you two have in common. Come along."

Jack took in this information as she hustled him across the ballroom, and he didn't like any of it, though he said, "If you admire her, she must be charming indeed," just to keep up his end of the conversation while he sorted facts. "Lead me to your charming American widow."

Laughter drew his attention as they approached the group of people standing next to the open balcony window. It was a sound that sent a chill up his spine, and a shocking, unexpected, jolt of heat through his blood.

Chapter 4

"Behind you!"

He pivoted and ducked at the girl's shout. The swift move was barely fast enough to dodge the downward arc of the cutlass that had been meant to take off his head.

"Damn!" he cursed, as he jumped away from another wild swing.

Hell of a bad day to lead a boarding party onto the deck of a Malay war junk, *he thought, as he had to deal with both the swordsman in front of him and the pitching deck under his bare feet. There weren't many of the Malay crew left, but the ones still alive were fanatical fighters. With a typhoon blowing in, he didn't have time for fanatics. He wanted to finish the raid and get out.*

"The prize had damn well better be worth the trouble!" he shouted. He backed across the pitching deck as the man continued to slash at him with the biggest blade he'd ever seen. If his pistol hadn't been knocked out of his hand a few moments before, he could have easily dispatched this primitive attacker.

When he reached the stack of three iron cages

lashed to the deck on the junk's prow, he scrambled
on top of them. All but one were empty. "Slave trade
must be slow," he commented. He balanced like an
acrobat as he ran the length of the cages. He barely
had time for a passing glance down at the girl whose
shout had saved his life. It was only when he caught
a glimpse of fair hair and pale skin that he remembered that her words had been in English. He
grinned, realizing just what cargo the Malay fighters
were protecting. He was laughing as he jumped, feet
slamming into the swordsman's chest. The Malay
dropped the oversized blade as he fell.

He snatched it off the deck and brought it down
across the Malay's thick neck. Then he swiveled and
brought the sword down as hard as he could on the
cage's lock. The blade shattered, but so did the rusty
old lock.

His men gathered around as he pulled the girl out
for a closer look.

"Thank you!" she said.

"Don't."

Their gazes met, locked, then she looked away, her
cheeks bright red. He knew what she'd seen in his
eyes. After a long moment she laughed, the tone mu-
sical, as clear and sharp as the salt wind that caught
the sound and blew it out to sea. It was a brave
laugh, slightly mad, defiant, yet reflecting the fear
he'd seen in her blue eyes. Beautiful eyes set in a
perfect oval face. It had been a long time since he'd
seen a blue-eyed woman. Longer still since he'd had
one.

He moved closer as he touched her cheek. He
breathed in the scent of her as he ran his thumb
across the ugly blue-green bruise that marked where

*someone had hit her. Her skin was warm, soft, flaw-
less. Only a fool would mar it. He wanted to touch
it, taste it everywhere, possess it.*

"You're not here to rescue me, are you?"

"No."

*She laughed again. The bright, bitter sound en-
chanted him. This was not a weak, hysterical spirit.
There was nothing fragile to her beauty, despite the
exquisite perfection of form and face. She laughed in
hell, and that made her priceless to him.*

*He ran his fingers through her hair. "The price of
innocence," he said, "is what someone is willing to
pay to destroy it."*

In and of itself, the woman's bright laughter
was an almost ordinary sound. Its timbre was
neither shrill nor forced: a genuine, unaffected
expression of amusement at some clever bit of
conversation. It was pleasant, rather infectious.

Malaria was infectious as well, Jack remembered, and it could send the same chill heat
quivering through one.

He saw exactly who he expected to see when
she turned their way, a tall, slender girl—no,
not a girl, a woman. Her golden hair did not
tumble wantonly around her lovely face. Her
hair was arranged in a fashionable coif, but it
was the same wheat honey amber color he remembered. She was not wearing a clinging silk
robe with absolutely nothing on underneath,
but an elaborate evening gown of stiff, shimmering black. The dark material served to outline every lush curve just the same, and to
accent the flawless paleness of her skin. She was
still perfect. She was still—Scheherazade.

Jack just barely managed not to say the name aloud. He just barely managed to catch hold of the facts that he was in a London ballroom, that the year was 1887, that if she saw him she'd scream, possibly faint, certainly denounce him as the fraud and villain he truly was. He wanted nothing more than to back away, to run for the door.

Instead, Lady Anne's arm tightened around his as she sensed his hesitation. He was totally helpless, totally detached from his body as she drew him to the woman. He felt as though he were floating toward his executioner and there was nothing he could do to stop it. When he saw the necklace, he stopped breathing.

He was damned, he knew it, but there was nothing he could do but watch and listen as Lady Anne spoke.

"Sherrie, my dear, this is Lord St. John Pen-Martyn, Earl of PenMartyn. We call him Jack."

Sherrie said, "Hello," before she actually looked at Jack PenMartyn.

When she looked at him her attention was instantly riveted on the masculine figure who stood so still and intensely silent before her. She did not actually notice the details of his appearance; it was the dark aura that radiated from him that riveted her attention. Her first impression was that a tiger had walked into the room and she was the only one who recognized the danger. She had an unfortunate habit of being drawn to danger.

"I shot a tiger once, in India," she heard herself say. "It was a mankiller. There was no other choice."

It was an odd and inane way of introducing herself to this stranger. She reminded herself to curb her too-active imagination. She didn't blame him when he took an abrupt step back. Only when he moved, swift and graceful, did she actually see the man. Tall, solidly made, with a strong throat and broad shoulders. His hair was blue black, his face as handsome as sin, his mouth wide and full and sensuous. She almost took a step toward him, her body obediently following his without any conscious volition. A response she hadn't felt in years kindled in her at the sight of him, until she saw the ice-cold blueness of his eyes.

It would never do to scream in the middle of Lady Anne's ball.

She'd given up screaming years ago, anyway. If there was one thing she could hide, it was her aversion to blue-eyed men. Fortunately, though the world was full of blue-eyed men, there were very few with the exact glacial shade of the man—the unknown man—before her.

She was able to stop the heart-jolting response to the stranger's familiar eyes before it had a chance to disturb her hard-won poise. This wasn't the first time this foolish response had tried to overwhelm her. She merely had to get past surface similarities, be briefly polite to the newcomer, then make her escape with the excuse that Lord Summers had asked her to dance.

Sherrie pretended she hadn't already spoken,

and held out her hand. It wouldn't have dared to do anything so cowardly as tremble. "I'm always happy to meet any friend of yours, Annie."

She was able, with more trouble than she wanted to admit, to force her initial image of the earl to the back of her mind. There were no tigers in the room, unless her imagination had conjured one out of memory and whole cloth. This earl was really just another mild-mannered aristocrat. He was probably one of the single gentlemen Lady Anne had promised Aunt Dora she'd trot out for inspection, even if she had to invade the gentlemen's smoking room. The poor fellow probably wanted to get the mandatory introduction to the rich American over with and get back to his brandy and masculine conversation as quickly as possible. She didn't blame him.

And for all the supposition she made up about the thoughts and history of the Earl of PenMartyn, she was desperately glad that they weren't alone. She was delighted that her hands were covered with white silk gloves, for if he touched her in any way, even if only to brush his lips perfunctorily across the back of her bare hand, she would know. And she did not want to know.

Though, of course, there was nothing to know.

At least he doesn't smell of cigars, she thought, dragging her mind down a sane and sensible path. Aunt Dora would never approve of a man who smoked for one of her girls. Judging his attributes with thoughts of matrimony for her cousins in mind, rather than the overactive prejudice of her imagination, she decided that she liked his height, the cut of his clothing, and the width of his shoulders. She especially liked the width of his shoulders, because they definitely had more breadth to them than those of the man she knew he could not be.

Faith and Daisy are tall girls, she thought. *It won't do to introduce them to the runts of any English litter, titled or not.*

There was a fleck or two of gray in his thick black hair, making it not quite so blue-black as she'd initially thought. She didn't suppose the girls would like that, but she found it distinguished.

His eyes, however, she continued to find disturbing. She didn't risk looking into them for more than an instant. This foolish reaction was entirely her own fault. If she had thought about it, she would have recalled that Britain was full of men with the Celtic ancestry that bred pale skins, light blue eyes, and silky black hair. The knowledge wouldn't have stopped her from coming to England, but she would have been more prepared than to have such a shocked reaction to the Earl of—

"PenMartyn," she said as she recalled the title. She still held her hand out, waiting for the requisite chaste brush of lips across her gloved knuckles. He didn't seem to notice. "Is that Welsh?" *Please, God, don't let him be Irish.* Not that her Irishman had been an Earl.

"Cornish," Lady Anne said, after the silence

drew out to an uncomfortable length.

Sherrie didn't know where to go from here. The man was clearly not interested in talking to her. In fact, he was barely looking at her. He stood there, large, imposing, expressionless, and statue-still. His gaze was fixed somewhere below her chin, though she didn't think he was ogling her bosom, despite there being quite a bit of it exposed by the cut of her gown.

When she finally realized what he was looking at, she touched the necklace clasped around her throat. "The six strands of white pearls are perfectly matched. The baroque black pearl in the center is quite rare," she said, as she ran a fingertip over the smooth undulations of the irregularly shaped gem. She had given this description a few times before. "The setting of the black pearl is carved from white jade. It depicts a tiger and a dragon. They are traditionally shown battling each other for the pearl of wisdom—which is not generally depicted as a black lump of oyster spit," she added, as the earl continued to stare.

She saw her rude comment and tart tone finally bring Jack PenMartyn out of his daze. A daze she'd probably caused with her initial odd comment about tiger killing. He must think her a very odd American duck.

Then he laughed. Actually it was more of a faint, rasping chuckle. It gave her the impression that he wasn't used to laughing. Which was a shame, since amusement served to make his already handsome features even better looking.

She didn't often take much interest in men's looks, but with Jack PenMartyn it was hard not to make an exception. When he took her hand and turned it so that his lips brushed not across her knuckles, but kissed softly in the exact center of her gloved palm, her knees went weak. That flesh did not actually touch flesh didn't prevent the searing reaction that shot through her. She could do nothing but stare transfixed as he stepped very close to her. Despite their color, there was nothing cold about the look in his eyes. She wasn't sure whether she was ready to flee, or rush into Cullum's embrace.

No. No. No.

They'd never met. She'd had this hallucination before. She was having the dreams too often, and they were invading her waking hours.

Fortunately, Lady Anne was there to remind them that they were hardly alone. The hostess's voice was full of forced cheerfulness as she filled in the charged silence around them. "As I mentioned earlier, Jack, dear, Mrs. Hamilton is a widow, but I don't think I told you about her adventures. She travels all over the world. She's been to India and journeyed as far as Tibet."

He was glad she was a widow. It saved him the trouble of having to kill any man who dared touch her.

The thought brought him up short, and back to sanity.

His reaction, after all these years, to Scheherazade VanHarlen—Hamilton—was a humbling experience for a man who took pride in his self-restraint. That she didn't recognize him should have been a relief. Instead, he was infuriated to the point that he was barely able to keep from stirring her memory in the most direct, carnal way possible.

He'd walked into a trap.

The demon that lived inside him laughed. Jack was just barely able to keep the civilized mask in place, to take one step away from Scheherazade, then another. He won the battle to keep his voice polite and calm when he spoke. He knew the polished, precise tone was nothing like the rough Irish-accented growl Scheherazade would remember. "My apologies, and deepest regrets, ladies, but you will have to excuse me. I can't stay. I'm not feeling at all myself at the moment."

The truth was, he was feeling more like himself than he had in years. No one here but Scheherazade knew just how dangerous his real self could be. He couldn't say another word, make another polite gesture. All he could do was manage not to flee in heedless, headlong panic when he walked from the room.

Chapter 5

❦❦

"*They've taken Primrose House for the Season—a mistake on their part, I think, since it's just next door to the silly man who's gotten everyone chanting . . .*"

It had been hours spent wandering in a fog of dark memories before he'd connected Lady Anne's comment with his task for MacQuarrie. That Scheherazade and Summers shared even that tenuous connection could be no accident. He was too steeped in Asian philosophy and culture, and too Celt in his blood and bones, not to realize that fate, *karma*, and some celestial force with a wicked sense of humor had brought him and Scheherazade back together at this time and place. Whether the *karma* was good or ill, it was still too early to say.

Jack told himself that it was a sense of protectiveness that brought him to Primrose House at three in the morning, dressed all in black and wearing crepe-soled shoes. He told himself it was a sense of obligation, that he was interested solely in seeing to a defenseless woman's safety, that seeing to her safety helped repay a debt. He would make sure she was safe, and then he would go.

He suspected he was bloody well lying to himself, but jumped the fence and made his way through the garden at the back of the house anyway. The night air was full of the scent of roses and lilacs, full of shadows thrown out by the cloud-shadowed moon. He wove his way easily from shadow to shadow.

There were several balconies overlooking the back garden. Jack had no trouble finding handholds on the painted brick as he climbed to the second floor and onto the largest of the balconies. He wouldn't have had much trouble getting inside the house even if the balcony door was locked, but she hadn't bothered with locking it.

She hadn't even bothered with drawing the curtains. There was a lamp burning on a table near the bed, its pink glass shade gave the light it cast a warm, feminine glow. He had no trouble seeing the sleeping woman inside the room, her pale skin vivid as pearls on velvet against the dark covers.

Eventually he eased open the unlocked door and went inside. He wasn't afraid of waking her. He knew that it was hard for her to get to sleep, but once she did, it practically took cannon fire to rouse her before dawn.

He told himself watching her sleep was a test as he slowly drew closer and closer to the bed. Such a wide bed, he thought, for a woman to be sleeping in alone. She'd thrown back the

covers, of course, she hated sleeping under
covers. And how well he knew the habits and
secrets of her nights. Her nightgown was un-
buttoned at the throat, and pulled up on one
side, revealing most of a long, shapely leg. She
was always so hot at night; sharing a bed with
her was like sleeping with a soft, sensual fur-
nace.

He hadn't expect the heat. Or the clean,
sweet, unforgettable scent of her flesh.

Jack reached a hand out, barely stopping
himself within a quarter inch of caressing the
naked flesh of her thigh. Feeling the warmth of
her without contact was maddening.

"Always so clean," he whispered, the words
so low that they were more thought than spoken. "So clean."

"At least take a bath first."

*His hands stopped as they reached for her. He
crossed his arms instead. He studied the expression
of mingled defiance and distaste on her perfect an-
gelic face. He'd noticed her gaze dart to the bed when
they first entered his cabin. A dangerous edge of his
temper began to flare. "Are you making demands of
me? Trying to back out of our bargain?"*

*She crossed her arms, her stance mirroring his.
She was dressed in rags, but she looked like a princess. "Call it a request."*

"A bath? Me?"

"Yes. You. And I need one as well."

"I've had one recently."

"Not too recently, I'd wager."

*He wanted her beneath him on the bed. He stood
and talked to her instead, in spite of the impatient*

lust that gnawed at him. He'd never thought that curiosity would prove stronger than appetite, but for now it did. "Wagering? What do you know of wagering? I assumed you were some kidnapped missionary's daughter." He took a step closer. She backed up a step, which brought her closer to the cabin's narrow bed. "That's a habit you'll have to break."

She blinked in confusion. "What?"

"Moving away whenever I come near. You have to wait for me. Come when I call. You belong to me now."

Fear almost overwhelmed the defiance in her eyes, but her response was immediate and tart. "For a month. I agreed to belong to you for a month."

He touched her bare shoulder. She trembled beneath his touch, but didn't try to jerk away. Good. "You won't regret it."

"I already regret it."

"It's better than a brothel in Singapore. That's where the Malays would have sold you. Where I'll sell you if you don't live up to our bargain," he reminded her. "How did you come to be in that slave cage? You're American, aren't you? How does an innocent American girl know about gambling?"

Her eyes flashed with anger. "Did you buy my history along with my body?"

"Yes."

She simply looked at him angrily for a long time, their gazes locked in a battle of wills as his ship sailed away from the edge of the storm. Gradually, as his own body tightened with need from being near her, he felt her skin grow warmer and warmer beneath his fingers, watched her cheeks and throat *slowly flush. He wanted her more with every passing second.*

Eventually, just as he began to bend his head to take her mouth, she answered, "I was visiting cousins, missionaries. We were traveling with some Chinese converts on their fishing junk when the boat was attacked. Everyone was killed, but—" He saw tears shining in her eyes. He would bet his soul that she wouldn't let herself cry in front of him.

"So they took the fishermen's catch, and you, and sailed away," he went on for her.

"Yes."

"And then I came and killed the scum who took you."

"From bad to worse," she agreed.

He put a finger over her lips. "Remember our bargain."

She shook him off. When she backed up a step this time, her legs touched the edge of the bed just as a rolling wave from the storm lifted the deck beneath their feet. She ended up sitting on the thin mattress. On the bed was right where he wanted her—for a month. For at least a month.

When she realized where she was, she stood up as though burned and moved to the center of the room. He laughed. Over his laughter, she said, "Yes, I'm American. I'm from Virginia City. That's how I know about gambling." She sounded as if that was explanation enough.

He had no idea where the place was. It might be Sodom itself, for all he knew. The cabin was small, he was beside her in one long step. His hands sought her almost of their own accord, lightly tracing her cheeks, her temples, the soft outline of her lips. He

*had never touched anything so perfect. So unspoiled.
Her body stiffened, her expression was full of disgust.*

"You agreed to be willing. Don't make me have
to remind you."

"You have to be clean," she snapped back. "We
both do. If I'm going to-to-do things—with you—be
your . . ." He watched her helpless hunt for words
with amusement and growing arousal. How was it
the very words and her struggle to understand them
could be arousing? She finally settled on, "Be your
inamorata—mistress."

"Whore."

Embarrassed shame turned to an instant of fury.
"Whores get paid. I know that much."

"Perhaps you aren't as virginal as I thought." He
hated to think someone else might have touched her.
It made his grip on her arms tight as he pulled her
close. "Are you?"

He had never seen anyone look more indignant in
his life. "Of course I am! Just because I know what
a—a lady of the evening—is doesn't mean I'm experienced in what they do."

"I'll teach you."

"I'm sure."

"You'll like it."

"Don't wager on it." She kicked at his shin. "Let
go of me. And take a bath."

He'd taken a bath. He'd asked if he should
shave as well. Her answer had been, "I'd rather
not see your face." Over the time they were together, he found that she didn't look at his face
that often, though she'd learned to pay exquisite attention to every other part of him. Nine

years later he was glad she hadn't requested he shave off his beard. He'd been so besotted he would have done anything she wanted. Fortunately, neither of them had been quite aware of the extent of his ardor at that moment. Nine years ago he'd been a randy young fool, obsessed by the only pure, innocent thing that had ever come into his life. With the passage of time he had—

Jack PenMartyn laughed silently, realizing that he'd broken into the woman's house like a thief. Never mind the excuses. He had come for the chance to stand here and watch her sleeping. Just to watch her sleep—and to remember what was best forgotten. Her next door neighbor was only an excuse. He might have thought he'd gotten over his obsession with Scheherazade, but apparently he was wrong.

He forced his trembling hand down to his side.

He shook his head, amazed that his discipline had deteriorated so far so fast, to the point that he used any excuse simply to do something he wanted. At least he'd caught on to the demon's tricks before any harm was done. He gathered his control back together as best he could, and slipped from the room without once having touched her.

He would never touch her again. He'd spent years learning to fight temptation, to subordinate his hungers, his temper, to focus all the dark energy that boiled out of his soul. He no longer indulged his appetites. He'd had his one last look. Any urge to see her again after tonight would be just one more craving he would deal with.

He left the balcony as silently as he'd arrived. He did not leave unobserved. Across the way, wrapped up in a blanket, with her big dog forcibly held across her lap, its muzzle deeply buried in heavy folds of wool, Minnie Hamilton sat and watched the stranger come and go.

Minnie had woken when Mama had come into her room after the ball. Her mother had brought gold and pink lamplight with her, and the wonderful smell of her special perfume. Though she scrunched up happily, Minnie pretended to sleep as Mama bent and kissed her cheek. Minnie then got up to keep her vigil as soon as her mother left. She and Lhasi settled on the balcony and watched light flicker in the bedroom across from the nursery as her mother prepared for bed. They'd stayed on the balcony, keeping watch long after her mother must have been asleep.

Minnie worried. Sometimes Mama had bad dreams, or couldn't sleep at all. She wanted to make sure her mother was well and truly peacefully sleeping before she went back to bed. It was only fair. Mama always stayed awake when she was sick. Minnie knew that if her mother couldn't sleep, she'd come out on the balcony. If Mama came out on the balcony, Minnie planned to wave at her and make her smile.

She saw the man moving through the garden before Lhasi even caught a whiff of scent or a hint of movement. She didn't think Lhasi was to blame, not as smart a dog as she was. Minnie didn't know why she saw him first. It was a very dark night, and he moved carefully, swiftly, from shadow to shadow. When she saw him she wasn't afraid. When Lhasi's head finally came up and she would have barked, Minnie forced the dog's head down. She soothed the big animal with her hands and the softest of reassuring words. Perhaps she should have warned the household, run for Ira to come with his big Colt revolver, screamed, and let Lhasi go after the intruder. She just couldn't do it, not even when he climbed up to her mother's balcony.

There was something sad about the way the man moved. Something lonely. Something familiar.

She should have been afraid. For her mother. For her own safety. Instead, Minnie studied him while he stood on the balcony for a long time before he opened the French doors and went inside. He didn't see her, but for an instant, when the moon briefly tore away from a patch of clouds, she got a clear look at him. She waited, keeping Lhasi quiet, until the man came outside again. When he was gone, she let the dog go and padded quietly off to her mother's room.

Mama never locked her door, Minnie was always welcomed inside. She went into the bedroom, only a little worried that something might have happened. Not even as worried as when she heard her mother having one of her bad dreams. She needn't have worried at all.

Her mother was stretched out on her back, the coverings thrown aside, just the way she always slept. Minnie climbed up beside her, and Lhasi jumped on the end of the bed.

Sherrie came partially awake as Minnie got into bed with her. She rolled over, and Minnie cuddled close to her as they shared the pile of pillows.

Before Sherrie could fall completely asleep again, Minnie said, "Mama?"

She still wasn't quite awake, but the serious tone in her daughter's voice called to her. "Hmm?"

Minnie hugged her, and said gravely, "I saw my daddy tonight."

She stroked Minnie's cheek as she murmured, almost talking in her sleep, "You were dreaming, honey. There aren't any pirates in London."

Chapter 6

"What's your name?"
He stood too close behind her, his hands on her shoulders. He had been clasping her hands a few moments ago, before his fingers trailed slowly up her arms. She could still feel the slow caressing movement along every inch of the bare flesh his rough fingers had skimmed, the lightest of touches leaving the deepest of sensations. She knew she was trembling, and that he could feel it. She hated that she was trembling, mostly hating that the reaction wasn't totally from fear and revulsion.

After a moment his grip turned harsh and he abruptly pulled her closer. The feel of his hard, bare chest against her back caused her to gasp. The hot touch of his skin against hers was too personal, the clean masculine scent of him too overwhelmingly real. She wished she hadn't asked him to bathe, hadn't given him the excuse to strip off his clothes and not bother to put them back on. He hadn't let her dress after her bath. In fact, he'd watched her the whole time. She hadn't looked at him, but had been too aware of his hungry gaze even to feel the water or the rough texture of the sponge she'd used to scrub off the grime. Or, rather, it had felt as if it wasn't water or a sponge that had touched her. He hadn't let her wrap the towel around herself after she'd dried, so she'd turned her back on him, pretending he wasn't there, that they weren't both naked. It hadn't taken him but a moment to come up behind her, to put his hands on her, to easily prove that pretending did no good.

He slipped a hand around her waist, drawing her even closer. She felt the fur on his chest brush against her shoulders. Felt the flat muscles of his bare belly. Felt his hips pressed to hers, and his hardness pressed intimately between them.

Oh, God.

His lips were against her ear when he said, "Answer me."

She recognized the sweet scent of poppy on his breath, and longed to turn her head away. That wasn't the bargain. She didn't move; in fact, she tried to let her tight muscles relax as she spoke. "Call me whatever you want."

His hand tightened, pulling them closer together. Lord, but he was hard! She made some small noise, and his answering laugh was both rough and soft— rough along her nerves, soft against her flesh.

"I want your name. I want to know who I own."

"Rent," was her immediate response. "You don't own me."

"I could," he said, and his hand moved.

"Scheherazade!"

It was her name, but the word came out sounding like—what?—A protest? A plea? For what? All she *knew was that she couldn't bear what his touch was doing to her.*

He laughed. God, how could a laugh sound so intimate? But his hand stopped moving. Not that the fear and fire that rushed through her abated one little bit.

"Cullum," he said. He stepped away. "Call me Cullum."

She turned, because she knew he wanted her to face him. That he had loosened his hold just so she could move the way he wanted. "I don't want to call you anything."

Cullum held out his arms. "Come to me, Scheherazade."

What choice did she have?

Sherrie woke with a start, but not with any real surprise. The dreams, and her overheated reaction to them, were too frequent these days to surprise her. She was hot, and sweaty, and flushed, but the dreams were not what sent sharp fear through her. They affected her deeply, but her reaction upon waking this time had nothing to do with the life she fell back into in her sleep—and, sometimes, when she was awake.

It was what she'd said when half asleep that shocked her to full wakefulness.

Had she said what she'd thought she had to Minnie last night?

"Oh, please no," she whispered, as she ran her hands through her disheveled hair.

Pirates in London? She had, hadn't she? Said something to her daughter—to the child she so fiercely protected—about her father having been a pirate. Minnie must never know. Never. She'd seen to it long ago that her child was safe—from rumors, from innuendo, from the truth.

The problem was, Minerva May Hamilton was too smart for her own good. Far too smart for Sherrie's.

If it hadn't been for the very odd, and large, and handsome earl of PenMartyn, she wouldn't have spent all that restless time trying to get to sleep last night, and blurted out some foolishness—all right, some truth—at an impossible statement of her daughter's.

She looked quickly around the bedroom, as if even daring to think about him would make the man appear before her in a puff of opium smoke. She was half tempted to say the name aloud, just to prove that he wouldn't appear. Since she wasn't prepared to have him in her bedroom, she didn't take the fanciful risk.

Sherrie swung her legs over the side of the bed and called out, "Minnie!" instead.

It was early morning, not too long past dawn, and she was alone. She must have dreamed that Minnie had gone to sleep with her. She breathed a sigh of relief and listened carefully, but didn't hear anyone stirring in the big house. The air was cool and damp. Rain pattered against the windows, but no breeze blew across the width of the bedroom from the French doors she thought she'd left open the night before. Of course, she thought Minnie'd come to sleep with her as well. She'd thought—well, she'd thought many fanciful things last night.

She shook her head and ran her fingers through the heavy, tangled strands of her hair. Thank goodness the night was over.

Sherrie stood and stripped off her nightgown, then hurriedly dressed. She'd barely finished donning a simple skirt and shirtwaist when the bedroom door was pushed slowly open. Lhasi bounded in first, and jumped on the bed. Before Sherrie could react to the big animal's liberties, Minnie rushed in and with a long leap joined the dog.

Minnie looked at Sherrie from the center of a pile of covers. "You're awake."

Sherrie crossed the room and sat on the edge of the mattress. "Sorry. If I'd known you planned on joining me . . ."

"Rejoining you," Minnie corrected. "Lhasi needed to go outside, but we came back as soon as she was done."

Came back. So she hadn't dreamed her daughter's being in bed with her. Sherrie refrained from sighing, because showing any of her trepidation might bring questions. Asking questions of her daughter about their late night conversation would only make the girl remember. Minnie was uncannily observant. Best just to pretend neither of them had said a thing. Sherrie nodded, and looked her daughter over.

Minnie was still in her nightgown, her dark braids frosted with a sprinkling of raindrops, a bit of mud showed on her bare feet. Her gaze was bright and curious. So curious that Sherrie had trouble looking the girl in her bright blue eyes for very long. She could see questions that shouldn't be there in Minnie's eyes. Or at least imagined that she did.

My eyes. Her skin and hair belong to someone else, but thank God her eyes are mine. Sherrie felt herself blush as the thoughts crossed her mind, and prayed they didn't cross her face.

"What's the matter, Mama?"

To distract them both, Sherrie answered, "Look at you. Ira's going to have both our heads if he sees you looking like a muddy urchin."

Minnie leaned against her dog's sturdy back. "No, he won't. Not when I explain that I was being responsible. Ira likes it when I look after Lhasi."

"Maybe," Sherrie conceded. She stood and held out her hand. "I still better get you cleaned up before it's time for your lessons."

"It's too early for lessons." Minnie and the dog followed Sherrie off the bed. Minnie gave Sherrie a hug, while Lhasi stood on Sherrie's foot, expecting to be petted. Sherrie pulled her daughter closer with one arm and scratched the dog's head with the other. She wasn't in the habit of denying any affection to those she loved. Physical contact, in fact, was something she craved and was happy to give.

Pity there wasn't a man in the world who could ease the growing craving to be touched, not as mother or friend, but as a needy woman.

Best not to think about womanly cravings, either. Those feelings were bound to settle down eventually. All she required was to find some new project to settle her restless energy on, some new adventure. Cravings for travel and adventure were ones she could satisfy, and quite adequate, thank you very much. She wouldn't have to live like a civilized human being for more than a few months. Once she'd help her aunt get the girls settled with proper English husbands, she and Minnie and Ira and May could be off to the wild, dangerous, fascinating corners of the earth once more.

A knock sounded as she thought of Ira and May Gartner. She wasn't in the least surprised when Minnie opened the door and the Gartners were there. The clock on the mantel showed that it was only six-thirty in the morning, but the four of them were used to greeting the dawn together. Ira held May cradled like a China doll in his arms, as he often did. He carried her into the room while Minnie closed the door once more. May could walk with the help of a cane, but Ira said he didn't see why she should walk if she didn't have to, and May acquiesced. She'd been ill for nearly a month, and Ira cared for his wife's health with fierce, tender devotion.

Ira settled May on the chaise longue by the fireplace, smoothed her red silk robe, and kissed her before turning to slowly look around Sherrie's spacious quarters. Sherrie watched him while the very tall, long-limbed ex-miner, ex-gunfighter, constant scholar and dear, dear friend carefully took in all the details of the room.

"Looking for escape routes?" she asked.

He smiled. "Don't I always?"

Ira had a delicious smile, a rich-as-cream deep voice, and the biggest, brownest eyes in the world. With his curly dark hair, broad shoulders, and beautiful hands, he was one of the most glorious men Sherrie had ever seen. Sometimes she almost wished May hadn't seen him first. She smiled to herself and recalled that it was Ira who had seen May first. It had just taken him quite a while to convince his adored "Lady May" that he was the man for her. He'd started by finding a Virginia City laundry operator to teach him Chinese—Mandarin *and* Cantonese. Then he'd volunteered himself as May's tutor, taking her from pidgin dialect to perfect English in a matter of months.

Sherrie never tired of watching the pair together. Now, *that* was true love. It gave her hope for the existence of happily ever afters. If not for herself, at least for those she cared about.

Minnie and the dog followed Ira as he crossed, graceful and silent, to the French windows, where he checked the latch. "Should have had a look around yesterday," he muttered.

"Mama's fine," Minnie told him emphatically. "I'm looking after her."

Sherrie and May watched Ira as he tugged one of Minnie's braids, then continued examining the room. They exchanged smiles behind his back.

"I don't think we have to worry about anything in London," Sherrie said. "But thank you for your concern."

"He worries," May confided. "Even when he shouldn't. You take care of yourself better than anyone." May waved a delicate, long-nailed hand. "Actually, my dear, Ira is—what is the word?—stalling?"

All gazes turned to May, sitting as regally as an empress in her dragon-embroidered red robe. Her sleek black hair flowed around her delicately high-boned face, her porcelain complexion was back from sickly green to its usual pearly glow. She was smiling. Her dark eyes glowed with amusement, and some emotion it took Sherrie a moment to recognize.

"You're looking distinctly smug, May Gartner," she commented. Sherrie put her hands on her hips and looked from May to May's husband. To her surprise, Ira was blushing. "What does May mean—about your stalling? About what?"

Instead of answering her, Ira took Minnie's hand. "Let's go out on the balcony and have a little talk, sweetie." He closed the French doors behind them once he and Minnie were outside, leaving Lhasi with her wet nosed pressed up against the glass.

"It's raining out there," Sherrie complained. She looked suspiciously at May. "What's so secret that he has to take Minnie out in the rain to tell her?"

May folded her hands in her lap. Tiny hands. Everything but her heart, intelligence and courage was small about May. "He's the closest thing she has to a father."

How well Sherrie knew that, and how grateful

she was they'd had Ira. "If Jerry had lived—"

"Ira would still be the closest thing Minnie has to a father."

"Jerry was still a better choice than . . ." She took a deep breath and made herself say, "Cullum." May's eyes widened in shock. "I made a promise to a very holy man to deal with my past," Sherrie reminded her friend.

"Deal with our shared companion you must, but not this morning. Later we will have a good, long talk."

A thrill of terror went through Sherrie. "I don't think I'm ready to talk about it."

"I think you are. You must. I will make you do it soon."

Sherrie couldn't stop the half-amused indignation. She wasn't really so sure she should talk about him even with May. May had tried to bring up Cullum before. Sherrie had always avoided the subject. Now what was she supposed to do because of her promise? Confess her sins? Bare her soul? To whom? Her aunt? Her daughter? The world? Herself? Why? For what? What would May advise? Sherrie didn't have to ask her friend that. May would advise the last thing Sherrie would ever do.

"Shared companion?" Sherrie asked bitterly. "Is that what you call him?"

"And friend."

"Yours." She caught hold of her growing ire, made her tone reasonable. "I suppose if anyone could like such a complete son of a bitch, it's you." She wasn't sure if what she'd just said was a compliment. Deal with her past? Of course. As soon as hell froze over.

May waved a hand at her, her glance going to the glass doors. "Hush. Do you want your daughter to hear?"

"His name?"

"Your swearing. We're trying to raise a proper young lady in this household, not that you're any help, Mrs. Hamilton."

Sherrie threw back her head and laughed. With all her annoyance forgotten she looked her friend in the eye once more. "Just what is it you and Ira have to tell us?"

Minnie wondered if she was going to tell Ira. She knew she should. She should say, "A man was in Mama's room last night, I let him escape, and I'm sorry." But if she told Ira, there would be too many questions, too much fuss. New locks on doors. Lhasi would probably have to sleep outside to guard the house. She couldn't do that to Lhasi. It rained too much in London.

Before she could quite make up her mind, Ira knelt in front of her. She liked that he always did his best to be on eye level with her. "I love you, honey."

She loved Ira. Then she remembered the man from last night. She loved Ira, but . . . "I know."

He put his hands on her shoulders. Warm, strong, safe hands. He spoke very seriously. "I'm always going to love you. You're my favorite pupil. My best friend. I like being your bodyguard and your nanny and your traveling companion, but things are going to change a little in a few months."

She was used to Ira being serious, but his tone made her very suspicious. "Are you going away?"

He gave her a quick hug. "No. Of course not. There's something else that you need to know. Something you need to get used to."

Minnie studied Ira's face. Saw that he was happy, despite being worried and serious. She considered possibilities. May had been sick a lot lately. Ira and May were married. "Mama's ladies' maid married our ranch foreman. When she got sick they had twins." Minnie saw that Ira was blushing. She cocked her head to one side and asked, "Are you and May going to have twins?"

Ira's blush deepened. He opened his mouth and closed it. Finally, he said, "Child, have I ever mentioned that you are sometimes a bit too observant?"

"No."

"No. Of course not." He hugged her again. She squirmed away.

"Are you going to have twins? Mama's maid hasn't traveled with us since she had the twins."

Ira sat down on the wet balcony and pulled her into his lap. "Probably not twins. But we are going to have a baby."

She knew Ira wanted her to think about it. Ira was her teacher. He always wanted her to think and learn and analyze. What she thought was that even though he was holding her the way he often did, she didn't feel like she belonged in his embrace anymore.

"I don't like it," Minnie said. "I don't like it one little bit."

He sighed. "I understand, sweetie."

Minnie stiffened in his embrace. No, he didn't. Ira had a father. She'd met him. A grave man with a thick white beard. Her cousins had a father. She wanted a father of her own. She always had. She loved her Mama, and she loved Ira, but he'd never been quite enough. Now she wouldn't even have Ira anymore.

"I don't love you," she told him. "I don't need you." She struggled. Much to her hurt surprise, he let her go. Minnie sprang to her feet and turned to face him. "You think I don't mean it, but I do."

"Honey—"

She didn't stay to listen, but pulled open the balcony door and ran across her mother's bedroom. Both Mama and May called her name and Lhasi followed at her heels, but she didn't hear Ira's steps behind her as she ran out into the hallway and back to the nursery.

She didn't care.

She had a father of her own. She'd seen him. All she had to do was find him.

Chapter 7

There was a very English breakfast set up on the cherrywood sideboard in the breakfast room, lots of heavy, hearty food in silver and china serving dishes. It was mid-morning, and after having been up for hours, Sherrie looked at the vast selection with eager appetite. The room was bright and cheerful. Yellow curtains flanked the high windows, and a floral-patterned wallpaper and blue Aubusson carpet added to the airiness of the room. Sherrie gazed upon the array that included kippers and kidneys and settled on a thin slice of poached salmon, strawberries with cream, a flaky pastry, and a good, strong cup of black coffee.

Once her plate was full she took the seat at the head of the table while her yawning cousins filed in and began looking over the repast on the sideboard. Aunt Dora was already at the table, her attention on a thick pile of envelopes. She was grinning from ear to ear, which meant that the envelopes all held invitations to balls and recitals and tea parties. Already it appeared that the girls made a favorable impression on the British aristos at last night's party. Thank goodness for Anne Beaumont's patronage.

"Good thing I saved Annie from being attacked by that wildcat last year," Sherrie murmured between sips of coffee.

Only thinking of Lady Anne and wildcats put Sherrie in mind of the ice-eyed earl in Annie's ballroom. The memory of his face, the way he moved, and his tall, tautly muscled form sent a reaction through her so strong it set her trembling. Breath burned in her lungs, tears stung behind her eyes, and for a moment, everything but the nine-year-long pain went away. The world swirled, full of great fire-tinted clouds of smoke and fog. A man came out of the red, reeking smoke: graceful, dangerous, blood on his hands, and his eyes full of ice, and a voice that wasn't there said, *"You'll do as I say, and you'll do it now."*

He had been a wildcat, all right. They had called him the White Tiger.

It took a great deal of effort to put her cup down without spilling it.

"Did you say something, Sherrie?"

Reality returned, and Sherrie discovered that the crisp linen napkin was no longer in her lap, but crumpled tightly in her fist. As she forced her hand to relax, she glanced out a window and noticed that the sun was shining on the rainwashed English garden outside. The air was scented by the fresh-cut roses in the table's silver centerpiece. It wasn't the middle of a tropical night, and nothing burned but her mind and heart and body.

Sherrie took a deep, rose-scented breath and banked down the constant fire. Then she looked at the cousin who had spoken. Daisy didn't look concerned. Good. Memory might be vivid, but it didn't necessarily take too much time out of her busy day. Which was fortunate, since she had quite enough at present to deal with, thank you very much. Sherrie might have promised to face her past, but she certainly wasn't going to do it over breakfast with her relations.

"I was just being grateful to our patroness," she told her cousin. Though she could have done without Lady Anne's introducing her to the earl with the disturbing eyes and wickedly handsome face.

After a quick, disapproving glance at her mother, Daisy said, "Yes. Of course." The young woman was frowning when she went back to eating her breakfast.

Daisy, Sherrie well knew, did not approve of this foray into British society. She'd come along for the chance to get to the British Museum, not to be a debutante. She'd been promised a college education if she didn't find a husband over here. Aunt Dora thought that was some sort of threat, or at least a disappointing second choice for her girl, while it was exactly what Daisy wanted. Daisy was sensible, scholarly, and the family diplomat. Daisy didn't quite approve of adventures that took place outside the pages of books, but was too circumspect to say so.

Sherrie glanced from Daisy to her younger

sister. Now, Faith—Faith was another story. They were equally pretty, tall, nicely shaped, both auburn-haired and brown-eyed. While Daisy wasn't particularly interested in her good looks, Faith reveled in hers. Faith wanted the wardrobe and fancy parties that went with snaring a titled husband. It wasn't that she was a silly, vapid girl. She was just . . . fashionable. Sherrie didn't suppose that was a crime.

Of course, spending time with the girls made her feel old, and certainly jaded. She loved them, but they had so little in common with her that even coming up with conversation topics at the breakfast table was a trial for Sherrie. Which was a pity, because right now she really wanted a distraction from the crazed inside of her own head.

She'd had a scene with Minnie in the nursery. A small one, because her daughter was doing her best to hide her very strong feelings about having to share Ira with a baby. Minnie had cried a little, and she'd reluctantly agreed to apologize to Ira. Minnie had even agreed that she was bound to get used to the idea of not being the only child in the household. She hadn't been very convincing. Sherrie hoped that all Minnie needed was time to adjust. Sherrie had wanted to take Minnie shopping today, to see the sights, to be with her and distract her and soothe her hurt. But Minnie insisted that she wanted to be alone. Sherrie finally agreed to let Minnie have today to be by herself for a full day of sulking and feeling sorry for herself.

Pity she didn't get that option. She was

happy for her friends, but this long-hoped-for pregnancy signaled changes Sherrie wasn't ready to deal with yet.

She was saved from trying to think of something innocuous to say when Daisy said, "Who was that man you were talking to last night?"

Sherrie froze at the question.

It was Faith who answered. "Lord Gordon Summers." Her eyes were shining, and her voice full of awe as she went on. "Isn't he gorgeous? And so wise, of course. He lives just next door, you know. What a wonderful coincidence. I really must go hear him speak. Everybody does. Attending lectures at his Golden Light Mission is the current fashion."

Sherrie breathed a sigh of relief and forced away the image that Daisy's question had conjured. But her palm still flared with warmth at the memory of the soft brush of lips, and that warmth permeated deep into her blood.

"I remember Lord Gordon," Daisy told her sister. "Quite handsome, very intelligent. Though *you* don't normally pay attention to a man's brains," she added.

Faith wasn't the least insulted. "Mama says a woman shouldn't marry a smart man. That they ought to be good at making money but let their wives manage everything else. Besides," Faith added with the sort of fervor she normally saved for visits to her dressmaker, "Lord Gordon isn't the marrying sort. He's a holy man."

"Of course he is," Daisy answered dryly.

Faith took no notice of her sister's skepticism.

"All the best people attend his lectures, so of course we will, too."

"If you like, dear." Daisy looked steadily at Sherrie. "But I was referring to the dark-haired man who came and went so quickly last night. He was so—different."

Sherrie's heart lurched and her mouth went dry. She didn't want to talk about the Earl of PenMartyn, but was also absurdly glad she wasn't the only one who'd noticed that he was, as Daisy said, different.

Before Sherrie could manage a coherent answer, Faith chimed in, "Oh, yes, I noticed him, too. So did Mama. She said that he was far too old for us and that we needn't bother, what with the way he was looking at you and all."

"Like he wanted to eat you," Daisy added.

"Mama said you made a handsome couple."

A surge of annoyance swept through Sherrie as she turned from the girls to face her aunt at the other end of the table. "You were gossiping about me?"

"Never mind about that, now," Aunt Dora said. She was grinning from ear to ear. "That's old news." She pushed back her chair and waved an ivory-colored square of vellum as she got to her feet. "Girls, nothing is as important as this."

Sherrie watched the woman's gleeful behavior in consternation. "What?"

Daisy and Faith rushed to their mother's side from opposite ends of the table, demanding to know what she was so excited about. Dora spoke to Sherrie as the girls read the invitation.

"Darlin', you aren't going to believe where we're going tonight."

Everything else that had vexed her this morning, including all mention of Jack PenMartyn, was forgotten as Sherrie caught the excitement of the moment. "Where?"

Dora Comstock gave a crow of triumph. "We're having dinner with the Prince of Wales!"

"You'll grow to crave it." Their bodies were perfectly fitted together, skin on skin, but he rose to his knees as he spoke so he could look at her. He hadn't had her yet. He hadn't even begun to have her yet, though he'd spent a long time touching her, tasting her, before laying her down on the bed. He'd never waited so long to take a woman before, never wanted to savor like this, to wait and make the roaring need grow into consuming fire. It was agonizing.

He wanted to see the agony and the fire in her eyes before granting them both any release.

So, instead of burying himself inside her, he made himself wait, watch, speak. Her hair was spread out in heavy gold waves across the pillows. Her creamy skin gleamed with a faint sheen of sweat, pale against the black silk bed coverings. He cupped her breasts, smiled as the peaks rose at the soft brush of his thumbs. Her breasts were full and so very soft. He watched avidly as her hands curled at her sides, bunching the black silk in her fists. The triumph of making her want him shot through him, hot as lust, almost as satisfying. "You crave me already."

Her answer was an angry snarl. "The way you crave opium?"

"More." He allowed himself only one pipe today, and wouldn't have had that much if he'd known his ship was going to catch up with the Malay raiders sooner than expected. How his innocent missionary American Scheherazade had recognized the distinct sweet aroma that permeated his cabin was an intriguing question.

"Why don't you just do it?"

That could wait.

Her breathless, angry demand made him laugh. "Do what? This?" He stroked her, hard hands moving slowly and with unaccustomed gentleness from her breasts, across and down her long waist to her belly, underneath, then up the insides of her firm thighs, and further up, between them. His fingers came away damp. "You're better than poppy smoke."

Her breathing was ragged as her gaze flashed to his face, and just as quickly slid away. It infuriated him that she tried not to look at him. Infuriated, and amused him. She wouldn't look at him, but he looked his fill at her. He loved looking at her. He loved her anger. She didn't give him tears, hadn't tried out any maidenly blushes or self-pitying whimpers of humiliation. She kept to their bargain, touching him where he told her, giving her mouth to him for the hot, hard kisses he demanded. She instinctively knew that reacting like a proper little virgin would do no more than amuse him, for a short while, at least.

She kept her fear to herself. She gave him fury, banked, controlled, but alive in every part of her, in every movement and reaction. Fury that he was going to train into unbridled passion.

How could he not want her?

"You'll never forget me," he told her. *"I promise you that."*

The bitch hadn't recognized him!

The fury that erupted with the thought was translated into motion. Jack sprang forward, then blocked a blow from Jhou Xa with an outthrust arm and a clawing downward motion. The Shaolin monk countered with a pivot, a feint, and a high kick that struck Jack in the chest.

Jack fought fiercely, but suddenly the much smaller man was all over him, swift as lightning, the blows from hard hands and feet just as painful. Within a few short, agonizing minutes, Jack was on his back on the padded mat on the floor with Jhou Xa's callused heel resting across his throat.

"The dragon has once more bested the tiger," the old man said in his heavily accented English. He did not sound in the least pleased about his victory. Master Jhou stepped back. "You were not paying attention."

Jack didn't argue. He worked on controlling his ragged breathing as he climbed to his feet. He made his tight, aching muscles relax. He bowed to the master who had so easily beaten him. He forced himself to pay attention to the stern words that followed.

"At your level of training such a display of emotion is inexcusable. I did not even recognize the animal who fought against me. You seemed sane enough when we started, the madness Chan warned me of entered your eyes. I did not journey all this way only on the word of my old friend Chan that you would benefit from my teaching to discover a crude, undisciplined child at the other end of a too-long road. Approach me with anger and pain in your eyes once more and I return to my monastery the very same hour."

Jack didn't doubt the old man for a moment. Complicated as the journey back to China would be for the Jhou Xa, he was as good as his word. Jack dared not risk losing control again. Of course, he knew that already, and not just for the sake of training with this highly respected master of the fighting arts. And not just for the sake of his sanity. He deserved madness, but the world didn't deserve what he could do to it during his fits of madness.

But she didn't recognize me! The wild part of him shouted in a howl of fury and anguish. *She took even that from me.*

He bowed once more as he shut out the sound of the inner beast's voice and cries of sorrow. Beasts deserved neither voices nor emotions. "It will not happen again, Master Jhou."

The old man gave a curt nod. He moved to the end of the practice area and raised his arms in a defensive posture. "Again."

Jack moved to the opposite end of the mat. He ignored the time and the appointments that waited for him in the world above his basement practice room. He had to control his actions here before he could trust himself in the world above, the world where Scheherazade lived. He cleared his mind of everything but steely purpose, concentrated on the exercise with Jhou Xa, and moved gracefully forward.

"Good morning, David," Jack greeted his friend as he entered the library. "Either you're exceptionally early, or I'm later than I thought."

MacQuarrie made a brief show of consulting his pocketwatch. "The hour's late for me, but early for your sort."

Jack noticed that the mantel clock read just past eleven. "Most of *my* sort haven't risen from their beds yet. We do stay up quite late this time of year," he said, as he caught a whiff of brewing tea and warm bread.

The butler—not the officious Moss, but dear, reliable Hawton—had left pots of tea and coffee on a side table, as well as a covered breakfast tray. Hawton tried not to cluck like a mother hen over the Earl of PenMartyn's irregular eating habits. Instead, he made sure appropriate food and drink was available whenever Jack seemed likely to spend time in any particular room. A visit like this from Inspector MacQuarrie was always cause for Hawton and Cook to celebrate.

Jack moved eagerly toward the food, and noticed MacQuarrie already held a plate in one hand. "Scones?"

MacQuarrie nodded. He got to business as Jack filled a plate. "I trust you had an enlightening conversation with Summers last night. Did you find out anything about his influence with the Prince of Wales?"

MacQuarrie obviously had no notion why

Jack smiled at his choice of words. "What?"

"Enlightenment. It's a Buddhist concept, but I doubt you were making a pun."

MacQuarrie frowned. "I most certainly was not. But what about Summers?" he went on. "You did observe his movements, I trust?"

Trust. Jack fought back the sigh as the word hammered into him, fought back the anger at himself. Not because it wasn't deserved, but because allowing himself any emotion was dangerous. Jhou Xa had shown him that already this morning. He had failed his friend last night and lost control of himself more than once in less than twenty-four hours. All those old weaknesses were battering against the cage where he'd locked them—betrayal, self-indulgence, temper, lust most of all. He was too good at all of them. He'd thought he'd put all his hungers aside. Then he'd seen Scheherazade, and suddenly he was starving. But no longer for food. He put down his plate untouched and moved to stand by the fire that chased the damp morning air out of the library. It did nothing to warm the chill that settled on Jack's soul.

"Jack?" MacQuarrie waved his hand. "Are you in the same room with me, laddie?"

Jack didn't recall MacQuarrie moving to stand between him and the fireplace. Before Jack could answer, the library door opened, and Lady Anne Beaumont sailed in just ahead of the protesting Hawton. "I've flustered your man," she announced, pausing just long enough to close the door in the butler's face. Then she turned around and said, "I didn't have time to send in a note with my calling card. Yes, I know I'm being far too direct for your gentlemanly taste, but desperate situations call for desperate measures." She held her hands out to him as she crossed the room. "I have an emergency of the most serious proportions, and only you can help me. Hello, young man," she added, with a sweet smile toward MacQuarrie.

While MacQuarrie stared in astonishment, Jack took Lady Anne's hands and led her to a chair. Her demeanor sent gnawing worry through him. "What is it, Annie? What can I do?"

"He's so good," she said to MacQuarrie.

"I'm not," Jack snapped, the anger not for Lady Anne, but for himself and the lie he led and called a life.

Jack stepped away from Lady Anne's grasp and made quick introductions. After the polite formalities were observed, MacQuarrie said, "I think I had best leave you and Lady Anne to her business, my lord."

"Oh, no," Lady Anne spoke quickly. "I interrupted *your* business. I'll be off as soon as I've secured Jack's help." She smiled winningly at MacQuarrie. "I'm sure I can trust the discretion of a man in your position, Inspector."

MacQuarrie looked both bemused and charmed. "No doubt you can, Lady Anne."

Before either of them could say any more, Jack said, "Annie, what's this about?"

She looked up at him, gaze full of earnest

concern that melted his rising temper. "The Prince of Wales."

Jack exchanged a quick glance with MacQuarrie. "What about the prince?"

Lady Anne looked from one man to the other. "It is a rather complicated matter," she told them. "And a political one."

"Then tell us," Jack said. It took effort to keep his tone mild and encouraging, when the temptation was simply to shake the woman's news out of her. Damn his quick temper, and damn temptation, and damn Lady Anne, too, if she didn't get on with it! Jack took a deep breath and added politely, "Please, Annie."

"I've had a small dinner party for the Prince of Havelstein planned for weeks. Every last, blessed detail planned. You know how the Havelsteins are about their precedence and their royal dignity. The highest sticklers in all of European society."

Small for Lady Anne meant no less than fifty guests, he was sure. "They don't come to just anyone's parties," Jack agreed. "Their attendance is quite a plum for you as a hostess."

"It's quite a pain, actually. Not that I would have it any other way," she added with a smile. Then her anxious demeanor returned. "But I don't consider myself a political hostess."

"The Principality of Havelstein is hardly of political importance. It's no more than a hundred miles square, as I recall."

"Most of those miles go straight up," Lady Anne added. "Very mountainous place. Cold as well. Probably why the royal family prefer visiting their relatives in London much of the year. As you may recall, my dear Jack, the Havelstein relatives reside at Windsor and Buckingham Palace. So the political complication to my little dinner party is the particular relative the prince has informed me he's bringing with him to my dinner."

"The Prince of Wales," Jack guessed. She nodded. "But Annie, I should think you'd be delighted."

"You obviously don't know Bertie."

He'd had the honor of meeting Prince Albert Edward a few times. The man was charming, intelligent, but restless and in need of some occupation other than being heir to a long-lived autocratic mother. MacQuarrie had good reason to worry about unsavory influences on a middle-aged man burning for the chance to start a life of his own. Still, he didn't see what Lady Anne could be worried about. "It's a social coup."

"It's a bloody nuisance. You try reorganizing the seating arrangements for this sort of an affair on such short notice, young man, and you'd soon get yourself a wife to handle such difficult and dangerous work for you."

Jack laughed and ran a hand restlessly through his thick black hair. "Yes, but—"

"But the point is, Havelstein is bringing Bertie, and Bertie is bringing that man."

"What man?"

"Lord Gordon Summers. Bertie's calling him his advisor on Eastern affairs—as if the prince needs advisors on having affairs."

"Summers? The prince is bringing Lord Gordon?"

"Won't come without, and Havelstein won't come unless Bertie's along. Months' worth of planning turned on edge just like that." She gave a loud sigh. "I've already done my social duty to Summers for the Season. I know Gordon's philosophy is the latest rage, so I was content to let him wheeze away about his religion last night. One night a year with the man is amusing, and after all, his sister and I did attend school together, so I owe the family something." She stood and placed herself toe to toe with Jack, looking at him as though it were all somehow his fault. "So, of course I need you at dinner as well."

She sounded as if it were all settled.

Jack couldn't imagine why. He'd performed *his* social duty by Lady Anne once already this Season. Last night's disaster had been enough. He'd seen too much, felt too much, almost done too much. He needed time alone to make sure his bestial nature was under tightly leashed control. If he couldn't kill the animal, he had to cage it. For Scheherazade's sake, he dare not go anywhere their paths might cross, and that meant any social gathering at any time during the Jubilee Season.

He started to decline Lady Anne's invitation, then he caught sight of the barely suppressed excitement on MacQuarrie's face. It recalled him to his duty to the man. He kept his promises. He'd promised to look into the matter of Lord Gordon Summers and his Holy Light or

Golden Light or whatever the man's mission was called.

"But what do you need me for?" he asked Lady Anne.

"Surely you can work it out for yourself, my dear."

He shook his head. "Afraid not, Annie."

"To counteract Summers' effect on Bertie, of course. The Havelsteins are notoriously strait-laced. Try to turn any talk about the Far East to more interesting aspects of the place if Summers starts going on about his chanting. You *do* have some interesting anecdotes about the place, I trust?"

After a noticeable hesitation, Jack conceded, "I do."

"Good." She headed toward the door. "I'll expect you promptly at eight."

For MacQuarrie's sake he dared not refuse. Surely there was no chance of meeting Scheherazade at the same dinner where princes were the guests of honor. Wealthy upstart Americans with husband-hunting relations did not get invited into the august presence of the likes of royalty, especially not patricians with overinflated ideas about the blueness of their blood, such as the rulers of Havelstein.

"Eight it is, dear lady. I wouldn't miss it for the world."

Chapter 8

Sherrie felt trapped, sensed it as soon as she walked through the Beaumonts' front door. She didn't know who had set the trap, but she trusted her senses well enough to know one existed. There was no physical danger, of course. She knew that even though she carefully scanned the overdecorated hallway and the overdressed crowd moving along the receiving line. She would almost welcome physical danger, as it was the easiest sort to deal with.

Of course, she wasn't surrounded by any dangerous people tonight, but by princes and dukes and their kin. These were people who *knew* their pedigrees were more important than all the gold in the world. She had no idea why Anne Beaumont had included her and her family at this glittering affair on such short notice.

She didn't necessarily disagree with the princes' opinions of themselves. She wasn't particularly intimidated by princes, either. Wouldn't have been even if she wasn't obscenely rich. She might be the daughter of a Dutch immigrant who'd struck it rich in the California gold fields, then moved on to strike silver, then gold in Nevada, and used that money to build ranches and timber and rail empires. But neither money nor position nor birth meant anything to Sherrie Hamilton. It was what a person did that mattered. It was up to each person to find out what was important to him and then take it from there. Wealth had been important to her father. Gaining social acceptance meant the world to Aunt Dora. If blood was what mattered to most of the people here, that was fine with Sherrie.

But while most people here already knew who they were and what they wanted, Sherrie had looked in the mirror earlier this evening and had had a disconcerting moment of not knowing who on earth she was. The moment passed, but the lost feeling burrowed deep inside her heart. She could feel it there now, like a physical weight. That, coupled with an odd, electric tingling of anticipation, had her as close to completely spooked as she could get.

When a hand touched hers, Sherrie very nearly jumped out of her skin. "Where are you, girl?"

She managed to get her feelings under control, and turned a smile on her aunt. "I have no idea."

Dora did not look pleased. "Well, don't get a fit of nerves on me now, Sherrie Hamilton. You're my ace card with these Limeys, darling," she whispered, as they moved closer to the two royal couples at the head of the line. "Remember that. It's your charm and, frankly, your money that's got my girls into parties like this. I need you."

Aunt Dora was right, they were here on a mission. She had her role to play. Sherrie gave her aunt a contrite look and fixed a smile on her face as another step brought her face to face with Prince Albert Edward himself. Queen Victoria's eldest, the heir to the British throne, smiled back as their gazes met. She curtsied. Someone officious told the prince her name.

Unexpectedly, the prince kissed her hand. "How delightful to meet you, Mrs. Hamilton."

"I'm honored, Your Royal Highness."

"I've heard a great deal about you from Lady Anne, Mrs. Hamilton, but find your appearance a source of delight. It's a delight to meet an adventuress who is not only bold, but beautiful. We must talk."

Did the man know another word besides "delight"? "I am at your disposal, sir." She regretted her choice of words even as she said them.

His eyes lit with merriment. His gaze also swept over her with a boldness she wouldn't have accepted from any other man in the room. "Happy to hear it, madam. Happy to hear it." He kissed her fingertips again. Lingeringly. "Until later."

Oh, dear. Sherrie held her temper at the man having dared to flirt with her in front of his wife, curtsied once more, and moved on.

Of course, it was just flirting. Quite harmless,

normally, but she was acutely aware of the low murmur of consternation that followed her while she was presented to Princess Alexandra and the royalty from Havelstein. Those few seconds with the prince were going to cause a bit of gossip. Aunt Dora would not be happy.

Then again, the gossip would no doubt garner a few more invitations from the fashionable and the curious, Sherrie decided, as she moved out of the line at last and into the reception room. The more places they were able to show off the girls, the better for the husband hunt. The realization didn't help her annoyance at being singled out when she wanted to hide. Wanting to hide, she squared her shoulders and walked into the room with her head held high.

The first person she saw was the Earl of PenMartyn.

The furiously jealous look he turned on her very nearly sent her to her knees as the trap sprang closed.

He had the most beautiful mouth in the world. It wasn't right or fair, but it was so. She shouldn't want to trace the contours of his lips as he slept, but she did. She shouldn't want to stay awake watching him as though it was some secret, newly discovered pleasure. She shouldn't be haunted by the memory of the feel of his mouth on hers, recall the texture, the taste of him. He had poisoned her with that mouth. She could feel the slow heat of it coursing through her blood and bones and tainting her soul. He'd marked her with his beautiful mouth. In the morning she'd be able to see the bruises.

Some of those bruises had never healed.

And he still had the most beautiful mouth in the world.

"Well, I must say, you've made quite an impression."

Sherrie turned a bleak gaze on Lady Anne as the woman put a hand on her arm. The woman's calmly amused expression brought Sherrie back from the precipice of memory. She caught her breath, and managed to turn the gasp for air into a self-deprecating laugh. "Yes. But on whom?"

When she looked back toward Cullum Rourke, he wasn't there. Jack PenMartyn, however, was no longer looking her way. He was standing next to Lord Gordon Summers, holding a perfectly normal conversation.

Oh, nonsense, Sherrie thought. The Earl of PenMartyn was magnificent to gaze upon, but the sight of him all decked out in formal attire was nothing to be afraid of, or even attracted to. The trap, after all, was of her own making. She'd noticed him glancing her way and had read some deep, heatedly sexual, horrible meaning into a casual look. It wasn't him, it was the ghost of Cullum Rourke she put between herself and any man she might be vaguely attracted to. She was going to have to exorcise that ghost, and soon, but not because of Jack PenMartyn.

Before Lady Anne could answer her question, Sherrie said, "Thank you so much for inviting us tonight. My aunt and the girls are so pleased to be here."

"Which implies that you are not?"

Sherrie blushed, but she didn't flinch from her friend's discerning look. She kept her attention firmly on Lady Anne, although she couldn't help but imagine that the earl was watching her. "I'm afraid I'm feeling a bit dizzy."

Lady's Anne's smile was decidedly triumphant. "What a lovely reaction you're having. I had one like that myself once."

Sherrie doubted it. "Really?"

"Oh, yes. The very first time I saw my dear Robert, the world just reeled."

"I hardly think that Prince Edward—"

"We call him Bertie. And I wasn't referring to your reaction to *him*. Oh, no." Lady Anne had Sherrie by the arm, her fingers clamped as solid as a vise. She kept Sherrie in tow as she headed toward Lord Gordon and the Earl of PenMartyn. "I really do insist the two of you get to know each other better."

So this was the trap she'd sensed. The one that had been set, not the one she brought on herself.

She couldn't wait for morning. She had to go. Now. While he slept, like the dead or the drugged, or both. Like a man at peace with what he'd done, what he'd do again and again for the next month. A month. Emotions boiled through her, her senses were flayed by the feel of his skin on hers, the taste of him was still fresh on her mouth. She couldn't live with the wanting.

She couldn't live.

Sherrie pushed down the desperation by fierce concentration on the danger presented here and now. She was to be the victim of one of the worst crimes a good woman could commit—first degree blatant matchmaking. Oh, damn!

"Annie," she said, with a cheerfulness that masked her very real anger, "You're incorrigible."

Sherrie wondered which of the pair had been picked as her future mate. Summers and PenMartyn were as different as night and day, but shared the kind of intensity that automatically drew the attention of others to them. Even Sherrie couldn't manage to look at the pair without a certain amount of feminine speculation, and she'd had plenty of practice at ignoring men.

Both men were tall, well built, handsome. Lord Gordon was long and lean, with fine-boned features, golden blond hair, and a fervent demeanor. Gordon Summers burned like the sun. Jack PenMartyn, more powerfully built, his coloring a mixture of Celtic black and white, was a cold dark night in contrast to Summers' openly passionate fire. Sherrie didn't think there was a woman in the world who wouldn't be attracted to one or the other of them. For herself, she found Summers' appeal too facile and easy. PenMartyn was the cool, controlled sort, the kind where the fire ran deep and strong, like lava flowing under a glacier. There was a certain kind of woman who enjoyed the challenge of finding out just what it took to melt the ice that covered all that dangerous fire.

Sherrie prided herself on *not* being that kind of woman.

"You'll thank me for this in the long run, my dear. Jack, my darling," Lady Anne said, as they came up to the men, "You are to act as Sherrie's escort, dinner companion, and general dogsbody this evening."

Chapter 9

Damn you to hell! Jack wasn't sure he didn't say the words aloud as the vehement thought streaked across his mind. The problem was, Jack didn't know which of the women he was cursing—Scheherazade, who didn't recognize him, or Lady Anne, who had no idea who he really was.

He did say, "Delighted, Annie," in a voice so normal it amazed him.

"Delight," Scheherazade responded, as Lady Anne left to pursue other hostess duties. "That seems to be the word for this evening." The years had made her rich, velvety voice deeper.

He took a step closer to the last woman in the world he should be near. The excitement of being close to her cut through him like a hot knife, though he told himself any emotion at all was his enemy. Enemies were for killing, especially the primal male need only this woman could rouse.

Perhaps he imagined that she wasn't as poised as she appeared. Scheherazade was no more pale now than when she'd first turned away from the Prince of Wales. No, it wasn't imagination. She did not look well—she looked upset and furious and very wary, though she covered it from those who did not know her well. But he should not flatter himself that he was the cause of her being upset. He'd watched while Bertie had made an obvious public overture to her. Such attention was enough to unnerve any sensible woman.

He managed to meet her gaze as if he were looking at a mere acquaintance. He even managed to remember her name. "I am completely at your service, Mrs. Hamilton."

"As am I," Lord Gordon added, stepping to Scheherazade's other side. "Lady Anne surely doesn't mean for Jack to monopolize your entire evening."

Scheherazade gave a bright and breathy laugh. Her attention shifted to the other man. "Surely not, Lord Gordon." Please not, she thought. The sapphire blue evening gown she wore was off the shoulder and sleeveless. The Earl was not wearing gloves, and the arm he touched was bare. She did not think Jack PenMartyn even knew he was touching her. She was barely aware of anything else. That her voice worked at all amazed her. "Perhaps you should both escort me in to dinner."

The eagerness with which she turned to Summers angered Jack more than the other man's daring to approach her. He should be grateful for any distraction. He said to Summers, "Ah, but Lady Anne does mean for Mrs. Hamilton to be at my side this evening." He looked back at Scheherazade. "Lord Gordon is here in attendance on His Highness."

"Not for the entire evening," Summers countered. "While he could only find a few hours' time this evening to listen to my opinions on the Asian delegations he is to entertain on Her Majesty's behalf, this is a social occasion as well. I'm sure we won't continue any meaningful discussion until after the ladies have left us after dinner."

Jack wanted very much to point out to the pompous fool that the prince already had competent advisors on Asian matters in the government. He wanted to tell Summers to leave Scheherazade alone, to stop looking at her as if she might somehow be available to him, to stop trying to impress her. Duty propelled him to pursue Summers' intentions despite what he wanted.

But it was Scheherazade who asked a question before he could. "You're teaching His Highness Buddhist scripture?"

"Not at all, my dear," Summers answered with a condescending smile. "It's hardly my place to attempt to convert the future head of the Church of England to another religion, no matter how much I believe in it. It is my firsthand knowledge of the Oriental mind that the prince wishes to draw upon. While His Highness and I have enjoyed philosophical discussions, I do my teaching for those who can benefit most from the wisdom of the East. Such as your young cousins," he continued. "I was quite pleased when they attended this afternoon's lecture, my dear."

"You were pleased and I was surprised. I thought the only thing on their minds would be tonight. Instead, Faith has talked of nothing but the *Lotus Sutra* since she came home."

Actually, Faith had done nothing but talk about what a wonderful way Lord Gordon had of speaking to each one in the room as if he were the only one there. How his wise gaze had rested on her more than once and seen deep into her soul. Faith had talked about his height, his hair, his eyes, his mellifluous voice, his gentle wisdom, and how she could hardly wait to hear him speak again. Never mind meeting the Prince of Wales, Faith was eager to come tonight just for the chance of being in the same place with her new teacher.

Daisy's report was that Lord Gordon wasn't a half bad snake-oil salesman and revival tent preacher, though she thought that Baptist fellow who swung through Nevada every summer did it better. Daisy had been a bit disappointed that there hadn't been snake handling and speaking in tongues, but she supposed the Brits were too reserved to provide that kind of entertainment.

Sherrie tried not to show her amusement at her cousins' differing opinions of Lord Gordon. "The girls tell me that you've just accepted an invitation to give a lecture on Buddhism two nights from now at a charity function. Faith has every intention of having the entire family attend."

He smiled indulgently. "Not just any charity function, my dear, but an evening of intellectual entertainment that will help raise funds for a children's hospital. Several ladies on the committee have persuaded me to speak in public. In fact, I'm told Lord PenMartyn here also helped arrange the event."

"I did not organize anything. I donated some funds, merely," Jack said.

"And the land for the proposed institution. He's quite a famous philanthropist, you know."

She wasn't sure she wanted to know any more of Jack PenMartyn's good points. She didn't want to know any more than the way to the exit when a man was thrust on her as a suitor. She kept her focus on Lord Gordon's interest in talking about himself. "I suppose there must be ambassadors from all over the world come to pay their respects to the Queen on her anniversary."

"Just so," Lord Gordon replied, with a wise nod of his leonine head.

Summers was a handsome man. He certainly drew the eye. Sherrie could understand Faith's enthusiasm for him. She found him easy to talk to, with his direct gaze, air of authority, and seemingly genuine interest in everything she had to say. The truth was, she didn't like him one bit. She'd watched him turn his charm on everyone he'd met last night, and had had it turned on her more than she'd wanted in the hours before the Earl of PenMartyn had shown up to ruin her evening. Sherrie supposed she could easily be wrong about Summers, but she didn't trust Lord Gordon Summers, not that she could put her finger on why. Still, she found it easier conversing with the charming lion before her than with the silent tiger at her side.

Jack's no tiger, she reminded herself sharply, but he was the man Lady Anne wanted her to marry. His eyes just reminded her too strongly of the past she was sworn to conquer. His eyes, his hair, his height, the dangerous grace in the way he moved. Other than that, he was perfectly harmless. Except that she was finding it very hard not to give in to the urge to sway toward him, to fit her body neatly against his, hip to hip.

She was finding it even harder not to burn up into a woman-shaped pile of cinders, now that his hand had moved from her arm to rest lightly at her waist. She should move away from Jack PenMartyn, but found it impossible to do so.

She concentrated very hard on her conversation with Summers. "You're advising the prince on these Asian ambassadors and their customs?"

"The ones I'm familiar with, yes. The East is a large place, as you well know."

Sherrie nodded. And Jack PenMartyn's fingers slid slowly, subtly, intimately up her spine. She could not move. She didn't want to move. No one had touched her like this in—she didn't want—she forced her attention to focus on Gordon Summers.

There was a catch in her voice when she

asked, "Wh-which countries are you informing His Highness about?"

"China, of course, my dear, and one or two of the other places I've visited. Are you familiar with an island country called Kuzay?"

Well, Khan Rhu Limpok did try to buy me once, she recalled. *And there is the small matter of that knife fight.* "I'm vaguely familiar with the place."

"After having spent some time there, I would not say that I'm sure Kuzay can exactly be called a country," Summers went on. "A mongrel collection of half-caste pirate scum from all over Asia is a more apt description."

Yes, that was the Kuzay she remembered. "So I've heard."

"The man who calls himself the ruler, the Great Khan, has made his way to London hoping to meet the Queen."

"Really?" The Great Khan couldn't possibly be Rhu Limpok, could it? Surely one of his rivals, or his sons, or even that hot-tempered great wife of his had done the old scoundrel in by now.

"Can you imagine the cheek of these pirates, wanting to present themselves to our Queen?"

Jack PenMartyn's hand came to rest on the back of her neck. She wasn't aware of anything but his touch for several moments. His fingers began to toy with the clasp of the pearl necklace she wished very much she hadn't worn. Not that anyone from Kuzay was likely to see it, or her, during their visit to London. It sounded as if Lord Gordon was doing his best to keep such socially unpresentable scum in their place.

Jack's hand moved away from her throat. The fire he ignited inside her remained.

"Are you all right, my dear? You look rather pale."

She is not your *dear.*

Jack would have been happy to slice the impertinent man's head off and present it to Scheherazade as a trophy, but he kept all but his raging thoughts still as the two of them talked. He filed away the information about a delegation from Kuzay. Later he would let himself consider what to do about having yet another piece of the past come stalking out of the night. Right now all he cared about was being close to Scheherazade.

Scheherazade. Lord, how hard it was not to lean close and whisper her true name in her ear. Names had power. Speaking hers would give him the power to bring her back to him, to remind her of the claim he'd made on her all those years ago.

A claim you renounced, he reminded himself, though for the moment he couldn't remember why.

"What's mine I keep."

"Leave me alone!" Her words were an insane shout above the storm.

He halted for a moment, watched as the girl was doused with spray when a wave crashed against the side of the ship. She looked like a miserable, half-drowned rat, and he still wanted her.

"I'll jump!"

"No."

"Don't touch me again. Not ever. I can't live knowing that—"

He laughed as he moved toward her, fast and furious. Rain lashed down, the heaving deck was slippery with water, but he moved with a sailor's barefoot sureness across the well-known planking. The girl's body might as well be naked, for all the protection the thin, soaked-through chemise afforded it. Her expression was wild in the irregular illumination of spears of too-close lightning. They'd outrun the dangerous center of the storm, but sailing through this was no easy feat. He left his men to minding the ship and kept his concentration on the girl. Her eyes were fixed on him as well. He knew for certain that her trembling came more from her awareness of his nakedness than from any reaction to the storm.

"I want to die."

"I don't care." If it hadn't taken him a moment to come awake from satiated sleep when she'd pushed herself off the bed and fled from his cabin, they wouldn't be out in the rain talking now. He still wasn't quite away from the memory of how it had felt plunging deep into the soft, secret heat of her, of claiming what no other man had known, of what he wanted no other man ever to know. *"What's mine I keep,"* he repeated.

Tears of fury streamed down her face, mixing with the rain. Fury that had little and everything to do with him, he knew. He saw the physical signs of what she was truly running from. She feared what he'd awakened in her more than she feared him. The wet, clinging material couldn't hide what she wanted to deny, the craving for passion that she

*wanted to die rather than face. He saw the taut
straining of her muscles, the panting breaths, the
telltale puckering of the tips of her breasts. He could
almost smell her heat. With one swift move he
grabbed her around the waist and pulled her back
onto the deck. Her hands came up, but instead of
fighting him off, she made a quick gesture of denial
and surrender before dropping them to her sides.*

*His laughter was hard and triumphant as he
swept her up and turned. Within moments they were
back within the shelter of his tiny cabin. Within another moment they were on the narrow bed. His
mouth was on hers, hungry and plundering. His
hands were on her, cupping her breasts, teasing the
taut nipples with the pad of his thumb, then suckling
them through the wet cloth. She moaned and cried
out, and begged. First for him not to touch her. At
first, and for a while. He tasted the sea salt on her
skin, all over, warmed the chill from her, turned it
into fire in her veins. Turned her into—*

You know what you turned her into, Jack
told himself with harsh anger, as he pushed the
memory away. He didn't want to think about
it anymore, but he couldn't stop the accusations
that shouted inside his mind.

He'd taken a confused, frightened, but spir-
ited girl and turned her into a creature trained
to satisfy his every sexual whim. *His* creature,
another, more demanding voice deep in his
mind reminded him. His superb, beautiful,
hungry, insatiable animal. His. Then. Now. Forever.

The knowledge that some man named Hamilton had dared to touch what was his, that Gor-

don Summers and the damned Prince of Wales
dared to look at her, sent rage boiling through
him. Tempted him to remind her quickly and
decisively just who her passion belonged to.
Nine years could make no difference between
them.

Don't be a fool.

Jack had no idea how even one reasonable
thought made its way to the surface of his
mind, but it was like a slap in the face and a
dousing of freezing water combined. He fought
down raging emotions, fought his way back to
some precarious measure of sanity, and discovered that only a few moments had passed.
Scheherazade and Summers were still holding
a pleasant conversation. No one had noticed
him go mad. The mask hadn't slipped. He
could even feel a pleasant, vapid smile tugging
up his lips.

Sherrie concentrated very hard on Gordon
Summers. Caught between the intensity of the
two men, she couldn't make herself move. Fortunately, Summers' natural charisma acted as a
counterbalance to the unwanted fascination that
drew her to Jack PenMartyn.

"His Highness is most interested in the Orient," Lord Gordon went on. "Which is where I
think your services would prove most helpful,
my dear." He chuckled.

Sherrie noticed that it was a warm, fruity, far
too self-satisfied sound. From it her imagination
conjured an impossible vision of Summers rubbing his hands together as he gloated evilly
over some wicked scheme. She knew her imag-

ination was being far too active this evening, though she blamed the silent PenMartyn rather than the verbose evangelist.

"I'm hardly qualified to advise a British prince on any subject," she answered Summers. She doubted Bertie would be interested in her opinions. Her cleavage most certainly, but not her opinions.

"You underestimate your appeal, my dear."

Sherrie bridled at last at Summers' smug expression and tone. "Lord Gordon, please, I dislike being spoken to in such a familiar way by someone of such a short acquaintance. I realize we Americans are considered somewhat informal and forward, but I assure you I am not."

Scheherazade's politeness had the quality of sheathed steel. Jack almost laughed. He almost took her in his arms. How damnably stupid it was of him always to be so affected by any show of this magnificent woman's spirit.

Rather than being put off, Summers looked contrite. "I certainly meant no offense." He looked meaningfully at Scheherazade's arm. "It was my understanding that you and I were of longer acquaintance than you and Lord Pen-Martyn. Perhaps you and he have met before? Perhaps in China? I understand that the three of us have travel in the Far East in common."

Jack noticed that his hand was clasped around Scheherazade's arm just as Lord Gordon spoke. The gasp that escaped his lips was of bereavement and horror as he dropped his hand and took a quick step away. He didn't know when he first touched her. He didn't know how long he'd been touching her. He didn't even know if she was aware he'd been touching her. He only knew that emptiness rushed back into him the instant he let her go.

But this was London. He was a different man; she was a different woman. The small world he inhabited watched them. Years of practice kept him firmly in the role of the Earl of PenMartyn. The logical response for the earl to make was to apologize for such forward behavior.

Before he could decide whether to apologize or simply flee, she turned to him. Her china blue gaze riveted his. For a flicker of a moment her eyes held a flare of searing heat, then hatred extinguished whatever other emotion there could be between them.

Sherrie jerked her gaze from the too-well-known blue ice eyes of the tall man before her. She took in the rest of him in a quick, hard glance. "You've been to China?"

He didn't answer. He didn't need to. In a rush, the truth became clear to her. Of course he'd been to China. Time had changed him, the setting was all wrong, but her first instinct had been correct.

Her veins ran with ice. She was beyond coherent thought. Her heart was a hard, burning knot in her chest. Tears stung behind her eyes.

It was Cullum. His shoulders had somehow grown broader, his features less harsh; his voice had changed. She saw him before her now in the guise of a gentleman. His hands were clean, the nails neatly trimmed, his scent was of bay rum rather than opium and sex. He wore a stiff

white shirt and the impeccably tailored dark
formal clothes that proclaimed his class. She remembered him in loose silk trousers that clung
to his hard-muscled thighs, an unfastened robe
revealing his thickly furred chest, a heavy
beard, and long, thick hair concealing all but
the wide, decadent mouth and hungry, hard
eyes. Only the colors he wore hadn't changed.

While he stood still as a statue, her gaze
swept once more from the Earl of PenMartyn's
highly polished shoes to his perfectly combed
hair. She still avoided looking into his eyes.

"Damn," she said, "but you always did look
good in black."

Without knowing how she made her body
move, Scheherazade VanHarlen Hamilton
turned and walked from the room.

Chapter 10

❧❧❧

"That," said Lord Gordon, "is the first time I have ever seen a woman turn into a tigress before my eyes." When Jack would have followed her he somehow found Summers blocking his path. "Magnificent woman," the fool blathered on. His eyes were bright, his amusement vast. "I can't imagine just what set her off, can you, PenMartyn? Something I said? Something you did?"

Jack did not know why he didn't simply break the man's neck and step over the body as it fell.

Gordon Summers watched the Earl of PenMartyn's reactions with barely concealed glee. He was delighted to find out that his guess that the American was the legendary White Tiger's woman was correct. He was amused to discover that at first the Hamilton woman had been unaware of Cullum Rourke's true identity. It was very useful to know that Rourke—St. John PenMartyn—still wanted his golden whore.

And she wanted him. She just didn't know it yet. *Not only is this going to be useful*, Summers thought, *it's going to be fun.*

He couldn't let himself be distracted by the anticipation of pleasure. He couldn't let Pen-Martyn get what he wanted just yet, either. Summers was in control. The lovers would learn it soon enough. Right now Summers chose to keep PenMartyn dancing attendance on him.

"It looks as if we're about to go in to dinner," he said. "The prince seems unoccupied at the moment. Perhaps now is a good time for me to have a word with him. If you'll excuse me, Lord PenMartyn?"

Just as he was about to push Summers aside to follow Scheherazade, Summers' words brought Jack back to reality. Back to the present, to Beaumont House. Back to his duty.

He couldn't leave. What he wanted didn't matter.

Jack remembered his promise to MacQuarrie, the reason he'd come to the party tonight. Duty was all he had left. He certainly didn't have honor. He knew just how flimsy a thing truth was. The only thing that kept him sane, civilized, of some slight value in this world, was duty.

Scheherazade didn't want him. He had no right to want her. She was probably about to bring the world crashing down around his ears. In the time he had left, he would find out what Summers was up to with the Prince of Wales.

Jack made himself at least *try* to stop thinking

about the only woman who'd ever meant a damn thing to him. He concentrated on what others needed him to do instead. He even managed to smile as he said to Summers, "Why don't I come with you?"

"What a good idea," Summers answered. He gestured Jack forward with an elegant sweep of his hand. "I'm sure Bertie will be interested in your views of the Orient as much as mine. You have such a unique perspective on it, having been in trade in that part of the world."

If only you knew. Jack kept the thought to himself and refused to be offended by Lord Gordon's mildly insulting allusion to the rumor that Jack had actually stooped to working for his daily bread while living in the East. What he'd worked at was no one's affair, though Scheherazade would probably soon make the sordid details public. "As you say, Lord Gordon. Unique. Lead on."

"What are you doing here?"
"Waiting for you. What—?"
May's question was drowned out as Sherrie slammed the bedroom door as hard as she could. The violence of the action gave Sherrie a certain amount of satisfaction. Not much.

Once the door was closed she turned back to her friend. "You were saying?" The words came out bright, brittle, sharp, dangerous. Just the way she was feeling.

May was seated on a chaise near the fireplace, a book in her lap. She did not get to her feet. That wasn't easy for her to do. But for a moment she did look like she wanted to run. She gently closed the book instead. "You are paler than a white ghost should be. And looking for something to kill, I think. What is the matter, Scheherazade?"

Sherrie walked toward where May Gartner sat. "What are you doing here? Where's Ira?"

May continued to look at her steadily, deliberately calm. "Don't be evasive. Tell me what's wrong."

"I'm not ready to talk about it yet."

"I was waiting for you," May told her. "We haven't had a chance to be together for a while. I managed to get through the day without being ill. So I was able to convince Ira to go off and have a look at London. I thought I would have time to read for a while before you came home, but here you are."

"Here I am."

"Did the Comstocks leave this foreign prince's party early as well?"

"No."

"I didn't think so. What drove you away from such an important evening?"

Sherrie wanted to be alone. She wanted to smash things. To scream out her fury until her throat was raw. She couldn't remember the details of how she got back to the Mayfair mansion, though she had some recollection of a solicitous butler helping her into her carriage. She did remember slamming every door she'd encountered on her route to her bedroom. She couldn't scream and smash things with May in the room. It might disturb her friend's delicate condition.

Sherrie reached up to unfastened the neck-lace—the damned heavy slave collar—and managed after two or three tries, hampered by her trembling fingers. Once the thing was off, she did not throw it across the room, but did let the priceless necklace fall onto the floor.

May wanted to know. And there was no one else she could tell. "He's here. In London. The bastard's in London."

The book dropped to the floor.

"Oh," May said, after the look of surprise faded from her eyes. "Good."

"Good?" Sherrie did not believe what she had just heard. "What do you mean, 'good'? I just told you that Cullum Rourke is in London."

"Good," May repeated. "Now you can stop looking for him in every remote corner of the world. It's time we all settled down."

Sherrie's mouth worked for a few moments without any sound coming out. Consternation joined the rage that had taken her over and dumbfounded her. When she finally found her voice, she shouted, "I have *not* been looking for him!"

"Of course not." May patted the space beside her on the chaise. "Sit down. Calm down. Tell me about Cullum."

Sherrie didn't feel like sitting down. She certainly wasn't going to relax. "You don't have to sound so happy about it."

She began to roam restlessly around her bed-room. She still desperately wanted to smash something. She clasped her hands tightly to-gether instead. Broken knickknacks, lamps, and furniture would merely alert the help to her state of mind. Besides, it was all rented. Destroying someone else's property was impolite and uncivilized. Crying was futile. So was screaming like a banshee.

She settled for answering May's curiosity. "He's calling himself the Earl of PenMartyn. Lord knows what he's up to. I don't know what he's doing in London. I don't know how long he's been here. I just know he's got to be stopped."

"Stopped from what?"

"I don't know. He has to be up to something!"

"Why?"

"Because he's a scheming, low-down, unscrupulous, English-hating, half-Irish pirate, not some earl from—Cornwall. I think he said he was from Cornwall."

"Perhaps he *is* an earl from Cornwall, wherever that is. Is an earl better than a duke?"

"No."

"You deserve at least a duke. Much more than Daisy or Faith. Perhaps Cullum can buy a dukedom for you. Or you could buy one for him."

"May."

"Of course you will go to Cullum and tell him you are sorry for all the trouble you've caused him. He will then make you his Supreme Lady. I will, of course, refuse to be his concubine, or even second wife, since neither Ira nor I would like that at all, though my father will not be happy."

May's tone was insufferably reasonable, and she looked completely certain of herself. Her attitude sent such a shock through Sherrie that she almost forgot her fury. Her reaction was so strong that she had to find a chair and sit down. "What *are* you talking about, woman?"

"You and Cullum will marry. As you should have nine years ago. I told him so then. I tell you now."

May had always liked Cullum. She had a reason to. "Just because he saved your life doesn't mean I have to be grateful to him."

"You love him."

"I hate him. Always have. Always will."

"Didn't you promise to give up such lies?"

Sherrie shot back to her feet. "Lies!"

May also rose, though her bound feet made it hard for her to stand for very long. "You have never loved another, have you? Not the man you married."

"You told me then that love wasn't necessary for marriage. So did Aunt Dora."

"I was wrong. That was before I met Ira. You should have listened to your heart."

"I didn't exactly have the time for that, did I?"

For a moment Sherrie's fury was washed away by a wave of pain. For a moment she was that confused eighteen-year-old girl who'd arrived home after months in a completely alien world to discover her parents dead from a cholera epidemic. To find herself heir to a vast fortune and responsibilities. To find herself pregnant. She'd been so alone, so lost, so confused and frightened.

And that, too, was Cullum Rourke's fault.

She'd survived. She'd made a life. But God damn the Irish bastard who'd forced it all on her. It could have been so much different.

"Oh, God." The words were a pain-choked whisper. Her eyes and throat stung with unshed tears. Bands of iron tightened around her heart. She fought her way back to the anger. Anger was so much cleaner, simpler, easier to deal with. She would not grieve. She would get even. Sherrie's blurred vision cleared. She looked at May. "Jerry and I would have made our marriage a success if he'd lived. We were friends. He was a good man underneath it all. Once the baby was born he would have settled down. We would have been fine. I would have been a dutiful wife."

"Why? For Minnie's sake? Or white ghost guilt for sins you imagined? For revenge against Cullum?"

"No!"

May was relentless. "Do you really believe you would have made a *success* somehow with that drunken, fornicating, very bad gambler who couldn't even shoot straight, even for Minnie's sake? You? The Tiger's Woman? You would have eaten Jerry Hamilton for breakfast and spit out his bones if he hadn't gotten himself killed three months after the wedding."

"Jerry was a better man than that slave-trading pirate who thre—"

Sherrie just barely managed to bite her tongue before letting the rest of the words escape. May would twist what she'd almost said into a weapon that could flay Sherrie to the core. She didn't want to fight with May about Cullum. She stopped arguing about Jerry Hamilton as well. He had been a fool. Sweet with it, though. Cullum Rourke had never been sweet. And neither was she.

"I'm tired," she told her friend. "Tired all the way through."

May seemed as willing to give up the argument as she was. In fact, the small Chinese woman looked as drained by their acrimony as Sherrie felt. May slowly sat back down on the chaise. She rubbed her temples. "All this makes my head hurt."

"I'm sorry." Sherrie went to the dressing table and began pulling pins out of her hair. "It makes my head hurt, too." When all the pins were out, she shook her head. Thick blonde hair framed her face, spread across her shoulders, and fell down her back. The face she saw in the mirror seemed years younger than it had a few hours ago. Young and vulnerable, the eyes full of freshly awakened passion. Lord, what that man had done to her! She deliberately rearranged her hair, placing the pins with only slightly trembling fingers.

"Was Cullum happy to see you?"

Sherrie didn't answer the question. She tried not to even think about it. She said, "I'm going to go look in on Minnie."

Sherrie strove to look and feel calm as she approached the nursery. Chances were very good, of course, that Minnie was sound asleep. If she wasn't, it would never do for Sherrie to appear the least bit upset in front of her daughter. The child was positively clairvoyant about the causes of Sherrie's emotions. The last thing in the world Sherrie wanted was to have her daughter suddenly start asking awkward questions about her father. Sherrie didn't know why, but despite all evidence to the contrary and all Minnie had been told, Minnie never quite seemed to believe that Jeremiah Hamilton was her father. Sherrie put it down to a child's longing to grow up with a father as well as a mother, but Minnie's suspicion of the truth was easily roused. Now that she was going to have to share Ira with his own baby, she was only going to get worse.

What if Cullum finds out about Minnie?

The thought struck her like a blow just as she reached the nursery door.

No! He won't have my baby!

Her worry about Minnie's asking questions was forgotten in her need to see and hold her child. Fear sent her rushing through the schoolroom at a run and straight into Minnie's bedroom.

Only to find the small bed empty, but for the large dog stretched out at the foot of the bed. Lhasi jumped to the floor and whined piteously as Sherrie ran in. Sherrie found a neatly folded square of heavy writing paper propped on the pile of pillows where Minnie's head should have been resting.

The note read:

Don't worry, Mama. I will be safe. I'm going to meet my daddy.

Chapter 11

❦

"Thank you, Hawton." Jack handed over his hat and coat, then took two steps toward the library before he stopped and turned back. "Moss?"

The butler gave a nod that was just a half degree below insufferably haughty. "Yes, my lord?"

"Where's Hawton?"

"An accident, my lord." Moss's tone of disapproval had the weight of the British Empire behind it. "Involving the Chinese—gentleman, my lord."

Jack wanted to be alone so that the calm, controlled, responsible part of him could write out a report of his observations of Summers for MacQuarrie. It shouldn't take more than an hour. Then he was going to surrender to the part of him that was a raving madman. He might drink himself into a stupor. He might find his way to the worst opium den in Limehouse and never come out. He might simply shoot himself. He didn't care. Soon, and somehow, all this empty pain was going to end. But for another hour he was the Earl of PenMartyn. He wouldn't be living the role of Jack Pen-Martyn if he didn't see to his household affairs.

He cocked an eyebrow curiously at Moss. "Accident? Chinese gentleman?"

Distaste practically dripped off Moss's tongue as he answered. "Hawton suffered an injured ankle, my lord. Something to do with the Chinese gentleman teaching him the proper way to kick."

"Apparently Hawton didn't get the hang of it."

"Apparently not, my lord."

"I see." The earl of PenMartyn was known for being a kind, fair, and concerned master. His shell automatically went through the motions. "Hawton is resting comfortably?"

"Yes, my lord."

"Thank you for assuming his duties this evening."

Moss showed a scant moment of surprise at Jack's courteous words, but a blink brought back the cold, disdainful mask.

Jack turned back toward the library. "I don't wish to be disturbed," he informed the butler. "For anything."

"Yes, my lord. One more thing, my lord."

Jack stopped at the door, but didn't turned back. "Yes, Moss?"

"The Chinese gentleman went out for the evening." Moss sounded incredibly suspicious. "He said he was going to visit friends. Or so I believe that is what he said, my lord, I confess

I find his accent most difficult to interpret. I tried to stop him, my lord."

"Why?"

"My lord, I thought—"

Jack opened the door. "Jhou Xa is my guest, not my prisoner." The Jack part of him wondered just who Jhou Xa was visiting. The madman was happy to have the monk gone. He'd had a holy man get in the way of his debauchery before, he didn't want to risk any interference now. Before closing the door and locking it behind him, he spared Moss a long, hard look. "When I say I don't want to be disturbed, follow that instruction as though your life depended on it. Because it does."

The man who opened the door had the most unfriendly face Minnie had ever seen. She was not in the least bit daunted by it. "I've come to see my—the man who lives here."

The unfriendly man was as long-legged as a Sand Hill crane, with a nose about as long as a crane's, too. He looked down his nose at her and said, "What the devil do you want, child?"

"I told you."

"Be gone, urchin, before I call the constables. His lordship will not have beggars at his door."

Minnie put her foot in the door when he went to close it on her. Maybe she was a little muddy from the ride, her clothes a bit torn, but she didn't think she looked like a beggar. She tried to look as haughty as the butler. "Tell his lordship Minnie Hamilton is here."

"Get back, brat. And you'll stop aping your

betters, if you know what's good for you."

Minnie hadn't known what to expect when she'd followed her father away from the party. Certainly not to have her way blocked by a servant. She was used to being spoiled by servants, not called names. She put her hands on her hips. "You're very rude."

"Insufferable." The man bent down and put his hands on her shoulders. "Be gone."

He pushed her back from the doorway, hard enough for her to tumble down the polished marble steps of her father's townhouse. She heard the door slam as she landed in a bruised heap on the walk. Undaunted, she sprang to her feet.

"Nobody treats Minerva Hamilton like that."

There were a lot of questions Minnie needed answered, from both of her parents. She'd decided to start with her father. She had no idea how long they were going to be in London. She might not have much time to find and be with her father. This was his house, and she was going to get in to see him tonight.

She looked around her, taking in the long, dark crescent of buildings that faced the brick street front. It was late enough so that only the occasional carriage or hackney cab passed by. She didn't see anyone else on the sidewalk, and very few lights shone in the windows of the townhouses that flanked her father's home. There was a park on the other side of the street. The house before her was four stories tall, with grated basement windows at street level. So there was no getting in through the basement.

No, she decided. Getting in through the front of the house was right out. Maybe she shouldn't have bothered jumping off the back of the carriage when the coachman pulled up in front of the street door.

"Should have gotten off at the stables out back," she decided. "Could have sneaked to the rear door through the garden. Now I'm just going to have to find the back alley and start all over."

Minnie was annoyed at the inconvenience, but too excited and eager to put her plan into action to be in the least bit frightened. She wasn't much good at being frightened in any circumstances. She'd been raised on adventure, and this was the adventure she'd been waiting all her life for. Nothing was going to stop her now.

"Stupid butler," she grumbled, and set about finding a way to break into her father's house.

Normally, Jack had a neat, legible hand. The two-page report he quickly wrote out for David MacQuarrie was barely readable. The way the words were scrawled on the paper indicated his agitation far more than any expression he allowed on his face. Outwardly he remained quite calm. He went about his actions with his usual concise, precise movement. He finished writing, folded the paper, addressed it.

He knew what to do next. He couldn't bear the thought of drink, or of opium. He had only one appetite left, one that drew him inexorably.

There was no way he could control it. No: there was one way.

Jack rose, took a cherrywood case off a bookshelf. Brought out the unloaded revolver inside. Picked up one bullet. Just one was all he needed. Going back to his chair, he sat down, put the round into an empty chamber, spun the barrel, then closed it. He wasn't particularly curious to see just how long it would take before the chambered bullet was fired.

He used the little room off the walled garden at the back of the house as a sort of office and library. At least it contained what few books he had, a strongbox, and a black lacquered writing table. There was a thick Chinese rug on the floor, all luminous blues and silvery greens woven in an intricate pattern. He knelt on the rug with Scheherazade, her peacock embroidered silk robe pooled around her, her naked flesh illuminated by morning light pouring gold in through a wide window. Her back was arched, her breasts pressed against his palms. Though her head was thrown back and her eyes were closed, he couldn't take his gaze from her face. He was completely caught up in the look of ecstasy on her features. He had been lost in the ecstasy they'd shared for days and days. He wanted nothing more than to hear her whimpering in need. He never tired of the sound. His pleasure in the act grew with every barrier he made her cross, with every fresh indication that she was totally his. His lips sought the soft skin at the base of her throat, then moved slowly to kiss, then nip gently on the side of her ear. He smiled into the thick fall of her hair when he finally heard the small needy sound he'd been waiting for.

"I love making you want me." He was kissing her hard before she could form words to swear at him. Inside he laughed, as much in amazement at Scheherazade's remarkable knowledge of unladylike phrases as in triumph. Need raced through him as their tongues twined and probed. In a moment he was the one who let out a savage animal growl of lust.

Only to thrust her away as he jumped to his feet. Every sense was alive with warning and fury as he spun to face the garden door. A throwing knife was poised in his fingers as he turned.

"Damn it, Grigori!"

"Cullum, old friend!" The great bearded giant of a man blocked the light of the doorway as he came inside. Spreading his arms wide, the big man stepped forward. Ignoring the knife, ignoring the girl scrambling into her discarded robe, the intruder grasped him around the waist and pulled him into a rib-rattling hug.

He pushed away. "How the devil did you get in here?"

"Climbed over the garden wall when your damned Chinee doorman wouldn't let me in."

"Maybe I don't want to be disturbed."

Grigori laughed. He ran a casual gaze over Scheherazade. "Heard about your new white slave girl. Everyone on the island knows you spend more time horizontal than even old Rhu Limpok, and he's got two hundred women in his harem." Grigori slapped him on the shoulder. "Don't worry, friend. The craving'll wear off soon enough."

But it hadn't. Jack knew it never would. The barrel of the gun rested against his temple.

There was a fresh, clean scent to the well-oiled metal, and it was cool to the touch. He applied gentle, steady pressure on the trigger until the hammer clicked home. Unfortunately, the bullet wasn't in the first chamber. Jack began to squeeze the trigger again.

"I asked you what you're doing here."

The big man laughed. "Came to spy on you, of course. That's what we spies do."

"Why?"

"Old Rhu Limpok's offering gold for a firsthand report on the looks of the beauty that's got the White Tiger in her thrall." Grigori's gaze swept insolently over Scheherazade once more.

She brushed hair from her face, tightened the belt on her silk robe with an angry jerk, and glared back.

He moved between Grigori and Scheherazade, making a show of slipping the throwing knife back into its sheath as he did so. "Why are you really here, Grigori?"

Grigori sighed. "Why must you always play the game so seriously, my friend?"

"Because I have better things to do than talk to you."

Grigori's laughter filled the room. He walked over to the writing table. He took out a revolver and put it down on the shiny black lacquered surface. "I like to play."

He followed the other man to the table. "I know."

Grigori put a bullet down beside the gun. "I have information for you. But first we play my game again, old friend."

"You're a sick bastard, Grigori."

Grigori's grin was both cruel and excited. "But it

is the only pleasure in my life." He glanced at the
girl. "The only spice for me is the uncertainty. You
want to know what I know, we play."

"God damn it." He didn't look away from Grigori's eyes. He reached for the revolver.

A soft white hand snatched the gun off the table
first. "Don't you dare!" Scheherazade shouted.
"Don't you bloody dare!"

"Stop that!"

The shout followed instantly on the sound of
shattering glass.

Jack was on his feet as a muddy bundle of
fury in torn clothing tumbled in through the
gaping broken window. The angry little girl
had a shoe in one hand. She threw it at him.
Jack was too surprised to move as the shoe hit
him on the shoulder.

The child had a scratch on her face and fire
in her eyes. How well he knew those eyes. He
was frozen behind his desk. She stalked forward, a young, hissing alleycat.

"I know that game. It's a stupid game.
Drunken cowboys and gamblers dare each
other to do it. Don't you *dare!*"

The little girl was crying.

Jack had never wanted to die more than he
did at this moment. Of shame. "It is a stupid
game," he agreed.

"You drunk?"

Her disapproval struck straight to his heart.
"I don't drink."

The girl dashed away tears. Her voice caught
on a sob. "Good."

Jack was around the desk in an instant. He

caught the child up in a tight embrace. No matter what other emotion or thought was going through him, he could only react to the overwhelming impulse to comfort.

The girl clung to him, as tight and as hard as she could. She sobbed and shook with reaction as he held her. All he could manage for a long time were incoherent comforting noises and to rock back and forth.

It was the child who brought him back to reality. After a while her crying stopped with one last sniff. She lifted her head away from his shoulder. "You can put me down now. Please."

Jack did so gingerly, almost reluctantly. It was only after she had backed away from him a few steps and was gazing up at him with an expression of bold curiosity that Jack glanced at the broken library window and said, "Do you often practice breaking and entering, Miss—?"

"I didn't mean to break the window," she said. "It was locked. So I hit it with my shoe and made a hole so I could get at the handle."

"I noticed."

She bridled at his sarcasm. "I wouldn't have had to if you'd been paying attention. I thought you might hurt yourself, so I had to *do* something."

"Thank you."

She nodded, as imperious as any young queen.

Jack was totally fascinated. He gestured her toward the chairs set before the fireplace. He had a million questions to ask, but felt the need to go carefully and cautiously with his young intruder. "You look exhausted. Would you like some tea? Warm milk?"

"I'd *like* something to eat," she answered. She sat down and looked steadily up at him with those disconcertingly familiar eyes. "Hot chocolate and cakes would be nice."

"Of course." Jack rang for the butler, then took the chair opposite her. He leaned forward and looked her over closely. She wasn't just muddy, but bruised and scratched, as well. "You're hurt." He jumped up again. "I'll call a physician." The girl's answering giggle set off another form of panic in him. "And hysterical. What can I—?"

"I'm fine." Her contemptuous snort was anything but the response of a delicate product of the nursery room. "I was hurt a lot worse the time I fell out the window at the Maharaja's palace. And the time I got lost when we visited the Bedouins. And I broke my arm when I switched from riding a pony to a horse, even though I'd already ridden a camel—but that was my fault, because I wanted to ride Streaker when Ira wanted me to ride Blossom first. A hot bath and I'll be fine," she reassured him, as he strode back to kneel in front of her chair. "Honestly. Mama says a hot bath is good for most everything. You just gave me a little fright," she went on. "I was enjoying the adventure until I saw you . . ."

Her lower lip quivered, but he sensed she would resent another hug right now. Not that he couldn't use a bit of comfort himself. Of course, he didn't deserve it. So he sat back on his heels. The fire in the grate was warm on his back. The girl before him filled him with a hundred conflicting emotions. He couldn't quite recall now why he'd been bent on suicide. He had far too much to atone for to allow for such an easy way out. More to atone for than he'd been aware of, apparently.

"How did you find me? No, wait. First tell me your name."

She answered his question first. "I saw you when you came to the house and climbed in Mama's window. I knew you'd be at the party tonight. That you'd be where Mama was. So I hid outside and waited. I recognized you by the way you moved. Then I hid on the back of your carriage the same way I did on Mama's on the way to the party, because I wanted to see you alone. I'm Minnie. Minerva. Hamilton. I don't know what your name is. Other than Cullum."

"She told you about me?"

"Oh, no," Minnie answered, looking calmly up at him. "Mama talks in her sleep."

"Yes, she does," he replied, before he realized that the child might have some inkling of where his knowledge came from. He welcomed the chance to turn from her as the butler came into the room. "Ah, Moss, good. Bring my young guest—"

"You!" Moss's face went bright red with anger at the sight of Minnie. "How the devil did this urchin get in the house? My Lord, I'm so sorry," he hastened to apologize. "I'll toss the little bugger out instantly. Or should I lock the creature in a closet until the constables can be summoned?"

Jack found himself looking between the outraged butler and his—toward Minerva Hamilton. "You two have met?" he asked her sardonically.

"I tried the door first," Minnie told him. "He pushed me down the stairs," she added.

"I see." Jack curbed the sudden murderous anger as he turned back to Moss. He *had* told the butler he didn't want to be disturbed. That didn't excuse Moss's behavior. "I want my carriage brought around. Then, after you've done me that small service, Moss, you may pack your things and leave the premises first thing in the morning. No man who pushes a child down a flight of stairs, especially this child, remains in my employ."

Jack dismissed the man from his thoughts as well as his service. He went back to Minnie, who was now standing next to the wing-backed chair. He took her hands in his. "You and I," he told her, "are going to see your mother."

Chapter 12

∽◯◯∽

"**H**e has her. I know he does. He took my baby."

"She left a note. No one took her."

Sherrie stopped her frantic pacing of the front hallway long enough to glare at Ira Gartner. Her heart ached, her mind raced, but terrified worry was all she could express. "You don't understand. You don't know what he's like."

"I do understand," he countered. "May's told me plenty."

"May doesn't . . ." She spun back around. "I don't have time to argue about this. I'm going after her."

Ira stepped in front of the door. "You're doing no such thing."

She'd been out that door once already. She'd been running blindly up the street when Ira had grabbed her from behind and carried her back to the house. If he hadn't turned the corner on his way home just as she'd come around it from the other direction, she wouldn't be stuck back here behind the solidly locked front door of the

124

Mayfair house now. "If you hadn't been out carousing, he wouldn't have gotten my baby."

"I don't carouse."

"But you weren't *here*."

"Neither were you. That's what you're upset about. Minnie's a headstrong, spoiled, little terror who's too smart for her own good," he went on. "She's as bad as her mother once she gets an idea in her head. And just as self-sufficient. If she went looking for someone, you can bet good money she knew where she was going, how she was getting there, and how to get back."

He didn't have to elaborate that Sherrie was the one who had run out into the night without any idea where she was going or any plan at all. That *she* was the one who hadn't a lick of sense, not her daughter. All she knew was that right now she lacked her daughter, and it was driving her crazy.

"Aren't you in the least bit worried!"

"Of course I am." He stepped forward and put his big, calming hands on Sherrie's shoulders. "All you have to do is say the word and I'm off to find this man myself. After I have your promise to let me deal with it," he went on, before she could protest that *she* had to find Cullum herself.

"But—"

"No. We can always call Scotland Yard. Have him arrested for kidnapping if you think you could prove it. But he didn't—"

"He—"

"Didn't take Minnie. This is all her doing."

"It couldn't be. She's just a baby."

"A baby with a very big, very protective dog." He glanced to where the Tibetan Mastiff stood, ears forward, tail lashing, by the staircase at the other end of the hallway. "Lhasi would be dead now instead of drooling on the carpet before she let anyone abduct Minnie."

"He's right," May said, from where she sat at the bottom of the stairs. Until now she'd silently watched Ira deal with the situation.

All this logic from her two best, most trusted friends, made Sherrie want to scream. Screaming would never work with Ira Gartner. May would probably use it as some sort of argument in Cullum's favor. Sherrie decided she wasn't really much good at hysteria anyway, though she'd been doing a pretty good job of it since finding her daughter's note.

"You're right. Blast you. Both of you," she added, with a hard look toward May.

Ira smiled, but the expression didn't reach his worried brown eyes. "I'll send for the constables if you want, but I think it would be best if I went around to this earl's house and collect her myself. And you're not coming with me, Sherrie."

"The devil I'm not."

"Let her go with you, husband."

There was a knock on the door before Ira could protest.

Even as the door he'd just knocked on was flung violently open, Jack knew he should not have come. He didn't know what madness drove him. The child would have been perfectly safe if he'd sent her home alone in his carriage. But of course that had not been possible. She was his child, his responsibility. He would have missed the pleasure of holding her in his arms when she fell asleep during the ride, the warmth and weight of her as he held her on his shoulder now. But to face her mother, to see Scheheraz—

"Minnie!"

One instant he was holding the sleeping girl, the next she was snatched away, his arms were empty.

"Oh, sweet Jesus, baby! Do you know how scared I've been? Where the devil have you been, Minerva Hamilton?" she added, with the fiercely protective anger only a mother could summon. The child slept through it all.

He faced Scheherazade, though her attention was solely on the child they'd made together. He knew exactly what madness drove him. Why he was here. Her spirit even more than her beauty called endlessly to him, the siren call was a part of his being. Before anyone could object, before he was even noticed, before he could fight off the necessity of being near her, he stepped through the open doorway.

The gaslights in the hallway made the place overbright in comparison to the night he'd just left. There were not enough shadows here. He needed shadows, but he needed to be near her more. The hall was wide, a gracious entrance to the rented mansion, yet it seemed overcrowded with people. He wanted to drive them all away, but he stood, mute and stone-still for the moment.

"Is she hurt?"

Scheherazade spoke not to him, but to a very tall, curly-haired man who came up from behind her. The man had large, long-fingered hands. He held them out and the child's mother surrendered the sleeping girl into his gentle embrace with an ease of familiarity that shocked Jack to the core. He could do nothing but watch in stunned silence that grew into cold, hurt anger as the pair consulted with each other in concerned whispers.

"She's fine," the stranger said, after a quick inspection. There was a hint of the old world in his rich voice, overlaid with the flatness of an American accent. "Just sleeping."

Scheherazade touched the girl's cheek. Her worried gaze flicked once more over Minerva from head to toe. "But that scratch?"

"She's had plenty worse, and you know it, Sherrie. She's fine."

"But—"

"Come on," the stranger said. With Minnie still held tenderly in his arms, he shepherded Scheherazade toward the stairs. The man gave Jack one brief narrow-eyed glance before he walked away. Scheherazade did not look his way at all.

Jack took a step forward as the pair left, but it was too clear that the man, woman, and child did not want or need anyone else in their little world.

The child had been so certain—

So had he.

For a few moments he'd allowed himself to dream . . . to dream *what*? That he'd fathered a child? That Scheherazade would welcome him with open arms because of it? Had those thoughts really somehow surfaced in the back of his mind? Could he have—

He laughed. The low sound was as dead and dry as the great Central Asian desert, and as life-threatening.

Bitterness brewed together with jealousy as Scheherazade and the man disappeared up the stairs. Her lover, no doubt. Not her husband. Mrs. Hamilton was a widow, he'd been told several times. Was the tall, dark-haired American the child's true father?

His stomach twisted in both rage and disgust. Did the bitch dare to keep a lover in the same house as her child? Was she that corrupted?

And if she did, who was responsible for such wanton behavior?

Not the American lover.

Even through guilt and outrage, he had to fight off reaction to an image of the tall American smoothing his long-fingered, gentle hands down Scheherazade's naked flesh.

At first he balled his hands into tightly knotted fists. Red rage came down on him, but he fought it back, fought not to take a step forward, not to rush up the stairs to do murder.

For the child's sake he would not kill—and for that reason alone. Jack reached backward blindly, found the doorknob, and twisted, though his hand was too slippery with sweat to gain any purchase on the slick metal surface.

He was barely aware of the sound of small hobbling feet as he turned to face the door. When a hand touched his, he shook it off. When a voice that was somehow familiar but different than he'd heard before spoke, he looked straight ahead, more aware of the polished grain of the dark wood than of the words she said.

"Cullum, wait. You've come too far to leave now. We all have."

Cullum. More weight came to rest on his ravaged soul. Here was someone else with the right to call him by that cursed false name! Someone else to whom he no doubt owed reparations for the sheer hell the man who wore that name had caused.

He sighed and turned to face whoever this accuser would turn out to be.

Her clothing and the arrangement of her jet black hair were the latest in Western fashion, but the tiny woman who looked up at him was a perfect Chinese beauty. Though she leaned on an ivory-handled cane, she did not appear the least bit weak. Her dark gaze was direct, concern combined with exasperation. She'd been in the hallway all the time, Jack realized, watching him, though he hadn't become aware of her until now. She seemed a stranger, and yet—

"Who the devil are you?"

The naked girl in his bed couldn't have been a day over fourteen. A fine-skinned Chinese beauty with tiny budding breasts and an ocean of heavy black silk hair falling around her face and shoulders. She kept her gaze averted as he dragged her from the bed, then fell forward when he let her go. Bound feet, he realized, bending quickly to help her up. She was no common whore, then. Only well-born Chinese girls were forced to live with the torture of purposely deformed feet.

"Look at me, girl." He held her by the shoulders to keep her from falling. "What are you doing here? How'd you get into my room?"

"Yes," Scheherazade said dryly, from where she stood by the door. "How did she get in here?" He saw amusement blended with resentment in his golden lover's expression when he turned his head to glance at her. "Just how many concubines do you have, Cullum? Do you plan to share your bed with us both? At once?"

Her bold words shocked him down to the bone. It amazed him that in just a fortnight his virginal prisoner had begun to entertain such decadent thoughts. Amazed, and aroused. But the notion of bedding both women at once was more than he wanted to contemplate, at least at the moment. He concentrated on the intruder.

"What are you doing here?"

He asked the question in Mandarin, realizing at last that the girl probably had no English.

He was wrong about that, at least a little wrong. Her answer came in hesitant trading pidgin. "M- my father sent me, Tiger Lord. A present. Your servant left me here to w-w-wait for you."

"Do you often receive such interesting presents? What sort of thank-you note does one send for the gift of human flesh?" He ignored Scheherazade's sarcasm. He ignored her when she added, "The

child's frightened. Let her go. I'll make up for it any way you like if you leave her alone."

"You'll do anything I like anyway," he reminded his concubine harshly. *To the Chinese girl he said,* *"What's your name?"*

"May?" he asked the Chinese woman before him. He put his hands on her shoulders. "My May?"

The smile that lifted her lips was both warm and cool at once. Her look was affectionate, but she lifted her head proudly as she answered, "Not your May. Ira's May now. And my own May."

He shook his head. He found it hard to think, almost harder to speak. "I must go."

"The man with her now is Ira, my husband," May informed him. "So you will not look at him as though he is the tiger's next kill. And the child *is* yours. And you are not going anywhere, my old friend. Not yet you are not."

"So that's Cullum Rourke."

"I don't want to talk about it."

Sherrie handed a folded nightgown to Ira as he finished gently running a damp washcloth over Minnie's face and hands. The girl was lying on the bed between them, limp as a rag. Her big dog paced back and forth at their feet, anxious and in the way.

"You don't have to talk about him," Ira said. "Not while he's in the house."

In the house. Sweet Jesus, Cullum was in her house! She shot to her feet. That monster had been with her child!

"He brought her home," Ira's quiet, steady, calm voice cut through her thoughts. "No doubt she gave him as much of a fright as she did you."

Ira didn't understand that Cullum wasn't a man who could be frightened. Just the opposite. He was the one everyone feared.

Lord knew she feared him. Even after all these years. She feared him more than ever. For Minnie's sake more than her own. Minnie, who had sought him out. Somehow.

"You should at least thank the man for bringing Minnie—who is doing an excellent job of pretending to still be asleep—home."

Sherrie thought she saw Minnie mouth a silent "thank you" at Ira's acknowledgment of her acting skills. She let it go. Sherrie wasn't ready to confront her child about her running off and into danger just yet. It was also better not to discuss Cullum Rourke with Ira in Minnie's hearing.

"Besides," Ira went on, "it might not be such a good idea to leave the earl out in the hallway for Dora and the girls to find when they get home."

"Oh." Sherrie hadn't thought of that. She could imagine how the servants must already be gossiping. The last thing she wanted was gossip about the Earl of PenMartyn and the Hamilton woman flying all over London. For the sake of Aunt Dora's daughters and her own, Sherrie had to keep even the breath of scandal from her door.

Which meant getting Jack PenMartyn on the other side of it.

She had no choice but to find the strength of character to face down Cullum Rourke for the sake of her family.

"If you think of him as the earl instead of the pirate, that might make it easier, Sherrie."

She spared a glare at Ira and gave him a grateful smile. "Wise man," she murmured.

"I know."

"You know me too well." He nodded, and with a stiff spine that had everything to do with willpower and only a little to do with corseting, Sherrie faced the door. She didn't let herself look back at Minnie, she just went. She found it better not to think about what she was going to do or say as she rushed through the house and down the stairs.

To find the front hall empty.

She heard the sound of a carriage outside, and, faintly, female voices. Her aunt and cousins were home. But where was Cullum? How was she to keep him from her family? Sherrie hurried forward.

May came out of the morning room as Sherrie reached the front door. "He isn't here," she answered, before Sherrie could ask. "Go to your bedroom. If the women see you, they'll keep you talking all night. Go. Before someone asks why you're so pale and frightened looking."

"I do not look frightened."

"Don't argue," May said, as she leaned against the doorframe. "Just go to your room."

The woman was worse than a scolding

mother, but Sherrie didn't argue anymore. She took her confusion—and, yes, her fear—and fled before the Comstocks reached the front door.

Chapter 13

~~~~~~~~

Sherrie didn't know what to do next after she had closed the door to her room behind her. Her impulse was to return to the nursery and sleep in the narrow little bed with her daughter. She leaned against the door and ran her hands through her hair. Hairpins were scattered across the carpet with an abandon that would have shocked Todd if the maid had been there to see it.

Sherrie couldn't keep the exhausted smile from her lips. "Mustn't shock the servants. That's the first rule of propriety, isn't it?"

"Probably not the *first*," Cullum's voice said, from the shadows by the French window, "but probably one of the most important."

No, not Cullum's voice, Sherrie thought, as she stood frozen in place, staring into the dim depths of the bedroom. Cullum's voice wasn't so smooth, so cultured—so aristocratically English. Cornish. St. John PenMartyn claimed to be from Cornwall.

"St. John," she heard herself say to the man

in the shadows. "What kind of name is St. John?"

He stepped forward, into the illumination of the one gaslight burning on the wall. There were dark circles under his eyes, and the blue-black shadow of beard stubble on his cheeks and jaw. Utterly familiar. Cullum, all right. Evening dress, perfectly-in-place hair, manicured hands, and all, this was the barbarian she knew. The same mouth that had captivated her. The same hands that had held her prisoner. The same hands that had—

"God damn you!"

"Yes."

"Who are you *really?*"

He'd caught his breath when her hair had come down. Need tightened in him at the sight of her standing there, defiant and vulnerable at once. She demanded, and he could do nothing but answer. "St. John is the name I was born with."

"What kind of name is Scheherazade?"

"The one my parents gave me."

"It doesn't sound very American."

"It's as American as any other in a land of immigrants."

"So, you're an Arabian princess."

"My father came from Amsterdam, and first struck gold in California. He found a book in a Sacramento store when he was working the California gold fields. It was the only book in the store, and he bought it with a gold nugget. He gave it to my mother as a wedding present because he knew she loved books. He couldn't read English then, but she

taught him with that book, reading to him the stories told for a thousand and one nights by Scheherazade to keep the man she was enslaved to from killing her. Scheherazade meant love to them.''

"Perhaps I should have you tell me stories. Perhaps we'll have a thousand and one nights together.''

"You promised to keep me for a month. That was eighty-six days ago.''

"You keep count?''

"Of course.''

He had kept his promise. Eventually. She was no doubt counting the seconds until he left her in peace now. He'd been mad to let May talk him into waiting here for Scheherazade. Just being in the room with her belongings, where she slept, for a few minutes had left him—

"You're really named St. John PenMartyn?''

Her words cut through his disconcerted thoughts, and her skepticism rankled. When had he ever lied to her? But then, when had she ever asked him anything?

"Yes.''

Sherrie's curiosity overcame all her other emotions. No, not quite. Fear was being overtaken by another response at being so close to him after so many years. She chose to call it anger. The growing fire deep inside her certainly burned with the same intensity as anger.

She took a step away from the door, a step closer to her nemesis. A step closer to the flames. She couldn't take her gaze off his face. "Then who's Cullum Rourke? Who'd you have to kill to get to be an earl?''

Perhaps he had never lied to her, but he had

told her many things that weren't true. At the time he'd lived them for so long that they'd seemed true to him. Now he told her, "I didn't kill anyone. My father and brothers died before me, while I was in the East. That left me with the family title. Cullum Rourke was the alias of a spy."

Sherrie came closer. Like a moth straight toward a flame, she accused herself. She'd stop Minnie from venturing so close to danger, but couldn't seem to stop herself. It occurred, in some logical but almost inaccessible part of her mind, that what she should be doing was demanding to know what this man was doing in her room, what he'd been doing with her daughter, what he'd told the child.

Instead, she heard herself say, "Spy? What do you mean, spy? You're a pirate!"

He wanted to laugh. He knew he smiled. Appalled as he was at the entire situation, as confused, as wracked by doubt at his ability to control himself, as surprised at the discovery of the child's existence, a part of him wanted nothing more than to collapse in helpless hysterical laughter. This was a serious matter. There was so much he owed this woman. She had every right to a straightforward, unvarnished, sober explanation before he took his leave of her.

Instead, he heard himself say, "And highly profitable it was, being a pirate, as well as fun. But it wasn't my first choice of career."

Sherrie's impulse was to throw something at him. Herself, for preference. She could do a lot of damage with teeth and fists and flailing feet.

But touching the man, any contact at all, threatened to unleash both heaven and hell and every kind of ungovernable, uncontrollable emotion. She did not deal in that sort of nonsense anymore. She was a grown woman with responsibilities, not some reckless girl lost in the middle of an alien land.

Not heaven. Don't you dare let yourself think it was ever heaven. She reined in her emotions with stern words, but her body remembered all too well the things her mind didn't want to contemplate.

For all her hard control, she found that just looking at the man sent waves of heat through her, made her knees weak and her hands ache—though whether to push him away or pull him close, she couldn't, wouldn't, say. Over the years she'd told herself that the devastating masculinity of the man who'd made her his lover was more her imagination, the hazy memories of a girl who'd been overwhelmed by an impossible situation.

It turned out he was larger than she remembered, taller, with wider shoulders, with an aura of male power. More handsome than she remembered as well, the rough, arrogant, wasted beauty transformed, refined. Just as arrogant, just as devastating. Her body, the traitor, remembered him far too well. The room seemed smaller with him in it, the space more intimate, certainly. And this was a bedroom. Sherrie's breath caught on a hard gasp at that thought.

But even as she tried to rid herself of temptation, he came closer, and her damned curiosity refused to let the questions go. "What kind of spy?"

"A British one."

He watched her hands settle on her hips, and her eyes flash, and wanted her. She'd only grown more beautiful with the years, her body more womanly, the girl's lush promise matured to perfection. He remembered how her skin felt under his hand only a few hours before. His fingers had danced along the long curve of her spine, stroked the soft, warm flesh of her throat. She had leaned into him, the fit as perfect as ever. So perfect that for the longest time he had noticed nothing more than that her body fitted to his made him complete. As with the yin and yang mandala, male and female halves fitted together to make a perfect whole.

And what a cruel joke it was for him to imagine even for an instant that their coming together was anything like perfection. For all that he knew what he felt was a lie, it didn't change a thing.

Desire for her raged in him as strongly as ever, undimmed by hours or years. He wanted to put his hands on her naked flesh.

You should always be naked, Scheherazade.

Jack was barely able to keep the thought from turning into words, barely able to keep his hands from tearing at the stiff layers of her ballgown and the undergarments that kept her body hidden from his sight. He wanted the soft heat of her beneath him, to stroke her long, sleek limbs, to mark her with his mouth and hands and plant himself deep inside her, to feel her hips rocking and arching up to meet him.

He wanted her as he'd always wanted her, but he would never have her again.

His hands were trembling when he clasped them behind his back. He curbed the arousal, denied the images of her and him on the bed behind him that swam in his brain. His voice somehow remained steady as he began to give her the explanation she deserved. "There's no one left alive who knows this, Scheherazade—"

"Sherrie." Her shudder of mortification was visible at the name he so loved calling her. It sent an equal shudder of remorse through him. There was harsh finality in her voice as she added, "Don't call me that. Don't call me that ever again."

She wanted no reminder of that time, or of him. Of course. How could he blame her? After all the things he'd forced on her? He would tell her what she wanted to know, though he broke a vow of secrecy to do so, and then he would go. He shouldn't even have come. Fool. Desperate, idiotic fool.

Jack nodded his compliance. "Sherrie."

She was shocked at the anger that flashed through her like a lightning strike at hearing the name she preferred from his lips, spoken in his educated, civilized, superior English accent. Jack PenMartyn had such a beautiful, deep, resonant voice. Damn him! It infuriated her for no good reason when all he said was "Sherrie," when all he did was respect her wishes. How *dared* Cullum Rourke behave in a civilized manner! How *dared* he respect what she wanted now!

What was the matter with her? She shook her head to try to clear it. "Go on. Jack."

Her contempt nearly froze him. And angered him. For all the coldness of his remorse, and though he knew how dangerous his anger was, he couldn't keep the hot glow of it from his gaze as he looked deep into her eyes. She didn't flinch. She never had flinched. But her eyes didn't lower or slide away from his as he was used to. The defiance in her steady look called to him. Called him closer. She backed a step, then stood her ground. How desperately he needed to touch her.

Jack stood very still. His head was swimming. He didn't know if he was close enough to smell her perfume mixed with the scent that was simply her, but he thought he was. He was surrounded by everything that was Scheherazade, here in this room where she slept.

Where he was going to sleep with her.

No. Get out, you fool! He shouted to himself. He came closer as he said, "I was a spy for the Crown when you knew me, playing the great game, as my Russian counterpart liked to call it. Surely you remember all those secret meetings I used to have? Surely you remember Grigori?"

Sherrie found that she was standing with her back pressed against the door, with Jack PenMartyn standing very close. There was very little air in the room, and what there was was heated, charged like the atmosphere just before a storm. There was the promise of lightning all around her.

"Of course I remember Grigori."

"Didn't you suspect he was a spy?"

"Of course. He was crazy. Craziest man I ever saw." She tried to fight off some very bad memories, but didn't succeed. "Damn, but I hated that man."

"Well," he said softly, and reached out to brush a strand of unbound hair away from her face, "you did kill him."

Sherrie closed her eyes for a moment, but not in revulsion at the reminder of that awful night. She remembered the blaze of the house on fire lighting the night, May's screams. She saw it all clearly, but was more aware of the man moving closer to her now, filling her world inch by inch.

Not that she'd ever been able to escape his world at all.

She lifted her gaze to meet his again. "I had to kill him. He was going to kill you."

His mouth was very close to hers. His lips lifted in the feral smile she knew so well. His hands were on either side of her, the palms flat on the wood of the door, pinning her in. "Scheherazade, I owe you my life."

She swallowed, or tried to. Her mouth was far too dry to permit it. The air burned in her lungs and throat. She still managed a defiant "That's right, you do."

"My foolish girl."

She put her hands on his shoulders, to push him away, she hoped. "I'm no girl." She couldn't tell him she wasn't his.

He didn't stop smiling as his mouth came closer. The growl that escaped her lips was one of deep, fierce anger, but she tilted her head up to him just the same.

Only a knock on the door behind her broke the old familiar spell that trapped them both.

Jack jumped back. Sherrie whirled around. She had to lean on the door to stand. She knew he retreated into the shadows on the far side of the room, though she didn't hear him move. She could feel his gaze on her without seeing him, a big hunting cat with its eyes on its prey.

She hadn't felt like this for a very long time— possessed, surrounded, vulnerable.

"Sherrie, honey," Aunt Dora's voice called through the thick wood. "You awake? Can we talk?"

She was a stranger to herself when she calmly answered her aunt. "I'm awake." Could she talk? Oh, lord, about what? Minnie's escapade? The man in her room? She was shaking like a leaf, yet she had trouble keeping herself from laughing. She was obviously hysterical, but couldn't let it become obvious to Aunt Dora. "I was just turning in. Can we talk in the morning?"

Aunt Dora's exasperated sigh sounded loudly even through the wood. "Why did you leave tonight? The Prince was asking for you. And that Lord Gordon person took up all of Faith's time after you left. He's not at all the sort of husband I want for my girls. Faith's all agog over him, and I won't have it. Won't do any good to tell her, that'll just make her set her cap for him more. I need you to be where he is, Sherrie, to distract him until Faith finds somebody suitable. He likes you. You keep him company from now on, do you hear me?"

Sherrie had no intention of opening her door, and Aunt Dora obviously had no intention of going away until she'd extracted a promise about Sherrie throwing herself at Lord Gordon for the sake of the family. And was that some sort of possessive, jealous growl she'd just heard from the tiger in the shadows?

Typical. Males. Never mind the species, males were always more interested in having a female when there were rivals to fight off. It was the rivalry they relished, the hunt more than the mating. Not that she was going to tolerate becoming anyone's mate. Besides, if Cullum Rourke had ever really wanted her—

Sherrie pushed bitterness away and rested her forehead against the door. "Aunt Dora, I'm tired. We'll talk tomorrow."

"But what about Lord Gordon? What about Faith's happiness? Her future?"

"I'll take care of it," Sherrie answered. "You know I will."

"You'll take care of Lord Gordon? See that he stays interested in a woman his own age? He's really a very handsome man, Sherrie, honey."

Don't you honey me, Sherrie thought angrily. She was so sick of people having to have their own way no matter what she wanted. So sick of being manipulated. Everybody she'd encountered tonight had wanted something from her. The damned Prince of Wales had eyed her like

she was his next meal. Lord Gordon hadn't
been much better. Lady Anne wanted to arrange her marriage. May and Ira wanted her to
run her life as they thought best. Minnie had
managed to drag Lord PenMartyn back to the
house, no doubt for the express purpose of seeing that her mama and father lived happily ever
after, as in some fool fairy tale. Now Aunt Dora
wheedled her into things for the sake of the
"family" and wouldn't leave off pestering until
Sherrie agreed.

And Cullum—Jack—God alone knew what
he *really* wanted, but it sure as hell involved
having everything his way and not a bit of it
hers.

She was sick of all of them.

"Go away," she said to her aunt. "Just go
away."

Aunt Dora responded with a loud, "Well!"
But she went. Sherrie heard her aunt muttering
about "Such rudeness!" as she stomped off to
her room. There'd be hell to pay in the morning,
but right now Sherrie didn't care.

She spun around to glare at Jack PenMartyn.
"You too."

She started to lift her hand for a dramatic gesture, but he was on her with a sleek, animal
bound before she could complete the movement. Sherrie couldn't find the breath to scream
as this black and white creature came out of the
night, out of her dreams and nightmares, and
pulled her close. His eyes were blue as midnight, full of merciless passion.

"Where were we, Scheherazade?" His voice

was a rough, familiar whisper. His laughter sent a dark shiver through her. "Ah, I remember," he murmured, just before his mouth came down on hers.

Chapter 14

What had broken his resolve was the oddest response to the tired slump of her shoulders, the weary curve of her spine, the resignation mixed with exasperation he heard in her voice. Somehow all that shook him more than any sensual look, any provocative movement. As he watched and waited in the shadows, the predator in him barely leashed, there had been a split second of sympathy for a woman pushed to her limits. Sympathy converted into conviction that she *needed* comfort, consolation, a source of strength—*him*.

That one instant of concern had been enough to break the chains that held the beast under control. When he moved, it wasn't to offer any gentle comfort.

The concern was a lie, of course, a flimsy excuse. All he wanted was what he wanted. She'd shown a moment of weakness, and he'd pounced.

Her mouth was as hot and sweet as he remembered, if not so instantly eager and yielding. He relished claiming her all the more because it required conquest, taking, coercing. Once he tasted Scheherazade, put his hands on her, there was no turning back. He kept his mouth hard on hers as he lifted her, swung around, and threw them both down on the bed.

Pillows scattered beneath her head as Sherrie landed hard on her back. Cool Irish linen sheets wrinkled and bunched as she grasped for purchase to lever herself from under the heavy, hard weight that bore her down. Everything around her became sensation. The mingled scents of citrus cologne and musky male sweat filled her nostrils. Sharp tiny flicks of sensation drummed against her arms and throat as her dress was torn and delicate beadwork scattered.

His hands were all over her. His mouth found a suddenly naked breast and suckled.

Oh, sweet God!

Her blood suddenly ran thick as honey, as heated as lava. If she didn't get away right now, she'd be lost.

If she got away—

"Get your hands off me!"

She bit and clawed and scratched, and his laughter was hot against her sensitized flesh.

The sweet smell of her overpowered him, familiar and new and unique. He couldn't get enough of breathing her in. The taste of her was all the wine he needed, giddy intoxication and hard-drinking quest for oblivion at once.

His hands were not as soft now as the last time he touched her, though they had seemed hard and callused to him then. The discipline of learning Shaolin fighting skills had hardened and honed his body until it was a finely tuned weapon. Not only his body was changed. The study of the warrior's arts made all his senses far different, more intense.

Despite the calluses, his highly trained awareness of body energy added new, deeper sensation to the familiar feel of Scheherazade's smooth white skin. He felt her life flow beneath his hands. He wanted to consume it, blend with it, bend it to his will, live within the give-and-take of all he could get and give to and from her strong, fighting spirit.

There was nothing spiritual about the overpowering drive to bury himself completely within the deep, hot folds of her sex. Just kissing her sent fiery sparks of his true spirit coursing through his bones and nerves. Every demanding touch brought the dark soul he'd driven down to its death closer to life again. Taking her, possessing her, filling her, feeling her tight and straining against his every hard thrust and begging for more would bring resurrection indeed.

Sweet release. The Tiger reborn. What a night this was going to be!

He laughed. He couldn't get enough of laughter. Too many years without pleasure had left it hard for him to know even how to make the sound.

How dared he laugh! How dared he touch her! Yet there was no mockery in the laughter, no sensation she didn't crave in his touch.

"Cullum, don't—" she began, only to find

her protest stopped by a harsh kiss.

She found herself responding with equally harsh fervor. It was her tongue that probed deeply inside his mouth, the same betraying tongue that had been trying to form words of objections betrayed her with hungry ardor. She found that her hands pulled his head closer without any volition. His hair was thick black silk beneath her clutching fingers. Her lips clung to his beautiful mouth and drank him in, in the effort to end all the dry years of thirst.

Her nerves sang, her need bloomed and burned deep inside of her.

Damn him.

Damn him to hell.

Damn her, too. He wasn't alone in this bed.

This sweet madness could not go on. Could not start again. It was too late for this. For them.

There was no them. He had never wanted a Them. All he wanted from her was—a fuck.

She thought letting herself think the ugly, obscene word would dash a thick blanket of shame over her growing excitement. Instead, the demon of lust in her laughed and stoked the growing burn of need. Sherrie shook with the effort at control. She told herself lust was just a craving—like opium, or alcohol, or gold. She could live without it.

How? her body demanded, as Cullum pushed up her skirts to stroke the insides of her thighs. Sensation rushed deep into the center of her with the speed and heat of tiny lightning strikes. She felt herself growing sleek and moist and pulsing. Her hips ground against the mattress, thrust to meet his touch. Her thighs parted with only the slightest urging of Cullum's questing fingers. His triumphant chuckle brought no shame to her. She wanted, needed, craved every touch, every dark, sweet sensation. Why would she fight this? How?

How? she shouted silently to her inner demons. *Just watch me!*

Sherrie forced her hands away from him. The movement was slow, a hard, near impossible act of will. To move away from Cullum was a hellish deed, one it seemed her very soul protested. Her reluctance shook everything she'd come to believe about herself. Her body didn't want to let her mind share any control of her actions. Lonely flesh wanted only touch and taste, knew only the drive of desire.

Desire wasn't enough. Desire wasn't a reason. Desire wasn't an excuse. Thwarted desire brought searing pain, but pain brought a clean, brief stab of sanity.

Sanity that lasted long enough for her to do what survival dictated. She'd traveled the world, put herself into potentially dangerous situations many times. She'd learned to take measures to protect herself no matter where she was, even in the master bedroom of a London mansion. The derringer secreted beneath the pillows fitted with the ease of long practice into her grip, once she finally managed to burrow her way beneath the fluffy pile.

Sherrie was amazed that her hand was steady when she rested the short barrel of the little gun against his temple. It seemed that years of practice gave her an advantage she hadn't expected.

"I should kill you right now."

Cullum lifted his head, slowly, until their gazes met. He laid his hand on her, on the mound at the juncture of her legs, cupping it. Heat speared through her from the spot. She moved the derringer with him, keeping it pressed against his temple.

His cheeks were flushed, a black wing of hair fell across his forehead. He looked younger than she remembered. His eyes were dark, feral, completely unafraid. "Yes, you should."

It was a dare, pure and simple. He was as reckless as ever, as sure of his power over her.

He grabbed her hand and twisted it down just as she pulled the trigger. Heat scorched her cheek. Feathers flew. The sound of the shot was absorbed in the layers of pillows beneath her head.

The knowledge that she would have killed him, and that he might have killed her when he turned the gun away, shook him, rattled what little sense he had left. But the extra edge of danger also added to his excitement. Excitement overpowered sense. He showed his teeth in a savage smile of triumph. He tossed the little gun to the floor.

"Naked, Scheherazade. Right now."

He pulled her up before she could protest. Up, away from the smell of cordite and the rain of feathers. Up, and out of the fear of death that had momentarily stunned her. If she had flinched, moved a fraction of an inch, the bullet would have—

She was barely aware of the fabric of her dress shredding around her, of layers being peeled away and discarded. She didn't know where the knife he used had come from, though she felt the flat of the blade, warm with his body heat, occasionally touch her skin. Her bare, naked skin.

She turned on Cullum in reaction, sliding through his hands to blindly grasp his shirt front. She pulled, tore. Buttons popped and flew in all directions. She wasn't going to be the only one naked when this was over with!

What the devil was she thinking? She wasn't thinking. She was just reacting. Oh, God!

Sherrie fell away, but he grasped her by the arms before she could roll off the bed. He dragged her back to the center of the mattress, forced her to kneel there on the ruins of her clothing, posed in a puddle of midnight satin and starkly white lace-trimmed linen. He leaned back on the pillows to enjoy the view, reclining like a sultan to take in all the naked secrets of his favorite possession. Like a pasha— or a pirate king.

But she wasn't his slave girl any more. And she wasn't afraid to take a good, long look at what she saw stretched out before her, either. He'd changed. The man of her memory was strong, powerfully built, but not so finely honed and finished looking as the man on her bed. He'd been impressive, but he hadn't been perfect.

She raked her gaze up his long, hard-muscled legs and powerful thighs, across the thickly

matted width of his chest and the rippling muscles of his stomach. His sex reared up from the
thick black thatch at his groin, thick and swollen and red against his belly. Ready for her.
More than ready.

She found her breasts growing sensitive and
heavy and the throbbing ache spread through
her insides once more as she looked at him. She
forced herself to meet his gaze. Only the act of
defiance turned into a trap as the need she
found in his eyes sparked an answering one in
her.

This bed became the only place in the world,
and they the only people in it. Years sheared
away. Desire that had been too long denied ex-
ploded fiercely around them. Flesh craved flesh,
and flesh would have its way.

He reached out, drew her closer, though he
kept her kneeling in front of him. His hands
skimmed up her thighs, came up to cup her
breasts. His thumbs slowly stroked the hard
peaks of her nipples, sending wave after wave
of sensation stabbing through her. Her hand
closed around the base of his shaft. He was soft
as velvet and hard as stone in her hand. He
drew in a sharp breath. Their gazes remained
locked.

"I should scream." It was her last grasp at
sanity, but it was hard to speak through the
heat that consumed her.

"You will scream," he told her. The slow
smile held heady promise.

"Or you will."

He threw his head back against the ruined

pile of pillows and laughed and laughed. His body shook as well, but not with laughter.

He was taut with need, and Sherrie reveled in how she affected him. She stroked her free hand across the width of his pectorals, followed the path of his chest hair with a sharp-nailed fingertip as it arrowed into a dark V on his stomach. The muscle and skin she explored were achingly familiar and all new to her. She was totally fascinated.

The small noises he made were sweet triumph in her ears, each breathy sound a reminder of the things that pleased him. Memory of how to please him was the only solid ground she had in this small world where they now lived. Even that was a thin crust over molten desire. Right now it still moved just below the surface, but any moment it was going to break, shatter her, consume her.

Desire would eat her alive and leave her broken, and she would revel in every helpless moment of it. Only he could do this to her. She hated him for it, but hate couldn't stop it from happening. Not after they'd come this far. Not tonight.

Her finger circled his navel as his fingers slowly circled the undersides of her breasts. His shaft throbbed thickly against her palm, demanding attention. She knew how to answer his demands.

Her hand circled and stroked him, long and slow, from shaft to tip and back down again. It brought him deeper into heaven, but it wasn't enough. He wanted her mouth on him, but not yet. Later.

He wanted his mouth on her. To hold her still as she struggled against the ecstasy he forced on her. How well he remembered her sweet, tangy, salty taste on his tongue. The way she cried out. Later. *Later*.

He would bury himself in her first, fill her, feel her soft heated insides ripple and give around his shaft with each hard thrust. Anticipation blended with her skilled attentions to leave him panting, slick with sweat, and oh so ready. A current of delicious burning pain radiated all through him up from his groin. He longed to get lost in the flow, let it drag him onward into insensibility. Not yet. He'd waited too long.

He slid his hands down from her breasts, to her narrow waist, to the flaring curve of her hips, reached around to cup the rounded globes of her buttocks. She was Scheherazade reborn. Different, yet still the same, more beautiful as a woman than as a girl. The changes were subtle, infinitely tantalizing.

He said something to her, the words a low, guttural growl in Mandarin. She gave a breathy response also in a language not her own as he shifted his grasp and rolled them into a new position, centering himself between her open thighs. Her long legs settled around his waist. She still held his erection in her grasp. He pushed her hand away, wanting no guide. He pushed her open thighs wider.

Then he held her open, gazed for a brief mo-

ment at the soft, swollen folds of her sex. He
touched her, traced a finger back and forth and
inside her. She was wet and ready for him. So
very tight. She jumped beneath his touch, making soft, panting, mewling sounds. His finger
came away covered in her moisture. Her scent
was sharp, heady, maddening. He couldn't wait
any longer.

They both cried out when he plunged deeply
into her.

Her first climax came the instant he entered
her, a shattering shuddering blooming rush of
elation that burned and faded, as swift and as
beautiful as a falling star. It was only the beginning. Prelude. Crossing one peak simply set her
on the rising road to the next.

The rhythm he set up was harsh, rapid, bru-
tal, and perfectly attuned to her body's demands. Her needs were the same as his. There
was no stopping it, no stopping him. She rose
to meet each demanding thrust. She cried out.
Clutched at him, beat at him with her fists and
her heels. She begged. But not for him to stop.

Through it all, the climaxes came again and
again.

And when it was over, after his body had
collapsed on top of hers, sated, sweat-covered,
muscles lax and languorous, she rested him in
the cradle of her arms, and for a few brief moments she tenderly stroked and patted his back,
the same back she'd left deep claw marks on
not an hour before. He nuzzled her throat, left
a memory of a gentle kiss on her shoulder.

Then the coil of fury and desire inside them

both began to tighten once more. Their gazes met in a flash of unholy fire. And it began all over again.

Jack woke to find the covers thrown back, though there was a hot and heavy weight resting across his chest.

There was a hand on his thigh.

What the hell had he done?

Stupid question, with an obvious answer. Not only did he know exactly what he'd done, but he was already aching to do it again. Even more than rolling her onto her back and having her right now, he wanted to drag the woman up and take her away with him.

As desire simmered in him, he stared at the ceiling, his fingers automatically combing through soft golden hair. A fantasy of locking Scheherazade away in a luxurious prison on his Cornish estate formed vividly in his mind. There would be no one and nothing that could come between him and his every voluptuary whim. He would make a world where only the two of them existed. He'd provide her with every luxury, pamper her, spoil her, keep her as lavishly as any empress sequestered in Peking's Forbidden City.

In return for such solicitous treatment, he would claim the right to rape her any way he chose, anytime he chose, and expect her to tell him she loved him for it. Oh, yes, making them both believe torture was love was the most important part of the fantasy. The prime rule of the game.

They'd been down that road before. How deliciously easy it would be to stroll that way again.

What a complete monster he was.

The child should have let him finish the game. He should simply have closed his eyes and let Scheherazade's bullet find its mark. Two perfectly good chances to rid the world of him had been wasted last night.

Scheherazade slept as soundly as she always did beside him. He'd used and debauched her until they'd both fallen unconscious, and now he was the only one driven restlessly awake by a nagging conscience. Once asleep, the woman could sleep through cannon fire, as he well knew.

Jack forced his mind to go blank. He pushed out thoughts. He pushed out images. Sensation remained, but he ignored everything that was not necessary to what he must do.

He inched slowly away from her. It was a difficult act of will and took a long time to accomplish. Gradually he was left with only the memory of her warmth clinging to his naked skin. Eventually he got to his feet. Slowly he found some remnants of his clothing and managed to cover himself. He did it all without letting himself look at the sleeping woman stretched out like a glorious sacrifice on the center of the bed. Once dressed, he went to the French window. He had come and gone this way once before. He left this way again. Though he knew he would not return, he did not look back for one farewell glance.

Chapter 15

⟲⟳

Sleep was a heavy, warm weight that bore her down, buoyed her, caught her like a creature in amber and went blissfully on and on. Sleep was dreamless and dark, delicious oblivion. Sherrie rose out of it slowly, making the transition to wakefulness in a slow, steady journey. Layers of peaceful abandon slid off her one bit at a time, as though she was swimming up and up through successive sheets of fine gauze and linen and silk. Out of sweet, warm darkness into the cold light of day. Dread caught up with her in the last stage just before waking. She'd reached a door she didn't want to open. She'd reveled in darkness, given herself up to all its sensual hedonism.

Come the daylight, there was hell to pay for the night.

Sherrie knew in the instant before she crossed into full wakefulness that the place beside her in the big, soft bed was empty. Stone cold empty. She was alone. Again.

She didn't want to wake up. She didn't want

to open her eyes and find that he was gone. Unlike some people, she'd had plenty of practice in doing things she didn't want to do. His absence didn't make her life any more complicated than his presence. His absence just made it easier on him.

Selfish son of a—

Sherrie came fully awake with an angry cry, reached out for the nearest object on the night table as she sat up, and threw a cut crystal water decanter against the far wall with every bit of furious strength she possessed.

The crash and shatter were a satisfying accompaniment to her wordless howl of pain. Shards of glass like sharp crystal tears shot off in all directions. Water soaked the dark wallpaper in a bloodstain pattern.

All the racket brought a flushed and frightened Todd running into the room. "Mrs. Hamilton? What—?"

Sherrie was out of bed before she quite realized she was naked. "A dream," she explained hastily to the reserved English maid. "I had a bad dream."

Which didn't explain the wrecked state of the bed linen or the bruises and bitemarks that left vivid evidence of intense lovemaking.

Todd blushed, and averted her gaze from Sherrie's nakedness after one wide-eyed look. "A dream. Of course, Mrs. Hamilton." She hastened to hand Sherrie her robe and slippers. "Please be careful of the broken glass. I'll get it cleaned up as quickly as possible. Shall I have your bath drawn, Mrs. Hamilton?"

"And the sheets burned," Sherrie muttered under her breath. That, and a long hot soak in heavily perfumed boiling hot water, ought to get the stench of Cullum Rourke off her and out of the room. Nothing short of burning down the house would even begin to erase the memories of what had gone on in this room last night.

No. That wouldn't do any good. The last time they'd been involved in a house fire the results had been nothing short of disastrous. Why tempt fate again? She had more to lose this time. So did he, she supposed. Not that she particularly cared about the Earl of PenMartyn's fate.

"A bath, yes. Thank you," she said to Todd.

"I'll attend to it immediately, Mrs. Hamilton." The maid gave a tiny nod and went phlegmatically about her business.

Sherrie watched the woman's competent movements and unperturbed demeanor with amazement that bordered on shame for her own melodramatic emotions and behavior. How *English* of her, Sherrie thought. Then amusement, and her sense of equanimity, began to reassert itself. She reminded herself that what the silly rich Yankee did was no skin off Todd's nose, now, was it? She would draw her wages no matter what fool things the American lodgers at Primrose House got up to—and the rich were always up to something, weren't they? Todd had her own problems and pleasures to deal with, her own life to get on with.

I am not the center of the world, Sherrie reminded herself. *Nor is Cullum.*

As if confirming this thought, Todd said, "Mrs. Comstock would like you to join her in the morning room as soon as you are ready, Mrs. Hamilton."

Maybe it was just as well she hadn't woken up in bed with Cullum—Jack—whoever he was this morning.

Sherrie wandered to the French doors and pulled back the curtains to look down on the rain-soaked summer garden. It was a dark, wet morning that gave her no clue as to the time. Years could have passed while she slept, for all she could tell from the gray English day outside. And which would she have preferred, to have slipped inexorably into the blameless future, or to slide back into the sinful past?

I wonder how he got out of the house? she thought, as her fingers traced a vague pattern on the thick glass pane. *Through here, or out the front door? And did he take Minnie with him?*

A jolt of terror went through her, to be immediately alleviated as her daughter and the dog stepped out onto the nursery balcony. Minnie waved wildly at her. Sherrie sagged against the glass door and waved weakly back. She had never been so grateful for the sight of her child. Or the sight of the big Tibetan mastiff, for that matter.

Of course, Lhasi wouldn't have allowed anyone in Minnie's room, or to spirit her young mistress away without a fight to the death. Or at least, not without making a fierce racket if the young mistress was prepared to run away happily with her newfound father.

Father.

"Father, indeed," Sherrie snarled. She was going to have to have a very long, serious talk with Minnie about the Earl of PenMartyn. She waved again, with more enthusiasm, and the movement caused a twinge of pain from a bruise Cullum had left on her shoulder. She was marked all over. Brands. Reminders of whom she belonged to? "Ha. Nonsense. He's a clumsy ruffian, that's all," she grumbled, and her deeply satisfied senses gave the lie to her mind's explanation of her well-used state.

Whatever the reasons, she was still bruised, and barely able to walk. She wasn't doing anything, whether it was to listen to schemes and lectures from her aunt, or to discuss the complicated facts of past, present, and future with her beloved child until she'd had a long hot bath and covered herself from neck to ankles in the thick, concealing clothing of a prim, proper, respectable widow.

Never mind that except for being a widow, she was none of those things. It was the armor and image she needed right now. That, and a bath for the aching aftermath of her first experience with a man in nearly nine years.

She turned from the French doors. "Hurry up with that water, if you please, Todd."

But Minnie came flying into the room before she could step into the tub of steaming water. Which was just as well, as grabbing up her daughter into a fierce protective embrace while the dog surged around her feet was far more important than soothing any sore muscles.

"Am I in trouble?" Minnie whispered in her ear.

"Oh, yes," Sherrie whispered back, and kissed her child's soft cheek.

She dismissed the maid with a glance, then settled on the bed with Minnie on her lap. "We need to have a long talk, young lady."

Lhasi jumped up beside them. Minnie giggled when the dog buried its nose in a pile of goose feathers and flicked them into the air with a loud whoof of air. Only then did Sherrie remember that the bed looked like a war had been fought in it, and that one of the battles had left a bullet hole in the pillows. She definitely looked and felt like a casualty of that war. She didn't want Minnie to see her like this. She didn't want her child to know about the battles, for surely there were going to be others before the ghost, and possibly the corpse, of Cullum Rourke could be laid to rest.

She stood and put Minnie down. Her child looked on curiously as Sherrie pulled up bedcovers and made sure her robe was fastened all the way to the top button at her throat.

"Can we see Cullum today?" Minnie asked, when Sherrie was done fussing.

Dark suspicion laced with fear swirled around Sherrie at Minnie's words. What had the man told her? When had he contacted her? She knelt by Minnie and took the girl's hands in hers. "How do you know about Cullum?"

"You talk in your sleep."

Shock rocked Sherrie back on her heels. Never in a million years would she have suspected that she was the one who'd given away her closely guarded secrets. "I do?"

Minnie nodded.

The world reeled around Sherrie even more. She wasn't ready to face the consequences of the night before, but her daughter needed her. So she'd tried to put rattled emotions aside for Minnie's sake. What Minnie told her left Sherrie more shaken than ever.

How long had the child known? How much of the truth did she know? How did Minnie feel about what she knew? How long had Minnie been keeping secrets from her?

Minnie stroked her cheeks. "Mama, are you going to be sick?"

Sherrie nodded weakly. "I think so, honey."

"Should I get Ira and May?"

"No, sweetheart, we have to talk."

Minnie settled down cross-legged in front of her. "You're angry because I ran off."

"Yes, honey. I am. Angry with you, angry with myself, and angry with the man who brought you home."

"Cullum."

Sherrie nodded slowly. She hated hearing that name from Minnie's lips, but tried not to show it. She held everything she felt inside, though the effort to show a calm face to her child tore at her. The reaction was so intense that her stomach clenched, knotted, and sent a more intense wave of nausea through her. She really was going to have to be sick soon, just to get some of the bile out of her system. She took a long, slow breath. "His name is PenMartyn, sweetheart."

"He told me. He doesn't like being called Cullum. He said to call him Jack."

At least he didn't tell her to call him "Father." "It was wrong of you to go to his house." And just how the devil had Minnie found his house? She didn't even know where he lived. Which wasn't surprising. She hadn't even known who he really was, either. Never guessed that Cullum had lied to her about everything he was even while blinding her with a spell of carnal decadence. Cullum Rourke had never even existed, and she had lov—

She was such a fool.

"I was very worried," she told Minnie. "It would have been better if you'd told me what you knew about Lord PenMartyn. We could have talked it over."

"It would have made you sad."

"Yes, it would. But I would still have talked to you about him."

"Can I see him again?"

The pleading in the girl's eyes and face showed Sherrie an innocent mirror of emotions she didn't want for herself, and certainly not for her daughter. She also knew how stubborn and reckless her child could be. It was up to her to protect Minnie, especially from the temptations she had trouble resisting herself.

"I'll have to talk to him first," she told her daughter.

She would have to, wouldn't she? For Minnie's sake. Now that he knew about having a daughter, what would he do? Would he want anything to do with the child? Would he attempt to use Minnie in some way? He certainly was not fit to be a father. She would have to make it perfectly clear that Minnie was hers and hers alone. That she would protect her daughter at any cost.

What she could not do at this moment was follow the impulse to forbid Minnie from ever again seeing the man who'd sired her. She wasn't going to break the girl's heart out of an automatic reaction of terror and mistrust for Cullum Rourke. She wasn't going to make any promises about letting Minnie see him, either.

She was, however, going to be very sick very soon. She struggled to her feet, gagged, and clutched her stomach. "Go to Ira, sweetheart," she said, as she fought off the gag reflex. "Have your lessons. Have him take you for a ride. We'll talk later."

Minnie hesitated, then nodded. As Minnie and Lhasi left the room, Sherrie clapped her hands over her mouth and ran for the washbasin.

"Sherrie, honey, are you listening to me? And why are you smiling like that?"

Her aunt's tone combined both annoyance and suspicion. Sherrie blinked, and the morning room came back into focus. She was dressed in high-necked black, with a large onyx mourning brooch pinned at her throat. A delicate china cup and saucer were balanced on her lap, the fragrant jasmine tea in the cup untouched, and grown cold. She wasn't quite sure where she'd been woolgathering, or for how long, but Aunt Dora was right. Sherrie had not been listening to whatever the woman had been saying about the quest to find her daughters suitable husbands having been sidetracked by Lord Gordon Summers.

But smiling? Surely not. She was too upset to be smiling at anything. Too angry. An hour ago she had been thoroughly sick. If she didn't have an obligation to deal with her responsibilities to every member of her family, she'd be out having target practice to improve her chances of getting off a decent shot at the man the next time she had the opportunity.

Just because her blood was singing with memories of uninvited, completely illicit love-making and parts of her that she'd very nearly forgotten existed were feeling particularly sensitized this morning didn't mean she had anything to smile about. Just the opposite. In fact, an anger was growing in her that burned with its own intense passion.

"I was not smiling."

"Oh, yes you were."

Perhaps she'd been smiling at the notion of seeing Cullum—Jack—an English spy's lifeless corpse falling at her feet. It was a pleasant conceit. She said to her aunt, "I was simply enjoying being alive on such a beautiful morning."

"It's raining cats and dogs."

"We're in England. It's supposed to."

"Speaking of cats, you looked like you'd been raiding the cream pitcher. I know that sort of smile," Aunt Dora went on inexorably. "Unless you were recalling some fond memories from your past, I wouldn't think you'd have reason to smile like *that*, either."

A telltale blush heated her cheeks, but Sherrie didn't look away from her aunt's deepening disapproving gaze. She folded her hands primly in her lap, hands that wanted to strangle the life out of the lying bastard. "Perhaps I was thinking of my dear late husband," she conceded. "Even a woman of my advanced years sometimes recalls conjugal relations with a certain affection."

Aunt Dora snorted. "Advanced years, indeed. You're just twenty-seven. Practically a girl."

As Dora's eyes lit with cunning enthusiasm, Sherrie realized she'd taken a completely wrong direction when she'd answered her aunt. "I don't know what you're thinking, Dora Comstock, but I know don't like it."

"Hear me out, child." Dora poured herself a cup of tea and took a sip before she went on. "What you need is a man."

I had one last night, thank you. A hot sweet memory of the experience rippled through her as the wayward thought insouciantly crossed her mind. The words very nearly found voice, but Sherrie ruthlessly suppressed both them, and the echo of passion.

The only passion she had any time for was passionate hatred. But passionate hatred wasn't wise, it made one reckless. PenMartyn was a dangerous, cunning animal. She would be a fool to hunt such a creature with anything but the calmest, coolest deliberation.

Sherrie laughed at herself even as the murderous thoughts surfaced. She let herself play with fantasies of violent, easy solutions for a moment more, then pushed them decidedly away. Fantasy was all very well, but she had far too much reality on her hands to entertain nonsensical notions for very long.

Just because much of what she had been certain about her and Cullum's pasts proved to be completely false didn't really change her life. It changed her, yes. Of course. She, personally, was quite lost, and that didn't matter one little bit to the needs of those who depended on her. She'd deal with her obligations. No matter where she went, she always took those with her. That was how she'd always survived.

"Do you know where those girls are now?"

Aunt Dora's question cut through Sherrie's thoughts, right to the heart of the matter. "At Lord Gordon's?" Sherrie ventured.

"Indeed they are. And Daisy was none too happy to go, I'll tell you. She couldn't very well let her sister go unchaperoned, and Faith wasn't going anywhere else." Dora shook her head. "Faith, my Faith, actually canceled a dressmaker's appointment this morning to go to church." Her eyes narrowed suspiciously. "I tell you, there's something very wrong with that child. And you have *got* to do something about it, and before Lady Anne and Mrs. Gadwaller and all those other people arrive for the tea party you're giving this afternoon."

"Tea party *I'm* giving? *What* tea party?"

"The one I organized after you ran out and I had to make excuses for you last night." Aunt Dora pointed a finger accusingly at her. "You owe me for that, young woman. Fortunately, everybody wants to meet the world-traveling Mrs. Hamilton, so I didn't have any trouble persuading a herd of women to round up their marriageable sons and bring them to tea. Now you have to get my girls away from Lord Gordon's in time to dress for the party."

"And entertain your party guests." Sherrie did not want to put herself on display and make bright conversation, but she owed this much to her aunt. "And get Lord Gordon's attention off my Faith. Lord Gordon's interested in you, Sherrie," she added. "You can use that."

Sherrie didn't dignify the comment with an answer. Instead, she stood and said, "I'll go get the girls."

Her aunt didn't try to stop her, or offer to come along. Sherrie paused only long enough to don a hat and shawl for some slight protection from the rain, then marched determinedly next door.

The servant who opened the door of Lord Gordon's house offered her a cordial smile and ushered her into a wide reception area where he asked her to please wait a moment. Sherrie heard chanting and glanced toward an open doorway. She caught a glimpse of a great many people, mostly female, seated on the floor and on a row of chairs near the back of the room. They wore saffron silk scarves and robes over their street clothes. Sherrie hoped she wasn't going to be asked to join the congregation. She'd stand out like a raven among parakeets in her somber widow's weeds.

Fortunately, the butler returned and said, "Lord Gordon asked me to show you into the library." He gestured, and she followed.

The first thing she saw when she was shown into the book-lined room was a portly bearded man who held a leatherbound volume in his hand.

"You have no idea how delighted I am to see you again, Mrs. Hamilton," the Prince of Wales said, as the butler closed the door behind her.

Chapter 16

"My lord looks as though he's been through the wars."

"I have, Dabney," Jack answered his valet. "I have."

He kept his head still and his eyes closed while Dabney continued to shave him. His head pounded and he was weary unto death. He'd dragged in and thrown himself down on the bed at six thirty.

Dabney entered his room promptly at six forty-five, as he did every day. Jack wanted nothing more than to kill the intruder, but he'd risen wearily and said, "Good morning."

Dabney then proceeded to wish him a good day, prepare his bath, lay out his clothes, and lather his face with mint-scented soap when Jack settled into the chair before the dressing table. Dabney wielded the razor with great skill, and took quite a bit of pride in keeping Jack's heavy beard under control.

Right now, Jack would have preferred it if the valet had wielded the razor to slit his throat, but knew it wouldn't do to suggest it to the man, even as a lame joke. So he kept quiet and suffered through the process.

He hadn't wanted to be bothered with the man's ministrations this morning. But Dabney's efforts to keep the Earl of PenMartyn presentable were part of Jack's everyday routine. Routine and pretense were the only weapons Jack had with which to fight himself at the moment. All his self-discipline was gone, so he fell back on habit until he could get some measure of it back. Perhaps if he pretended hard enough to be the Earl—

"Quite a bit of excitement last night, my lord," Dabney commented, as he wiped the last of the lather off Jack's face.

Jack glared at the man. "Moss deserved to be sacked."

Dabney poured a splash of bay rum on his hands and patted Jack's freshly shaved face. "Indeed, my lord," he responded. "I was referring to Mr. Hawton's accident."

"The devil you were."

"As you say, my lord." Dabney handed Jack his clothing one piece at a time. "But the circumstances of Moss's exit from the staff did result from Mr. Hawton's accident." He adjusted and fussed with Jack's attire until he had the Earl looking the way he wanted him. After considerable silence, Dabney went on, "One hears that there was an urchin involved, my lord. It's a bad business, turning away urchins. Especially knowing how you feel about the poor— deserving and otherwise." Dabney tsked.

"Moss never was our sort, but as he was Cook's nephew and as he had such fine references, we thought we could bring him around."

Jack found himself reluctantly but irresistibly drawn to ask, "Oh?"

"He had absolutely no idea of what it is we do here at PenMartyn House, my lord."

"What is it *we* do, Dabney?"

"Look after you, my lord, while you look after everyone else. Even Cook said good riddance to the man, and has laid on a fine breakfast for you just to show she bears no ill will over the affair. She was hoping to bake some ginger cookies for the urchin as well, but Masters says you delivered the child to Primrose House. Very good people, Americans. No doubt the child will find a good home with the Hamilton widow."

Masters was his coachman. Servants knew everything, and they talked too damn much. As Jack gaped at his valet in shock, an errant thought crossed his mind that Scheherazade's staff were just as aware of the night's activities as his were. Only his people were under the mistaken impression that the earl had gone about performing one of his good works. That he'd rescued an orphan and given her to a lonely woman to raise. They had this horribly false image of him as being a good man. They shielded him, protected him, cared for him with a loyalty he didn't deserve.

"Dabney," he said, unable to contain his disgust with himself, "I spent most of last night in an orgy of lust and degradation."

"Yes, my lord," Dabney responded placidly. "A man needs to relax and enjoy himself sometimes. You don't do that often enough. Shall I have breakfast brought up, my lord, or would you prefer to be served downstairs?"

The very notion of eating was out of the question, though Jack managed to push enough food around his plate to keep Cook from worrying that her efforts to please him had been in vain. Fortunately for Cook's self-esteem, both MacQuarrie and Jhou Xa joined him in the dining room to share the bounty on the sideboard. While the Chinese monk dined on fruit and pastries, the Scotsman made free with heaping piles of toasted bread, sausage, eggs, and salmon in cream sauce as well.

Jack wanted nothing more than to be alone, but he also welcomed the company. It helped keep his attention on something besides the craving to return and claim Scheherazade. It wasn't just the woman he wanted to claim, but the little girl and all the years since the night they'd conceived the child.

Why hadn't Scheherazade told him, then?

And what a greedy fool he was, to think he could insert himself into mother's and child's lives at this late date.

"Why so morose, Jack?"

Jack might have welcomed company, but had forgotten there was anyone but himself in the world, and he wasn't quite sure for how long. When he did look from one companion to the other, he wasn't surprised to see MacQuarrie and the monk regarding him curiously. There was also a faint air of disapproval about each of them, as though each was prepared to have Jack fail him in some way. Or perhaps he had already failed and each man was waiting to be able to confront Jack in private about his own particular agenda. And there was his secretary standing in the doorway, trying to look unobtrusive and get his attention at the same time.

What did all these people want from him? Would the world never leave him in peace? A moment before, he'd welcomed company; now he simply wanted to tell them to go to perdition and walk away from it all.

But doing exactly what he wanted was not to be allowed. Not ever. Couldn't be allowed. He knew too well what happened when he let himself—

"What is it, Sanders?" he demanded of the secretary. "And have some breakfast while you tell me," he added, because politeness was a habit, and the man was as thin as a pencil and about as stiff. Sanders wouldn't expect to eat with an earl even if he was dying of starvation. Sanders knew his place. Jack enjoyed upsetting the balance of the Way Things Were Done. It was one of the few pleasures he had allowed himself.

Until last night.

He would not think about last night. But he wanted to. He could feel the beast inside him slavering for another taste of degradation.

"No thank you, my lord," Sanders said from the doorway. He made an elaborate show of looking at his pocketwatch. "Your lordship has an appointment with the Children's Hospital committee at ten-thirty." He cleared his throat. "That is five minutes from now, my lord. Your solicitor would like to speak to your lordship about some changes you indicated wishing to make in the endowment for the home for disadvantaged young ladies."

"Is that the house you set up in Whitechapel?" MacQuarrie asked. "The one for keeping prostitutes off the streets?" He shook his head. "Do you really think it's possible to reform a whore once she's had a taste of the life, Jack?"

"I know it's possible to turn a girl into a whore against her will," Jack answered coldly.

He didn't add that he knew from personal experience. God, but he was a hypocrite! Perhaps something of his true nature showed in his face, for MacQuarrie suddenly seemed to feel the need to concentrate on his salmon and set about finishing his plate rather than continue any conversation.

Jack looked at his secretary once more. "Anything else?"

"Sir Geoffrey from the Foreign Office would like a word, my lord."

Jack gave a curt nod. "Schedule an appointment with him. Thank you, Sanders. I'll be with you shortly."

The thin man left hastily, as though fearing the earl would invite him to dine once more, and the world would abruptly end if he were to yield to the temptation of taking the Earl up on it.

"Save yourself," Jack murmured very quietly. "The sky is falling."

With Sanders gone, MacQuarrie ventured a reproachful look at Jack. "What's this about the Foreign Office? You aren't planning on going off to play spy before this business with Summers is done, are you?"

"No, of course not," Jack answered. He was tempted, of course. Very tempted. It had been a long time since he'd had any contact with the Foreign Office, and the life no longer appealed to him. But an assignment somewhere on the opposite side of the world from Scheherazade was just what he needed. He was never far from her no matter where he was. He carried her in his soul. But to be physically near her was impossible. Completely.

MacQuarrie pushed his chair back. "And how is the Summers matter coming?" He spared a glance for the Chinese monk, then looked back at Jack. There was a clear question about whether they could talk in front of the foreigner in the Scotland Yard man's eyes.

Jhou Xa chuckled very softly before Jack could answer. He spoke to Jack in Mandarin. "Tell him I have little English, and less interest in false holy men."

Knowing Jhou Xa as he did, he realized his words indicated that the monk had a keen interest in both and was as curious about Jack's opinions as MacQuarrie was.

Jack very much wanted to tell both men to go to the devil—where he would join them presently. Instead he passed Jhou Xa's words on to David MacQuarrie.

MacQuarrie nodded, pushed his chair back and got to his feet. "I need to make a report to my superiors, Jack. So if you could just tell me what passed between Lord Gordon and the Prince last night and your plans for further investigation of the man's schemes, I'll be on my way."

The problem with dealing with Summers meant Jack might have to see Scheherazade during the course of the investigation. That was simply not possible. "You have nothing to worry about from Summers," he told MacQuarrie. "Nothing at all. I assure you." He didn't know if it was a lie or not. He did know that the ends justified the prevarication in this case. And what a Cullum-like notion that was! It didn't matter. He had to protect Scheherazade from his intruding on her life again.

But could he let duty and honor slide in the course of that protection? He could certainly try.

"I couldn't discern Summers exerting any influence on Bertie," Jack told MacQuarrie. "Nor do I see it having any importance if he should. Even if he were using mesmerism on the prince to make him say black is white, what good would it do Summers? It's not as if Her Majesty's government or Her Majesty ever pays any attention to the heir to the throne."

MacQuarrie scratched his jaw. He looked worried. "So it is your considered opinion that Lord Gordon Summers is a harmless crank?"

Jack nodded emphatically. "It is."

"I hope you're right, my friend."

So do I. Jack got to his feet and patted MacQuarrie reassuringly on the back, all bluff and hearty—and false—as the inspector turned toward the door. "A passing interest on Bertie's part. He's had them before. Usually involving ladies of high station and easy virtue," Jack added. "He's probably between mistresses just now."

"Aye," MacQuarrie said. "That's likely. No doubt the prince will lose interest in Summers the moment he finds a new woman."

"Let's hope that's soon," Jack agreed.

A moment later the dining room door closed behind the departing MacQuarrie. With one conversation done and a morning's worth of appointments still awaiting him, Jack turned impatiently toward the Shaolin monk. Jhou Xa watched his every move with his usual discerning, alert calm.

"It is not like you to lie. Though perhaps those were not quite lies," the monk said with soft reproof. "There must be something very wrong indeed for you to be so misleading with a friend."

Jack didn't try to explain any of his reasons. Instead he asked, "Just what is it you want with me this morning, Master Jhou?"

The monk did not looked pleased at such direct questioning from a student, but he answered. "You have heard that a delegation has come from Kuzay for the Queen's celebration."

Jack frowned. "I've heard. It has nothing to do with me."

"I spoke with them last night." The monk stood.

Jack was surprised. "How does a Buddhist monk come to be acquainted with such outlaws?"

Jhou Xa smiled. "I am acquainted with you." Jack gave an agreeing shrug. The monk went on. "I, too, am an outlaw, if you recall. The Manchu rulers of China outlawed the Shaolin monks, and we scattered to many places. That is how you met and came to study with us after you left Kuzay."

"After I *escaped* from Kuzay."

"Members of my order have found refuge there in recent years. They have helped us. It is our duty to help them if the need arises."

Jack didn't want to hear about duty. "What does this have to do with me?"

"Rhu Limpok wishes to speak with you."

"Rhu Limpok will see you."

The court official had brought enough guards with him to make it obvious that his words were not a request. They surrounded the compound that contained his house in a way that was ominous and quite unexpected. "Why?" he demanded of the messenger.

"Because he wills it," was the answer he received. He didn't like it. Not one little bit.

He liked it even less when the messenger added, "And you are commanded to bring your golden concubine with you. Rhu Limpok will look upon her."

There had been no choice but to acquiesce to

the whims of the ruler of the pirate island. It had been the beginning of the end. The end of his assignment, and the end of his interlude in paradise with Scheherazade.

"Rhu Limpok might want to see me," Jack told the monk, "but I don't intend to see him. Not now. Not ever." He bowed formally to his teacher, but his expression was implacable when he went on. "Don't ever mention that man's name to me again."

Chapter 17

As he left the dining room Jack was surprised to see both Hawton and Saunders waiting for him in the hall. "I thought you were waiting in the library," he said to his secretary. "And you should still be off that sprained ankle, shouldn't you?" he added to the butler.

"My ankle is fine, thank you, my lord," Hawton responded. "I was just on my way to inform you of the visitor."

"The visitor Mr. Hawton showed into the library," Saunders said.

"A young lady," Hawton elucidated. "She insisted that you would wish to see her."

"Alone," Saunders added. Which explained the secretary's presence.

Jack barely noticed either of them after being told a woman was waiting in the library. A woman who had insisted on seeing him alone.

Scheherazade? Here? Could it be possible that she'd come to him?

His heart hammered at the thought. His blood raced with fire. He hurried to the library.

Minnie Hamilton, her face and expensive clothes all proper and clean, her glossy black hair done up in long, ribbon-tied braids, turned away from looking at a shelf of books as he came in. "Hello," she said, and regarded him warily as he shut the door softly behind him.

Jack waited a few moments before he spoke. It took time to get his emotions under control, and there were a great many emotions to deal with. Far more than he was used to. There was an ambivalent combination of disappointment and relief to sort out. Then there was the mixture of elation, confusion, and irritation at finding this unattended eight-year-old—she must be about eight—child standing before him once more. While he didn't manage to get all of these feelings under control, he did sort them out enough to present a calm demeanor as he stepped forward.

He stopped a few feet in front of her, put his hands behind his back, and asked, "What are you doing here, child?"

He didn't know if she intended to mirror his gesture or not when she put her hands behind her back. She looked up at him. "I wanted to ask you a question."

What was he to do? Run from a small girl? He wanted to. He wanted to run very far away before having to face the truths this child would demand from him. Truths he wasn't prepared to face himself. Truths he hadn't known about and hadn't yet been able to think about. She'd obviously been thinking about them for a long time, though. She deserved answers now, not whenever he was ready to give them. Jack supposed Scheherazade might not agree with that, but Scheherazade wasn't facing Minnie Hamilton right now; he was.

Heaven help them all.

"I have questions for you, too," he told the child.

"Can I go first?"

Jack smiled faintly. "Before you lose your nerve?"

A flash of annoyance crossed the child's face, but she nodded.

"Would you care to have a seat? Shall I ring for refreshments?" His politeness was more a play for time than any civilized behavior. He tried to put himself at ease as much as Minnie. This was not going to be a pleasant interview.

"Thank you." Minnie took one of the leather chairs by the fireplace. "I can't stay very long. So we better just ask each other our questions."

Jack took the seat opposite her. The fire drew the dampness from the room. Dampness that was partially caused by a draft from the window Minnie broke to enter the house last night. The curtains were drawn across the window to cover the patched glass. The electric chandelier was switched on, lighting the room rather more than Jack liked. It was easier to keep secrets in the dark, but this wasn't the time for secrets, he supposed.

He braced himself. "Very well," he said. "You first."

Her words came out in a rush. "Why did you leave by the window?"

He was completely astounded by this unexpected question. "What?"

"You know where the front door is," she went on in a reasonable, practical tone. "But you left by the window again last night. You could have stayed for breakfast."

The heat of shame coursed through him, along with a growing sense of outrage that the child had so carefully monitored what had gone on in her mother's room. He didn't want to remember what had happened in that room, in that ruined bed, last night. He hated the thought that Minnie was even vaguely aware of such evil. For her own sake she needed a good talking to about the dangers of being too curious.

He stood, looming over the small figure. "Minerva—" he began sternly, but felt so serious a lecture called for something more. "What is your middle name, child?"

"May."

May. Of course. "Minerva May." He took a deep breath. "Minerva May PenMartyn, you are too curious for your own good. Too willful. Too enterprising. And no doubt quite spoiled and headstrong as well."

She slipped out of her chair to stand gravely before him. Her eyes were round as plates. "I'm your daughter."

He wasn't sure whether her reply was an explanation for her behavior, or childish delight in his easy acknowledgment of their connection. His answer came in a heartbeat when she threw herself gleefully into his arms.

His arms circled her, the gesture as needy and automatic as hers. He didn't know how long he held her, warm and soft and fragile, clasped to him. Soft and warm she might be, but the child was strong. She held to him as fierce as any tiger cub.

When he did let her go it was because some measure of calm had returned to him. He recalled that theirs was a reunion of strangers no matter how welcome it was. She did not know him, and it would be best if she never did. He knew he was not fit to be a father, though his possessive soul cried that she was his and what was his he kept.

Fortunately, he had experience fighting that demon, and he was able to loosen his embrace, to gently pull her tightly clasped hands from around his neck. He sat back on his heels so that they were eye to eye. "What other questions do you have for me, Minerva May?"

The girl smiled, and he saw himself in her. Even through the wave of pleasure at this resemblance between them he wondered how her mother could bear the constant reminders of the man who'd fathered her daughter. Then again, perhaps Scheherazade had never noticed his smile.

What sort of mother was she, this woman who was heaven in bed?

His musings were interrupted as Minnie said, "You answered my questions already." She bounced once, with delight, he thought. Then she looked toward the door. "I have to go, Papa."

He rose as she went to the door. "Papa?"

She turned back questioningly, expression anxious. "Can I call you Papa? Or—?"

Jack ran a hand along his jaw; he could already feel his heavy blue-black beard beginning to return despite Dabney's best efforts. He worried that the stubble might have scratched his daughter's tender skin. Children were delicate things. They had delicate bodies, and even more sensitive feelings. He had worked among London's orphaned and abandoned children, and seen how the lack of parents devastated and warped them.

"You may call me Papa if you wish," he told Minerva. "If your mother agrees," he added, after a moment.

Jack supposed it was only fair to give Scheherazade's wishes in the matter some consideration. Despite his vow to keep away from Scheherazade, there was more to be settled between them about the child than could be dealt with by their respective solicitors.

"I'll take you home now, Minerva."

She shook her head, obviously not anxious to have her mother know she'd been to see him. And just how was it that Scheherazade allowed the girl out on the streets of London by herself? It was improper, and certainly dangerous. Did the woman care so little for the bastard he'd forced on her that she—?

"You have business," Minnie told him. "I heard your secretary mention appointments to Mr. Hawton. Mr. Hawton is very nice."

"Yes, he is. My business can wait. You can't go out alone."

"I'm not alone. Ira brought me. He's waiting outside."

Ira. So that's how she got here.

Jack remembered the excessively tall, broad-shouldered American with his dark curling hair, high-arched nose, and wide, full lips. He remembered the outsized hands that had held Minnie with practiced tenderness, and the sharply intelligent brown eyes that had assessed him with one quick, intent look before he'd whisked Minnie away.

Anger and suspicion seethed in Jack at the thought of Ira. Just what was this man to his daughter? Or to Scheherazade. May had claimed Ira as her husband, but May was ever a peacemaker, always Scheherazade's ally and confidant in the harem quarters where he'd kept them. *"May's coming with me."* Scheherazade had declared it on the day she'd left him, and neither he nor May had argued.

It was logical and right that May would still be in any house where Scheherazade dwelt. But it wasn't his concubine's friendship that worried him at the moment, but this Ira's influence on his daughter.

Something was going to have to be done about this Ira. But not here and now. The last thing Jack intended to do was disturb Minerva in any way. He would take the subject up with Scheherazade, and soon.

He kept his tone jovial as he said, "Then you

had best be going, my dear. You wouldn't want to keep Ira waiting any longer."

If she had thought that retreating into the crowded meditation room would rid her of the attentions of the Prince of Wales, Sherrie had been sadly mistaken. Prince Albert Edward simply followed her when she excused herself from the library and hastened to join the saffron throng.

They weren't chanting now, but listening in rapt silence as Lord Gordon stood at the front of the room before a gold statue of a seated Buddha and lectured his converts. Sherrie found a place at the very back of the room, in hopes of remaining unobtrusive.

She didn't have to worry on that account. Space was made for her and the large man who trailed after her, but only one head turned at their entrance. Cousin Daisy briefly caught Sherrie's gaze, a look of long-suffering annoyance mixed with the light of hope that Sherrie had come to rescue her and drag Faith from the clutches of religious bliss. Sherrie gave Daisy a brief nod, but took a seat rather than march forward to take her cousins home. Since she had no real reason to make a scene, Sherrie supposed it was best to wait until an opportune moment to make a getaway with the girls.

In the meantime Sherrie tried to forget the prince's presence by looking curiously around the room. There were gold Imperial Chinese dragons painted on the ceiling while the filigree lamps suspended on chains overhead were more of an Ottoman design. The patterned rugs in deep reds, creams, and indigo blues were Persian, the shoji screen near the windows was Japanese. There were two serenely smiling Buddha statues in the room—the one Lord Gordon stood in front of, which was Chinese, and a second one standing near the door that Sherrie guessed was Burmese, or perhaps Thai. There was also an alabaster statue of Kuan Yin, the Chinese goddess of compassion, and a bronze statue of Hindu Shiva the Destroyer, in a pose that showed him dancing for the end of the world. The shining copper incense burners were from India, and there were wall hangings depicting arcane Tibetan symbols.

Amid all the religious clutter were prosaically English touches such as huge potted ferns, a hunting print over the fireplace, and a mantel clock in the shape of a train engine. There was a stag head mounted above one of the wall niches. The room was full of fragrant smoke, fairly reeking of a mix of sandalwood and patchouli.

Sherrie found the overall effect an assault on her senses. She supposed that the decor, with its odd hodgepodge mixture of Asian symbolism and English bad taste was supposed to be some sort of comforting introduction to Oriental philosophy, where the Mysteries of the East were revealed in safe, familiar surroundings.

And in the middle of it all was the Great Teacher. He stood before the gathering as a virile, handsome, titled member of the ruling class who smiled lovingly upon his students. And he talked. Lord, how the man could talk, and in such a mesmerizing, mellifluous voice!

Sherrie didn't pay too much attention to what Lord Gordon Summers said. It was the tone that irritated the hell out of her. She found herself becoming more annoyed at the image he projected. Everything he did revealed that he saw himself as an intrepid and wise master of the British Empire who had returned from great adventures in the East to bring back all the secrets of the ancients, secrets that only he could interpret and reveal and share at his Golden Light Mission. Only Westerners could truly appreciate the wisdom of the ancients, even though that wisdom had been hidden in the East. The ancients, according to Summers, had just been waiting for a pale, blond, titled, well-connected, educated Englishman to come along and finally get their wisdom right and graciously pass it on to the rest of the pale, fair, white world.

For a fee, she supposed, though Summers didn't go so far as to pass the hat. There were probably a great many ways of manipulating what he wanted out of his followers. Or maybe he really believed that he was a great, wise teacher come to save the Western world.

As far as Sherrie could tell, she and Daisy were the only people in the room who didn't agree with Summer's assessment of himself as the wisest man on earth. Even the Prince of Wales had a benign smile on his face the entire time Summers spoke—though she suspected that Bertie's smile had a lot to do with his having a hand on her knee, a heavy touch that she didn't notice until near the end of the sermon.

When she did notice that the prince was taking liberties, Sherrie promptly pushed his hand away. "Your Royal Highness, please!" she whispered.

"Apologies, m'dear," he answered, sounding more hearty than apologetic. "We wouldn't want to move too fast, now, would we?"

"No," she answered. "We wouldn't." She suspected that her dry tone was completely lost on the Prince of Wales. He was too involved in acting out a script he knew by heart, and took no notice that she hadn't auditioned for the role of American Widow of Easy Virtue in the production. "I don't do amateur theatricals," she murmured.

"What's that, m'dear?"

My dear. M'dear. First Summers and now the prince. Why did these puffed-up British males seem to think that there was anything dear about her? That their attention was somehow flattering? How did one tell the heir to a throne to leave her be? With Rhu Limpok's son she'd used a knife. But that probably wouldn't work in this situation.

She supposed that there *was* a protocol which governed the circumstances, which were not at all to her liking. He, no doubt, expected her to be flattered by his overtures, to give him coy, encouraging glances. Even if the heir to the throne was a notorious womanizer, she made it a policy not to get involved with princes. Or kings, maharajas, grand dukes, or great khans. Especially not great khans.

"She is indeed golden, my friend, and as lovely as rumor says."

Cullum was standing behind her with his hands on her shoulders. His grip tightened until it was very nearly painful at the Khan of Kuzay's words. His touch was reassuring and frightening at once, proof that he held onto what was his.

"Thank you, Highness," Cullum responded.

"She pleases you, my friend."

"Frequently, Highness."

The men laughed, and she pretended not to hear. She kept still and quiet in Cullum's embrace, eyes humbly lowered. She had yet to grow used to being spoken of as an object, a female whose flesh was readily available for inspection and comment, but she strove not to show any emotion.

Rhu Limpok gestured and a servant came forward. The servant held an ebony case toward Cullum. The lid of the case was open, inside was the most spectacular thing she'd ever seen. A treasure in pearls and carved jade.

"This is as beautiful as your golden one," Rhu Limpok said. "And far more priceless."

"I think the woman's price is for me to judge," Cullum answered. She heard the anger in his clipped, precise tone, felt it course through him, communicated to her from the hard touch of his hands on her shoulders.

"I judge what is priceless here. I have decided to give you the necklace, my friend."

"In exchange for what?"

"Your golden one."

"I think not."

Rhu Limpok ignored Cullum. "The necklace is a fair trade. It was made in India. A raja's gift for the English queen, though the jade carving is from China in ancient times," Rhu Limpok said. He laughed. "It came to me instead of the English queen. The six strands of white pearls are perfectly matched. The black pearl in the center is quite rare. The white jade that surrounds the black pearl depicts the tiger and a dragon that battle each other for the pearl of wisdom."

"Which is not generally depicted as a black lump of oyster spit," Sherrie murmured to herself, and noticed that her fingers touched her throat, as though searching for the necklace that wasn't there.

Why did she keep the thing when it was nothing but a symbol of slavery and degradation?

Because Cullum's hands had fastened it about her throat. At the time it had been a symbol of triumph, of their victory of life over death.

That's why, you idiot, a voice in her head stridently informed her. You remember what that moment felt like, don't you? What his hands felt like? The fierce triumphant glory of the kiss you shared?

I remember, she answered the insistent voice. *I can't forget, but I want to.*

Liar, her conscience responded.

Sherrie deliberately lowered her hands to her lap, and clasped them tightly together. Her nails bit harshly into the backs of her hands.

Even through the sharp pricks of pain she could still feel his hands on her, his mouth clinging hot and sweet to hers. *As though it had been yesterday?* The words inside her head were a venomous snarl. *You idiot, it was.*

Nothing had changed. Everything was the same. Except her, and him, and the world. The pirate and the girl were long gone, and it turned out the pirate she remembered was even more false and treacherous than she'd thought. How he must have laughed at her even then, as the arrogant Lord St. John had his way with the ignorant American. Bastard.

Beautiful, magnificent bastard.

"My dear, are you well? Is it the incense? You seem a million miles away?"

She turned to the prince. "Only a few thousand, Your Highness."

"We shall have to do something to focus your attention here." He stood and held out his hand. "Come and I'll introduce you to some of the ladies."

The service was over, people were moving around, but it didn't appear that anyone was headed for the door. Most were clustered around Lord Gordon. She didn't need the prince's help to identify many of the members of the congregation. She'd met most of those present at the social functions she'd already attended. There was Lady Ottilie Tanager, whose husband was something important in the Finance Ministry. And Dame Agnes Blythe, whose husband, brother, and son were all generals. She was accompanied by a daughter-in-law, and a daughter who was engaged to Sir Basil something, who built ships and owned coal mines. Mrs. Bosworth's husband published newspapers, and Ginny Ambersworth's family owned land, lots of it.

Sherrie couldn't help but notice that scattered among all these women from powerful, prosperous families there were also converts in simpler clothes and hairstyles, women with humbler bearings and self-effacing attitudes. In fact, Sherrie spotted her own maid in the group of worshippers as Todd took off the saffron shawl she'd worn during the service.

Sherrie didn't try to catch Todd's attention as her maid moved toward Lord Gordon. She looked quickly away when Lord Gordon took Todd's arm and walked her away from the group for some individual words of wisdom. Sherrie felt it would be intruding on the woman's privacy to pay more attention to the lady's maid. How Todd spent a half-day off was none of her employer's business.

Besides, more important than dealing with the prince and a large portion of the women of the British ruling class, she had the wrath of her Aunt Dora to think about. She'd come here to bring Faith and Daisy home. It was more than time to gather them up and get them out.

"Excuse me, Your Highness."

Chapter 18

❧❧

Summers wasn't at all happy to have the servant approach him with the Hamilton woman in the room, but he showed no annoyance. He smiled at her, the same gentle, loving, knowing smile he used on duchess and drab alike. He looked deep into her eyes in the way that never failed to let a woman know that he cared deeply for her, that—at least, for as long as he needed her—she was the only woman in the world. Without a word he took the maid's arm and drew her aside. His followers would respect his wish for a private word with one of his daughters, so he had no fear of interruptions.

And his most distinguished guest, his most royal highness, was too taken up paying court to the new woman he fancied to bother him, either. Later, of course, Bertie would express his pleasure at the encounter with the woman that Lord Gordon had promised him the night before. Bertie was delighted by such simple things.

The prince wasn't a stupid man, but he was spoiled. He wanted a new toy, and Lord Gordon was happy to provide it. Prince Albert Edward was used to his gentlemen friends providing him with "opportunities" such as this one today. He was used to his friends providing him with their wives, if that was what he fancied. The wives were generally quite happy for the opportunity to further their own and their husbands' ambitions by doing whatever was necessary.

It was a perfectly workable system and Lord Gordon Summers had no intention of changing the rules, merely using them to his own advantage. He didn't see any reason why those wives and daughters and sisters—and maidservants, for that matter—shouldn't use their native gifts to manipulate the men who thought they ruled the world into doing exactly what he wanted.

Of course, he was working on the men as well, gathering followers. He was an advisor to many, a good friend to all. The growing group of powerful men who came to his private evening services were becoming quite attached to lessons in meditation. He taught them a way to enlightenment that required the use of very limber, very naked young women and illustrations from the *Kama Sutra*.

There were other inducements as well, other pleasures, other addictions he could nurture and exploit. He was very good at what he did, and it was all coming along quite nicely, really.

Best to concentrate on the moment, though. The Buddha was right about that. He smiled his benign smile on the maid, and spoke ever so softly to her. "Yes, Amelia? What have you to tell me, my dear one?"

The woman's already loving gaze lit with even deeper joy. Her voice was so low that he almost had to strain to hear. "He was at the house last night, Master."

"Indeed?" he whispered back. "You are sure?"

She nodded. "A footman recognized him. He was in *her* bed all right," Todd went on with whispered contempt. "They went at it like animals. I know. I had to clean up the mess."

He nodded and gently stroked her hand. "You poor dear."

"The room stank of what they got up to. So did she."

"You must pray for her, my dear. Pity her. Continue to serve her so that you may bring her to me. We will redeem her together. She and Lord PenMartyn share a very deep, very damaging *karmic* connection. Only with our help can they sever it and find peace." He added a fatherly sternness to his gentle tone. "You want them to find peace, don't you, my dear?"

Todd lowered her gaze. "Of course, Master."

"Bringing these two hurting souls peace will be very hard. I need you. They need you, Amelia."

"I won't fail you."

"I know. Continue to watch, and bring your news to me." He put his hand on her head in blessing. "Remember your own soul as well.

Say your *sutras* and do no harm. Now leave me, I must speak to others.''

The maid drifted away with a beatific smile. Lord Gordon noticed that Sherrie Hamilton and her cousins were gone from the room. It didn't matter. Faith was his. Todd and several others at Primrose House were his. Sherrie Hamilton would be his soon. He had great things planned for her.

As for the Earl of PenMartyn? Summers smiled, and there was nothing benign about it. He had great plans for Jack PenMartyn as well.

''Scheherazade.''

The whisper came to her on the rose- and lilac-scented breeze, though she told herself it was just her imagination. Sherrie's pace faltered for a moment as she neared the entrance of the gazebo. A chill ran down her spine, but she told herself that was her imagination, too, caused by the wind or a cloud crossing the recently emerged sun. She looked around the garden that was still damp from the morning rain. It was bright now with late afternoon sunlight, a fragrant, shining, peaceful place. What shadows there were she had brought with her. She wouldn't be intimidated by her imagination. She didn't have much time to be alone, so she continued determinedly along the brick path that led to the gazebo in the center of the garden.

The guests for Aunt Dora's tea party were due to arrive very soon. She didn't have much time to try to find the composure she needed to make herself seem charming, calm, and cultured.

Sherrie would have preferred to spend the rest of the day with Minnie, but had been informed that Ira had taken Minnie and May on an excursion. She wished she could have gone with them.

"Scheherazade," the whisper came again.

A shadow moved inside the rose-covered structure, and suddenly he was there in the doorway. His broad-shouldered form was framed by soft pink and white rose blossoms on the trellised gazebo. The setting didn't make him look any less dangerous. Neither did his dark, expensively tailored clothing.

His icy blue gaze caught and held hers before she could turn to run. When he held his hand out, Sherrie moved toward him without thinking. He took her arm and drew her into the privacy behind the climbing roses.

Sherrie regretted her reaction the instant he drew her inside, but once she was in the cool, fragrant interior of the building, it was too late to turn and run. Because he stood before the entrance. To get out she would have to get past him first. They both knew she was trapped, and she knew that she'd allowed it. But why? What was it about this man that still drove her to such risky behavior? At least he had released his hold on her arm once they were inside.

She backed away from him, coming to a halt when she encountered the wrought-iron bench set in the center of the gazebo. With no escape and nowhere she could run, Sherrie stood her ground and confronted him.

"I should scream."

He crossed his arms. "Why?"

"For form's sake?"

"Or as a signal to let the games begin? You should have screamed when you first saw me." He added, "I always enjoy it when you scream." Jack felt his control start to slip away the moment they were alone. She appeared innocent and fragile and young in the lacy cream dress she wore, and the surrounding wall of flowers added to the impression. When she blushed at his words, he couldn't stop the predatory smile from quirking up his lips.

"We need to talk," he went on. "In private." He took a step closer. "You know how dangerous it is to be alone with me. How improper."

He knew the danger he posed to her far better than she did. But for what they needed to discuss, they must be in private. "I won't let you scream, of course." What he'd meant to say was that she had no need, though the words had more truth than the good intentions behind them.

She didn't cower, of course. She responded with the fire he expected. "You clean up pretty, *your lordship.*" She crossed her arms and looked him over the same bold way he used to look at her. "But you haven't changed a bit."

He inclined his head and spread his hands out before him. "I know."

He wasn't smiling when he said it, not gloating. His serious expression puzzled her. For a few moments he had looked like the dangerous, seemingly relaxed hellcat-with-sheathed-claws Cullum of old. Now he stood ramrod erect, with his hands at his sides; the fire had gone out of his icy blue eyes; all expression had left his handsome face. He looked—not so much as if he'd assumed a mask, but an entire new identity.

"What are you doing here, Lord PenMartyn? Don't tell me that my aunt invited you. Of course!" Sherrie was appalled and indignant, though she supposed she should be grateful at such an easy, mundane reason for his presence. "Aunt Dora thinks this earl masquerade of yours is real."

"It is."

"She thinks that you're just another respectable suitor for the girls. That you're a fortune-hunting English nobleman. You stay away from my cousins. It's bad enough I've got to keep shooing Faith away from Lord Gordon. I'm not going to have you involved with them, too. It's hard enough to keep this family in order without adding the likes of you to the mix. I'll do anything I have to to take care of my family," she warned him. "If you lay a finger on one of those girls—well, the next time I shoot at you, I won't miss."

He ignored her rash threat. "Don't be ridiculous. I have no interest in either of those young ladies."

"Maybe I should just shoot you before you get the chance to develop any interest."

"Maybe you should." He grabbed her by the

shoulders, but she spun away from his grasp, and would have fallen head first over the bench if he hadn't put his arm around her waist to steady her. She automatically leaned against him, molded her body to his. She threw her head back against his shoulder. "Damn you, Cullum."

His lips touched the vulnerable, exposed skin of her throat. Her scent was far more intoxicating than the sheltering roses. His hands found her breasts beneath their coverings of lacy-covered cream silk and the restrictive corseting. He heard her gasp, felt the tips of her breasts become pebble hard against the pads of his thumbs. He felt himself hardening as well. The emptiness in his soul was overshadowed as the insistent ache began in his groin.

There was a time when he would have simply bent her forward over the top of the bench and had her then and there. A time when taking his pleasure with her was his right, his privilege, whether she was ready for him or not ... but then, that had been their agreement. Her part of the bargain was to open herself for him whenever and wherever he pleased. He couldn't recall a time when she hadn't been ready for him, begged him to do what pleased him. What pleased them both.

How he missed that power. With his hands on Scheherazade once more, he couldn't recall why he'd given it up.

He had touched no woman for nine empty years. No one was Scheherazade. Until last night.

Until last night he had gone to bed alone. He'd held no one close. Now his arms moved to enclose her in a vise-hard grip. He felt her stiffen with sudden apprehension. The shiver of fear made him smile. His lips moved from her throat to just beside her ear. "Did you sleep with him? Did you go to his bed?" She held perfectly still as he crushed her against him. His whisper held the rough, lilting tone of Cullum Rourke. "Did you?"

Her confusion was palpable. "Who?"

Her reaction fed his anger. And his possessiveness. How many men had she been with? How many in—Nine. Long. Years. He concentrated on the one that mattered. "Your . . . husband." Damn it, what had the man been called? "Hamilton."

She squirmed against him, struggled against his unbreakable hold as though she'd just woken from a dream. "Let go of me."

"Answer me."

"It's none of your—"

"Did you?"

"Yes!"

"While you carried my child? Did you sleep with him while you carried the baby I planted in you?" *Did you love him?* No. That was an answer he didn't want.

"Why do you think I married him, you damned fool?"

He released her and stepped back when he heard her answer. His senses reeled from the revelation. Of course. Of course. Here was proof of another degradation he'd driven her to.

She'd married not for love, but to protect her child from being labeled a bastard.

Her eyes flashed angry fire that caught and held him. He almost lifted his hand to shield himself, but he couldn't move, couldn't look away.

She stepped toward him, her elegant hands balled into tight fists. "Did I sleep with Jerry? Yes. Is it any of your business? No. Did I enjoy it? Would it bother you to know that I did enjoy being made love to by my lawful wedded husband?" She spoke each word slowly, with vicious savor.

His throat was dry. His lungs burned, pain lanced through his head, and his heart hammered painfully against his chest. He wanted to go deaf. He didn't want to speak, but the word dragged itself out of him anyway. "Yes."

"Well, I didn't. Not once. Not ever. I did my wifely duty—and I felt *nothing*. You did that to me."

"I'm—"

"Sorry" wasn't a strong enough word. And it wasn't even true, not completely. Part of him, a large, ugly part of him, was delighted that no man had ever given her pleasure but him. That he still owned that part of her.

"You're what?" she demanded.

He couldn't answer her. He couldn't let the subject of Hamilton go, either. "What happened to him, this husband of yours?"

"He was shot."

"Shot?" Jack gave a short laugh as he remem-

bered the derringer under her pillow last night.
"By whom? You?"

"He was murdered during a card game in a
saloon."

It sounded like an episode in one those
American penny dreadful novels. Yet it was no
doubt true, and nowhere near as outlandish as
some of the incidents he and Scheherazade had
lived through. "And what did you do about
this murder?" He didn't think she was likely to
have simply assumed her widow's black and
settled into a proper, quiet period of mourning.
He told himself he had no right to know about
her life or her feelings, but he was intensely curious just the same.

"I didn't do a thing." She didn't know why
she answered. It was none of his business, but
she went on. "I was pregnant at the time. Mar-
shal Callin wouldn't arrest the gambler who'd
killed Jerry, said it was a fair fight, and everybody knew Jerry had been heading for that bullet for years. It was Ira who accused the
gambler of being a cheating murderer and
goaded the killer into calling him out. Ira was
faster on the draw."

Ira. The mention of the man's name, and her
account of this Ira's heroics reminded Jack of
why he'd sought out a private word with
Scheherazade. Perhaps it should be this Ira person he had words with.

"And where is *dear* Ira just now?" he asked.

"At the Tower of London." She didn't know
why she told him. "He took May to see the
sights."

Jack was appalled. May was delicate, physically weak, and shy, her appearance completely
alien. "May will be stared at."

How strange—he sounded as if he cared.
"She's used to it by now. She just bravely stares
back. Ira's been very good at convincing her
that being different is just fine. He's rather different himself, you may have noticed."

He took deep offense at her belligerent tone.
She sounded as if she expected him to make
some anti-Semitic comment, as though religion
and race were the reasons he objected to the
man's presence in the Hamilton household.

"And is my daughter with them?"

Sherrie feared and resented the Earl of
PenMartyn laying claim to her child. She also
resented his arrogant, condescending tone
when he spoke of Ira Gartner. He seemed to
think that Ira was just another servant he could
order around. "Of course Minnie is with Ira,"
she told him. "Where else would she be?"

The woman dared to smile at him as she
spoke, a thin-edged, dangerous smile, showing
contempt at his concern for Minerva's welfare.
Her attitude did nothing to placate his temper.
"You allow the man to act as her nanny?"

She laughed. "Ira is Minnie's tutor, and her
bodyguard. She needs both, the way we travel
the world."

"Dismiss him."

"What?" She didn't believe her ears. Who did
this man think he was to march into the life
she'd created and disrupt it with a few curt

commands? And what a foolish question for her to pose.

"You heard me. And this world traveling of yours, it stops right now."

"Excuse me?"

"It's not good for the child."

"Who are you to tell me what is good for my child?"

Jack was preparing to roar the answer at this impossible, foolish, stubborn woman when a voice from the entrance behind him said, "I hate to interrupt your conversation, Sherrie, honey, but it's time for you to come in now."

"I thought we might find you two here," another voice added.

"Later," he whispered, before assuming a pleasant, smiling mask and turning to face Scheherazade's aunt and Lady Anne. "Later."

Chapter 19

❦

"**T**hat did not go particularly well," Jack murmured to himself behind the shield of a lifted teacup.

Unfortunately, he had run out of the time and the necessary privacy to repair the damage done by his high-handed arrogance in dictating the matter of Minerva's upbringing. Instead of showing his concern for his child's welfare he had quickly managed to alienate Scheherazade even further.

If that was possible. Her final question, *"Who are you to tell me what is good for my child?"* echoed in his ears. Who, indeed? Someone who cared deeply for the charming, headstrong child? Or was his paternal concern for Minnie merely an excuse for forcing himself on Scheherazade once more? He didn't know. God, he didn't know.

He did know that he was pleased that she'd stood up to his presumptuous demands, that she had not taken kindly to his giving her orders. It was a relief to know that his hideous, inexcusable behavior the night before had not broken her spirit.

He gazed over the top of the cup, but not at the women in his conversational circle. His attention was drawn inexorably across the terrace, down to the tables set in the rose garden, and to the beautiful blond woman dressed in cream lace as she moved with gracious assurance among her guests. Mrs. Sherrie Hamilton was the tallest woman among the thirty or so people attending the gathering at Primrose House. The most elegant, the most graceful, the most—everything.

Jack was barely aware of anyone else, and knew she was equally aware of him by the occasional, almost furtive glances she aimed his way. He supposed she wanted to have him thrown out, or hoped he would flee in fear of her exposing his wicked past. He stood his ground, he didn't know why, and hid as best he could amid vapid conversation and the clattering of cups and saucers.

The fine china was a flimsy shield at best, but he supposed the group of mamas and their eligible daughters that surrounded him would provide adequate defense against anything more violent than a bitter look Scheherazade might throw his way.

He didn't know why he stayed for the tea party, or why Scheherazade let him. No. Of course he knew. For propriety's sake. They both played the respectability game.

"What was that you said, Lady Phoebe?" he

asked, aware that he was required to reply to something the woman had said.

"I was wondering what you thought of Mrs. Hamilton's rather amazing history. It's all quite beyond belief, don't you think?"

For a moment he feared they'd been caught out. He very nearly grabbed the woman by the front of the gown that covered her ample bosom and demanded what she knew.

Before he could move, Dame Julia Leslie said, "I've read the memoirs she's published about her travels in India and the Holy Land, and I'm anxious to know what she'll have to say about life in Tibet. A fascinating woman, for an American. She has a sharp, wry eye and a clear way of expressing a woman's view of the places she's been. That was why I was so anxious to meet her." She smiled at the group, and added, "I didn't even mind bringing my son along to meet her cousins in exchange for the privilege of a conversation with Mrs. Hamilton."

"You dream of being an adventuress, Julia?" Mrs. Caxton asked. She giggled, and her two daughters followed suit.

Dame Julia smiled. "Not I, but I can appreciate the achievements of those who choose a less conventional path. Besides, I hear that between the Comstock wealth and the fortune Mrs. Hamilton plans to settle on the girls when they wed, having one of them in my family might be a very good thing. You know how much work that old castle of ours in the Highlands needs."

"Julia, you're shameless!" Lady Phoebe

looked scandalized, though she had both her daughter and her niece with her in the group that surrounded the eligible, wealthy Earl of PenMartyn. She turned her attention back to Jack. "What do you think, my lord?"

"I think," Jack answered honestly, "that I had better read Mrs. Hamilton's memoirs."

For it had just truly dawned on him that nine years had passed since he had last seen Scheherazade VanHarlen. The women's comments, plus what he had learned from Scheherazade in the rose arbor, sparked a new depth to his constant interest in the woman he could not and should not have.

He gazed out across the terrace in wonder at the beautiful woman who was the object of his obsession. She was currently deep in conversation with Lady Anne Beaumont. *Who are you, Sherrie Hamilton?* he wondered. *And what difference can it possibly make to me?* he added bitterly, knowing it was too late suddenly to care. Not that the bitterness and regret dampened his growing curiosity one little bit.

Later. Sherrie couldn't get his last threatening word out of her head. What did he mean by *later?*

He was up on the terrace, watching her. She could feel his gaze even though he seemed to be deep in conversation every time she let herself look his way.

"And who are all those women?" she murmured, and was quite appalled that the irritated words came out before she even knew she was thinking them.

Lady Anne replied cheerfully, "Your cousins aren't the only ones on the marriage market, my dear. Most of the mothers in Britain are after him for their girls, and as you can see, those girls aren't arguing."

Sherrie stared at the group on the terrace. She was completely aghast by the very notion. Indeed, there were at least three young girls among the admiring, simpering women clustered around the Earl of PenMartyn. She was appalled. "What would any child see in him?" As if she didn't know. All right, the man was tall, broad-shouldered, and devilishly handsome.

"Indeed," her friend replied. "I think a match between the two of you is the only fit one for either of you." She rubbed her hands together. "It will be the wedding of the Season." She shook a finger at Sherrie. "I won't have you running off to America, or eloping to some other foreign place. We shall hold the wedding in my ballroom. You will look splendid in a Worth gown that will exactly match those lovely pearls of yours. We will have Minerva as a flower girl. She's going to love Jack, you know. He adores children."

Sherrie didn't take her gaze away from the man her friend intended her to marry while Lady Anne's words conjured up images of the perfect wedding. To the wrong man. He was poised, his expression polite and friendly as he chatted with the admiring women. He appeared civilized, intelligent, vital, and vibrant. He exuded a controlled power and sexuality that couldn't help but attract, fascinate. Sherrie could see him at the wedding Lady Anne described, standing sure and protective next to his adored bride. She could imagine a doting, devoted husband, lover, friend.

She could imagine quite a bit, and let herself, at least for a few moments.

She was quite enthralled, and more than a little horrified at her reaction to Lady Anne's plans, but balked at the mention of Minnie. That brought her back to reality as a jolt of fear raced through her.

She turned on her friend. "What do you mean, he adores children?"

Lady Anne either didn't hear the frightened accusation in her voice, or chose to ignore it. She looked pleased at Sherrie's showing any interest in Jack PenMartyn. "His charity work, for one thing—the orphanages, the children's hospital he's helping to finance. It's all quite admirable. And of course, people are always coming to him when their wild wastrel sons get in any sort of trouble. He's done a great deal to help turn the lives of some young men around. Jack says he knows all about how their minds work."

If there was one thing Sherrie was certain of, it was that the man Lady Anne so admired knew all about how a wild wastrel young man's mind worked. So did she. "They don't have minds. They have unholy urges."

Lady Anne's smile didn't dim a bit. "That's

almost exactly what Jack says. You two are going to deal wonderfully well together."

Sherrie looked at her friend for a moment in utter panic as she fought back the urge to tell Lady Anne everything, to reveal just how well she and Jack PenMartyn had dealt together. The hysterical urge passed quickly, pushed down as it always was by the knowledge of how dangerous the truth really was.

"The first thing you must do is get him to retire completely from the Foreign Service," Lady Anne went on, bent on her arrangements for the future. "I'm not supposed to know about it, but my Robert is his superior. My dear husband has shared some of his knowledge with me, knowing I won't pass it on. But," she touched Sherrie's arm. "Some of the stories I've heard about Jack's exploits make my hair stand on end."

"Exploits?" Sherrie asked, with her heart in her throat.

Lady Anne looked very encouraged by Sherrie's interest. "Am I impressing you? He's quite the secret hero, you know."

Sherrie glanced once more at the cool, suave, much-admired Earl, surrounded by a bevy of adoring women. *If only they knew about some of those exploits*, she thought. She also knew that his secrets were safe with her. Because his secrets were also hers. If it had been just her own reputation at stake she might have shouted his crimes and infamy from the rooftops. Just to see how he would respond, if for no other reason. She could survive the social ostracism that would follow without too many regrets. But what of Minnie? What of her aunt? Her cousins? Her love for them forced her into unwilling complicity with Jack PenMartyn, forced her to live with her own hypocrisy. Damn the man!

Lady Anne put her arm through Sherrie's and guided them toward the terrace. Sherrie let herself be led, knowing that people would notice and comment if she appeared to snub someone so beloved as the Earl of PenMartyn. She also knew, and damned herself for it, that she went because she wanted to. Being apart from him was harder than being with him. She hated making the admission, but she didn't have the emotional energy to lie to herself at the moment.

Why should she lie to herself, anyway, when she had Jack PenMartyn to do it for her?

Sherrie quickened her pace when she saw her cousin Daisy join the group around Jack. Daisy, the sensible one, Daisy, who was young and beautiful and wealthy, smiled at something Jack said. Jack smiled back.

"Oh, no," Sherrie murmured, as protective fury overtook her. "We won't have any of that if I have anything to say about it." She shook off Lady Anne's grasp and hurried forward.

"You said we would talk later," Scheherazade said quietly from behind him. "Let's make later now, shall we?"

Jack wanted nothing more than to be alone with her, and knew it was the last thing either of them needed. For her reputation, for her safety's sake, he should make some excuse and leave. He turned to her and said, "My time is yours, Mrs. Hamilton." He held out his arm. "Where may I escort you?"

Sherrie knew they were trapped by all the curious gazes of her guests. She couldn't simply march off the premises with the Earl of Pen-Martyn. "Why don't we take a short walk through the maze?" she suggested, and let him touch her. It was a light, almost impersonal grasp. Or so it would seem to those who watched. She knew it was as unbreakable as an iron band. "Excuse me for abducting the earl," she told the surrounding ladies. "I promise to return him to you presently. Daisy, why don't you join your sister? She's talking to Sir Daniel. I suspect she's preaching about *sutras*. You may need to rescue him," Sherrie added, as she noticed the glazed expression of the young man standing a few feet away with Faith. "I'm sure he'll find your company much more entertaining than your sister's."

"And that Daisy will find Sir Daniel's company infinitely more interesting than mine," Jack murmured, as he led Sherrie toward the boxwood and lilac bush maze at the end of the garden. "You never were very subtle, Scheherazade," he added. His voice was pitched so that no one else could hear. Her expression didn't change, but he felt her flinch at his use of her given name. He fought the urge to touch her, to run his hand through her hair as he asked, "Does no one ever call you by that name? Do you hate hearing it from me so much that it makes you tremble?"

He didn't know what he wanted to hear. That she wanted to hear her name on his lips? That she wanted the reminder of the hell he'd put her through?

Sherrie didn't answer him. She didn't say anything until they stepped inside the entrance to the maze. She reminded herself to keep her voice down as she turned to face him and hissed, "Stay away from my cousins!"

Jack knew he should simply reassure Scheherazade that he had no interest in the girls, but he took offense at her accusing tone. Her attitude offended the pride of the Earl of Pen-Martyn. "I assure you, madam," he responded haughtily, "that their dowries—"

"You're not getting your hands on them, or their money."

"They are quite lovely," he conceded. "In fact, they rather resemble their elder cousin. I'm sure they'll do well on the marriage market, but I am not the marrying kind."

"No, you're the debauching kind."

"You would know."

She paled at his hard words, words that she had stung out of him. He couldn't stop himself from matching angry word for angry word in a cold, aristocratic drawl. His tone was a disguise for the fact that she drew blood with every cutting word she spoke. That he deserved to bleed didn't make him able to bear the pain in defenseless silence. He added, trying to reassure her through his own torment, "I have no interest in debauching the innocent."

"Liar!"

He had meant to be comforting. Of course he had gotten it all wrong. She didn't want or need to hear those words. "Of course," he agreed with her. "A constant liar. A manipulator. A user. Guilty of whatever you say, but I am no fortune hunter. I have quite enough fortune without needing to marry your cousins to get more. Nor do I want to seduce their innocence away from them."

"And we both know how you got that fortune, don't we?" she spat back at him. "Pirate. Opium runner. Slave trader. Mercenary."

He nodded. "Yes. I hunted them all, and took a percent of every cargo I confiscated as my bounty. I grew quite wealthy cleaning up the flotsam and jetsam the Royal Navy couldn't touch."

Sherrie was speechless. Her mind raced, but words totally failed her. How could he say these things to her? How could he admit that his life had been a lie? A fabrication? That he had only been pretending? That nothing they shared had been real? The things he'd done with her still felt real to her. He had taken her away from everything she knew, changed her irrevocably, then set her adrift without a backward glance. Cullum Rourke did what he wanted and thought nothing of the consequences, and she had belonged to Cullum Rourke.

She wanted to scream. She wanted to take him by his starched shirt front and shake the explanation out of him. Why had he done what he did to her? Why the bargain? The captivity? Why the endless, boundless hours of shared passion without a single word of explanation, of reassurance? Why had he played games with her body, her heart, and her soul?

"I could say it was the opium," he said, as though he knew exactly what she was thinking. "I could say it was the drink. I could say it was the loneliness, and getting caught up in believing the role I played for too long. I could make any number of excuses, but the truth is, I did exactly what I wanted and enjoyed every moment of it, and didn't give a damn about anything but my own pleasure."

They looked into each other's eyes for a few moments after he spoke. He didn't ask for absolution. She didn't offer it. She supposed he didn't want any. He had done what he wanted and that was that. Maybe he thought protecting the British Empire earned him any reward he chose, including taking any woman he briefly fancied to his bed.

"But I'm an American," she said.

A look of confusion filled his ice-blue eyes, but she broke eye contact with him before he could speak. Though she wasn't looking at him, she felt the angry tension grow in him, and felt him rein it in. He was putting on his party mask again, she supposed. She made an effort to do the same.

"We should go back, my lord," she told him. "My guests will be expecting me."

"And you wish to be safe among them," he answered.

He managed to make his tone cordial, but the tiger was there, claws showing but sheathed in the reminder of her safety. The beast was leashed for now, but it strained to get out. If he let it have its way, he would drag her to the center of the maze, throw her to the ground, and repeat last night's performance. His true self didn't care about propriety, about her guests, certainly about her safety. His true self cared only about mating, and with no one but her.

He knew that nothing had been settled between them. Of course, nothing could be. It would be pointless to ask for a forgiveness he did not deserve. "If you don't want me to ravish you again, we had better go."

Sherrie didn't know whether his words were threat or promise. It took all her strength and self-control to nod her head, let him take her arm once more. She walked back out of the maze more shaken and confused than when she went in.

Chapter 20

Aunt Dora, Lady Anne, and a delegation of other matrons waited just outside the entrance to the maze. From the eager looks on their faces, Sherrie got the impression that they were gathered to await the announcement of her impending engagement to Jack. She didn't know what Lady Anne had told these people, or how much her aunt had encouraged them, but they were in for a disappointment if they expected Jack PenMartyn to ask her to marry him.

Hell, the man didn't even bother to ask her if she wanted to go to bed with him before inviting himself on in. About the only ceremony she was likely to attend with him was his funeral. About the only thing she would formally ask him to do with her would be to participate in a duel. Of course, the Earl of PenMartyn would never fight a lady. The coward had his title to hide behind.

Just the way you have your widowhood to hide behind, a stern voice in her head reminded her.

A voice that sounded remarkably like May's, but was undoubtedly her own conscience. *You're as much a hypocrite as he is, Sherrie Hamilton. Now, aren't you?*

Aunt Dora spoke up before Sherrie could respond to her own difficult question. "Lady Anne's been telling me all about you, young man," she spoke to Jack. "She also tells me I'm not supposed to ask if you're going to be welcomed into the family just yet. I know you've only known Sherrie a few days and wouldn't dream of proposing so soon. But you English expect us Americans to act rashly and indiscreetly, and I hate disappointing my guests." She held up her hands as everyone, including Jack and Sherrie, laughed. "So," Aunt Dora went on. "Are you two going to get hitched?"

"Mrs. Hamilton was just informing me that she is American," Jack said. "But I doubt that she is rash and reckless enough to accept even were I to propose marriage."

Sherrie hated that he sounded bright, cheery, and urbane. Everyone laughed again. She hated that he was charming and universally admired—just because he was kind to orphans and saved the world on secret missions didn't make him admirable. Or maybe he was admired because he was handsome, wealthy, and eligible. And just what was an earl doing being eligible at his age, she found herself reluctantly wondering. Didn't he have a duty to his title and family name? Shouldn't he have an heir and a spare by now? He'd told her last night that he hadn't had a woman for nine years. A man with his appetites going without a woman? She didn't believe it.

And yet—

She remembered how desperate and demanding he'd been when they'd made love. She remembered the taut straining of his muscles, the way he'd shaken as he'd buried himself inside her, how he'd controlled his desire, forced it to last. She remembered how wild and needy they had both been, and felt that need growing inside her again.

It was because he was touching her, she decided, and made herself step away from his side. Moving did no good. She could still feel him touching her, even though his hand dropped from her arm the instant she moved. *What does it matter if there is no physical contact,* she thought, as the familiar ache filled her. *He's been touching me for nine years.*

Sherrie moved next to Lady Anne. Jack graciously offered his arm to Aunt Dora and they all walked back from the maze to the buffet tables set up just below the terrace. Conversation was light and easy, and soon came to center on the multitude of events planned to commemorate the Queen's Golden Jubilee.

"Just how much is the Queen participating?" Aunt Dora asked. "In America we read about how reclusive she is. But what does the press know about the truth, anyway?"

"Dame Julia is a lady in waiting to Her Majesty," Mrs. Caxton told Aunt Dora. "So if anyone can tell us how much Her Majesty plans to participate, it's you, isn't it, Julia?"

"I do know her schedule a bit," Dame Julia admitted. "Her Majesty does lead a quiet life. There are several charity benefits she is considering attending." She looked significantly at the Earl of PenMartyn as she added, "And, of course, there is the ceremony next week to award several Prince Albert Medals, but that will be a very exclusive affair."

Mrs. Caxton looked slightly exasperated. "Anything involving Her Majesty is always very exclusive. In fact, I haven't seen the woman since my girls were presented at court."

Aunt Dora sighed enviously. She looked hopefully at Sherrie. "Isn't that lovely, honey? I'd love to see my girls presented to the Queen." She laughed and added, "I'd love to meet the Queen. Wouldn't you, Sherrie?"

Actually, Sherrie wasn't particularly interested in meeting the Queen. She'd met one queen already. It was an experience she wasn't eager to repeat.

"You will bow before the Great Wife, Lui Jai, Marvelous Lady, Queen and Consort . . ."

The titles and honors went on, but she didn't pay much attention to the pompous eunuch's sing-song pronouncements, not when there was a foot resting on her back, shoving her face into the thick pile of the rug in front of the cushion covered dais. She could barely breathe with her head forced to the floor. Besides, she could hardly hear over her own sobbing and the thunderous rush and roar of her heart. Still, the high-pitched voice went on.

She didn't care about Lui Jai's titles and status in

Rhu Limpok's harem. All she cared was that she was in Rhu Limpok's harem, and that it was Cullum Rourke's betrayal that had trapped her here in the depths of the pirate khan's palace—and soon into his bed.

For a necklace. Cullum had sold her for a handful of pearls!

Despite his promises, despite the words of love he spoke in the dark, in the throes of passion—his breathless, panted words revealing his longing, his need for her—the liar! When it came to it, Cullum's greed and avarice won out over his fancy for her. After all, she was just another girl, a commodity to be sold, given away, traded for a bauble. Priceless pearls, Rhu Limpok called them, but that was as much a lie as Cullum's words of love. They were only worth her body, her heart, and her soul.

She wanted to die.

And supposed she would soon, one way or another. If she couldn't arrange it for herself, she was sure that someone else in this violent, intrigue-soaked palace would arrange it for her.

She knew for certain that she was going to die when she was pulled to her feet. She noticed through her tears that the room was full of beautiful women dressed in vivid silks: small, delicate, Asian women from a dozen lands. She stood out like a sore thumb among them: a big, yellow-haired, broad-footed creature with pale eyes and a big, high-bridged nose. She didn't know what the Khan of Kuzay could see in a foreign devil white ghost female like herself.

"You are almost too ugly to look at," Lui Jai said, echoing Scheherazade's thoughts. "Men are strange,

with too much appetite for that which is not good for them."

The Great Wife stared at her with utter hatred. Cullum, May, and Cullum's servants had all told her stories about the notorious Lui Jai. She was said to be more ruthless and wicked than her pirate lord. If not the power behind the throne, she was the brains and backbone.

"My lord is a man of too many whims," Lui Jai said, as she looked Scheherazade over. "Most of them are harmless ones." She waved a long-nailed hand; her jeweled nail guards glittered in the light of the lamps that surrounded the dais. Lui Jai shook her head. "I will not have a foreign devil woman here. Bad enough Rhu Limpok allows the Tiger to roam the waters around Kuzay. Who knows what you will whisper to my husband while in his bed. How you might try to influence him. I don't like your ways, or your looks. You do not know how to show me the respect a Great Wife deserves. No. You cannot be here."

Scheherazade was relieved to see that the Great Wife did not want her in the harem any more than she wanted to be here, and Lui Jai had the power to see that her stay would not be a long or pleasant one.

"You will die tomorrow," the Great Wife told her. She sighed. "But first you will go to my eldest son's bed. He wants what his father wants, but has agreed that one night with the Tiger's woman will be more than enough to satisfy his curiosity."

"Come to me."
The prince stood next to a very large bed. It was

made of elaborately carved mahogany, with red silk coverings embroidered in silver and gold. The room itself was rather small, though it had doors that were opened to a moonlit garden, which gave some illusion of space.

"No . . . I don't think so," she answered the prince's command.

He held out a hand and smiled. He was young, handsome, but for the scar that slashed across one cheek. She supposed he was handsome even with the scar, that it made Rhu Limpok's eldest son look dashing and dangerous. The prince wore only a pair of belted trousers made of clinging silk, his chest and arms were corded with wiry muscle. There was a large gold-hilted dagger stuck through his belt. No sheath. Very dramatic. Very threatening. She was not particularly impressed. Terrified, yes, but not impressed.

He shrugged. "My mother said I should have you drugged."

"A boy should always listen to his mother," she responded. She knew being meek, submissive, and pleasing wasn't going to do her any good, so why bother? If she was lucky, showing her claws might get her killed quickly. Otherwise she would have to wait until after she was raped.

He moved toward her, smiling; his thumb caressing the golden dagger hilt.

She backed up a pace only to come up against the door a pair of guards had shoved her through a few moments before. They were still there. She could faintly make out the sound of their voices in the corridor beyond. They seemed very amused by the idea of the prince bedding a foreign devil. She couldn't see anything funny about it.

As the prince drew closer, she warned, "I'll kill you if you touch me."

She didn't blame him for laughing. It was pure bravado. She was taller than he was, but he was most definitely stronger, and a well-trained fighter. He knew there was nothing she could do to save herself from him.

He grabbed her. She screamed, as much with surprise as terror, as she was tossed onto the big bed. He landed on top of her an instant later. She had the knife out of his belt an instant after that. She wasn't sure what instinct was at work in her. She thought she wanted to die, but the need for self-preservation took over before she could think about it.

He was strong, he was fast, but he didn't expect it when her knee landed in his groin. Maybe no woman had ever tried to fight him before. She had an instant to push him off her when he reacted to the blow. By the time she was on her feet, he was after her. She ran for the entrance to the garden.

Only to be shoved aside as a large body came barreling through the doorway. Scheherazade was knocked to the floor. The dagger went flying. She looked up, terrified, waiting for a guard's sword to come slamming down and take off her head. Waiting for the prince to grab her and throw her back on the bed.

The last thing she expected was what she saw. It wasn't a guard who had come racing in from the garden. Two men struggled across the tiny room locked in vicious hand-to-hand combat, the dark, wiry Asian, and a much larger westerner.

"Cullum!"

"Hush, woman," he complained, breathless with exertion. "There's only so much I can bribe the guards not to hear."

She scrambled to her knees and snatched up the fallen dagger. By the time she got to her feet the fight was over.

Cullum turned from where the unconscious prince was sprawled on the bed. He looked down at the knife in her hand. "I thought you could use my help, but if you'd rather I left . . ."

It took her a moment to realize he was joking. Then she chuckled. Then her senses filled with wonder, her heart with relief, and her eyes with tears. "Oh, Cullum."

He swept her into his arms. "Are you hurt? When I heard you scream—"

"I'm fine." She touched his face, traced her fingers along his lips, met his eyes for one of the few times since he'd captured her. Her heart beat wildly as she whispered, "I thought you traded me for the necklace."

He cupped her face with his hands, brushed his lips across hers. "I wouldn't trade you for my life." He kissed her, and all the fire she'd thought had turned to ash at his betrayal ignited once more. The kiss didn't last nearly long enough before he broke away, and said, "We have to go. Through the garden. Quickly."

He kept the necklace, though.

Sherrie touched the pearls clasped around her throat as she looked into the dressing table mirror. She realized that she had completely lost track of where she was for a few moments while Todd finished carefully arranging her hair.

When she came back from her memories, Todd was done. "Thank you." After she dismissed the maid, she got up and went to perch on the end of the chaise where May was seated. She spared a glance at the mantel clock. "I promised Minnie I'd have dinner with her in the nursery."

"I know."

"He sent her a letter." She hadn't heard a word from the Earl of PenMartyn since yesterday's tea party, but this morning a thick vellum envelope bearing a fancy gold seal had arrived addressed to Miss Minerva Hamilton.

"I know that, too."

"Minnie can't think or talk about anything else. Not just a note to his 'Dear Minerva May,' but he invited her on a picnic. Did you know that?" May nodded. "A charity affair—with orphans. Taking them on an outing in the countryside. It's disgusting, him using unfortunate children to lure Minnie away from me."

"You were included in the invitation. Ira and I received one, too."

"He's up to something!"

"He wants to see his daughter, and the woman he loves."

Sherrie concentrated on her frustration at the placid smile on her friend's face to keep from thinking about love. May, of course, saw nothing wrong with a father inviting his child on an outing.

Sherrie knew it would do her no good to tell

a Chinese woman that a child didn't belong to a man just because he'd sired it. In fact, it would do her no good to tell a Western woman the same thing. Sometimes she thought she was the only woman in the world who believed that men didn't have a God-given right to do whatever pleased them because they came equipped with a dangling bit of muscle and skin they couldn't control, and generally used to think with instead of their brains.

May was pregnant. She hoped to present her husband with a boy-child. Presenting her husband with children was her duty and her joy. "You probably want me to present Cul-Ja-Him with a son, don't you?"

May patted Sherrie's shoulder. "I want you to be happy."

"I'll take that as a yes." She twisted her hands together in her lap. "I can't stop thinking about him."

"Why do you sound so desperate now? You never can stop thinking about him."

Sherrie didn't deny it. Possibly for the first time ever. "The problem is, I don't know what to think about him."

May laughed. "That, my friend, is an improvement."

An improvement over what, Sherrie wondered. "Am I supposed to stop hating him just because Minnie has decided she adores her 'Papa'?"

"You've never hated him. And Minnie has excellent judgment of people, doesn't she?"

"Minnie," Sherrie agreed, "is frightening." The child had an almost preternatural gift for understanding and evaluating people. Sherrie didn't think her daughter had inherited the ability from her side of the family. In fact, she'd put the girl's almost psychic discernment down as something Minnie had inherited from her father.

"He lied to me." Why did she have to keep coming back to that? She should be more worried about the man's intentions toward Minnie than about an old betrayal. An old betrayal she'd just discovered. That's why it hurt so much. She was used to all the old pain he'd caused her, but this was a new, raw wound.

"Men lie," May told her. "So do women. Good men lie when they must."

Sherrie glared at her friend. "Did he have to? I don't think so. He says he did it because he wanted to."

May glared back. "Did the lie do you any harm? Does the lie change anything that happened? Didn't he save you from the Malay pirates? Didn't he keep you safe on Kuzay? Didn't he let you go?"

"Yes—but—the context . . ."

May made a sharp, dismissive gesture. "You're just looking for another reason not to forgive him."

Sherrie shot angrily to her feet. "Another?"

"It's been a long time, Sherrie. People change. I have, you have. He has. He changed that night. You know exactly when it happened. He changed. He found redemption, and you can't forgive him for it."

She didn't want to hear this. She wasn't going

to listen to this. She had an hour before she had to leave with her aunt and cousins for an event where she was probably going to have to face Jack PenMartyn again. She was full of dread, anger, anticipation, and something she hated to identify as longing, at the prospect of seeing him.

She smoothed out the skirts of her emerald green gown. "I'm going to go see Minnie now."

And spend the next hour discussing dear "Papa," no doubt. Sherrie gritted her teeth. Whether it was May or Minnie, there was just no getting away from the man. The worst thing was, she didn't even know if she wanted to.

Chapter 21

"There are an awful lot of diamonds in the audience tonight, my friend," David MacQuarrie said to Jack, as the inspector peered out from the side of the stage. His voice was pitched to carry over a Mozart piece being played by the quartet of skilled amateur musicians currently on the stage.

"And a few pearls," Jack added quietly. He saw her in the audience, just visible beyond the bright limelights placed on the edge of the stage. Sherrie—he forced himself to think of her as Sherrie—sat second row center, with her family around her. She was vivid and lovely, her fine, fair skin set off by a deep green gown, her long throat accentuated by the sheen of the dark-hearted pearls.

Her blue eyes flashed with fury as she held the necklace out to him. Behind her the fire that had lit the night was finally burning out. Her face was covered in soot and shadows, making her eyes seem even brighter.

"Keep them," he told her. His hands and arms

and face stung like hellfire, but he kept the pain from his voice. "Please."

"Why? Because I earned them?"

"As a memento." Please keep them, *he thought.* "To remember me." Please forgive me, *he thought, but didn't have the courage to say aloud. He barely had the courage to do what must be done.* "Just take May and the necklace, and go."

She didn't bother arguing with him anymore.

Why did she still wear them? He wondered. Was it anything at all to do with him? For him?

God, what a vain, foolish thought!

Perhaps it was simply for vanity's sake that she wore the necklace, but a part of him hoped that she wore the pearls because she wanted to keep the link with him alive. He had no right to hope, but he couldn't seem to stop it.

That hope tempted him to join her, there was an empty seat by Sherrie Hamilton's family group. Fortunately, he would have no chance to yield to temptation this evening. He had been asked to come backstage by Lady Julia Leslie, the charity event's main organizer. Besides, MacQuarrie was along for the evening as his guest. He would not abandon duty to be with her tonight.

The Scotland Yard man was along on official business. MacQuarrie wanted a look at Gordon Summers, a chance to observe personally the man he worried was up to no good. MacQuarrie claimed his copper's nose was never wrong. He smelled something amiss about the leader of the Golden Light Mission even without any hard evidence. Jack was convinced his friend was mistaken, but he acceded to Mac-Quarrie's request to get the inspector closer to Summers in a way that wouldn't "tip the cove off." Since Summers was scheduled to speak this evening, bringing MacQuarrie to the theater seemed like a good idea. So they waited backstage, barely hidden by the velvet curtain pulled back from the proscenium arch, just enough to peer at the audience without being seen. Summers was scheduled as the next person to do his bit for the children's hospital fund-raising event on the stage.

"Perhaps he has some sort of mass mesmerism planned," Jack joked.

"Maybe he does," MacQuarrie answered. He didn't sound as if he was joking. "Maybe his lordship plans to wave his arms and put the ladies in a trance."

"Then he'll take their diamonds," Jack elaborated. "Heaven help the man if he tries to abscond with Mrs. Hamilton's pearls, though."

MacQuarrie nodded. "Rumor has it the lady carries a gun."

Rumor was correct. Though Jack assumed the rumor was founded on the belief that a gun seemed the sort of thing an American from the Wild West should have. He wasn't about to tell David MacQuarrie that Sherrie kept the gun under her pillow, not in her reticule. Then again, perhaps she did carry a derringer in her evening bag. Possibly in her bustle. He had spent much of last night and today reading her memoirs. He wouldn't put anything past the woman.

She shot tigers in India, he thought proudly, as he stole one more look at her. *She actually rode through the forbidden mountain passes into secret, sacred Tibet and spoke to the living incarnation of the Buddha of Compassion. She's done so much since last we met. And there she sits now with her aunt and cousins, as regal and protective as a mother swan among her cygnets.*

"What an amazing woman."

MacQuarrie overheard him and responded, "Mrs. Hamilton? Oh, aye. Though the lass next to her in the yellow dress is more to my taste."

"Really?" Jack asked his friend. MacQuarrie blushed as Jack gave him an assessing look. A devil of mischief overtook Jack's other demons. He smiled, and said teasingly, "The lass in yellow is Daisy Comstock. I can introduce you to the young lady, if you like."

"What?" MacQuarrie asked, aghast. "What? Introduce the likes of me to an heiress?"

"Why not?"

MacQuarrie didn't deign to answer such an outlandish question. "This is the oddest thing I have ever been in a theater for," MacQuarrie commented, as the music ended, effectively changing the subject. "Toffs entertaining toffs? *Wot's the world comin' to, guv'nor?*"

Jack's attention was drawn from the subject of Sherrie Hamilton and her family. He continued to smile at his friend. "What have I told you about that fake Cockney accent of yours?"

"You have told me, my lord," MacQuarrie replied, in round Oxonian tones, "that you have a facility for regional dialects, but that I do not."

"I wish you would remember that." Jack clapped the taller man on the shoulder. "You should hear my Irish accent. It's quite good." Though MacQuarrie didn't know it, Jack had just revealed something about his hidden past that he had spoken to no one about in years. He wondered if he had just made some sort of break with that past, first thinking of her as Sherrie, now this. He was almost tempted to reveal more. Did he dare? Would catharsis do any good? Or would it just bring out the beast?

Jack forced his mind back into the moment. He and MacQuarrie stepped back from the side of the stage, partly to get out of the way of the exiting musicians, mostly to be out of Summers' line of vision when he came on stage after being effusively introduced by Lady Julia.

Jack forced himself to concentrate on the strikingly handsome blond man who walked easily out to face the crowd. Summers was smiling, self-possessed. He looked at home behind the limelights. More than that, he looked like he not only owned the wealthy, influential audience, but that he had every right to. From the way the audience responded with loud clapping and cheering when he came before them, it appeared that they agreed.

That Summers quieted the adulation with a gesture caught Jack by surprise. Summers waited for a moment in silence, looking slowly around the expectant crowd. He held them in his hands and he knew it, and his eyes glittered with greed. Jack's hunter's instincts roused as he thought, *It's not their diamonds this man wants, it's their souls.*

But what did Lord Gordon Summers want with the souls of all those rich, influential converts?

He exchanged a look with MacQuarrie as Lord Gordon began to speak. "I begin to see what you mean," he whispered. "I think I've missed something about the man. Something dangerous."

MacQuarrie put a hand on Jack's arm. The gesture spoke volumes about his trust in Jack, his faith in Jack's abilities. A trust and faith Jack never completely shared.

Whether Jack believed in himself or not didn't matter. MacQuarrie's faith in him would force him to do whatever was necessary to stop Summers—from whatever it was Summers was up to.

After the first minute or so, Sherrie completely lost interest in what Lord Gordon said. It was no trouble at all for her to tune out his platitudes about love and kindness and improving the world by following the Way—*his* way, specifically. She found him banal and boring. It was the reactions of those around her that she found disturbing. Faith sat straight in her chair, a rapturous expression on her face, nothing in her eyes but a reflection of Lord Gordon Summers' face. Faith certainly wasn't alone. All around were lords and ladies, peers and ministers and captains of industry who reacted with just as much fervor, applauding and cheering whenever Lord Gordon paused for a moment.

If he passes the hat, she thought, *there won't be a diamond or a pound note that's safe from him.*

Sherrie exchanged skeptical glances with her aunt and Daisy and Lady Anne, but everyone else around them seemed to be caught up in the man's mesmerizing aura. It was as if they formed a small island of sanity. She was almost frightened to appear unaffected by Summers. A chill raced up her spine, as an odd, disturbing vision flashed through her mind of his ordering his followers to turn on the nonbelievers among them. He gave no such command, of course, though she was shaken by the suspicion that if he did, he would be instantly obeyed.

Fortunately, his little talk didn't last too long. In fact, the standing ovation for him went on longer than Summers' speech. Sherrie prudently rose from her seat and clapped with all the enthusiasm she could muster. *Always be polite and follow the customs of the natives,* she reminded herself.

Once the noise had finally died down and the audience had returned to their seats, Lady Julia came sweeping grandly out onto the stage to make the next introduction. The handsome matron was a vision in a dove gray gown, rubies at her throat and dyed egret feathers in her artfully arranged hair. Sherrie admired Lady Julia's style, but she did feel rather sorry for the egrets.

"Dear friends," Lady Julia said. She spread her hands wide and smiled warmly, clearly enjoying her turn as mistress of ceremonies for the evening. "Soon the Welsh choir that Lord Carfanon has graciously brought to London will serenade us."

There were faint approving murmurs and a slight ripple of applause from the crowd. Sherrie had heard about the magnificence of Welsh choirs and looked forward to this part of the entertainment.

"First, however," Lady Julia went on. She gestured toward the wing to her right. "I would like the man who has made the building of the Victoria and Albert Children's Hospital possible with his generosity and hard work. Lord St. John PenMartyn, will you please join me on the stage? Come along, Jack," she added with a laugh, when seconds went and the applause began to die down.

There was a ripple of good-natured laughter from the audience, and more applause as Jack PenMartyn came striding out on the stage at last.

Sherrie couldn't move. She might as well have been bolted to the seat. She just sat there and stared, never mind that the second standing ovation in the last several minutes was going on around her. She was actually grateful when the people in the rows ahead of her stood. At least she was hidden, if only for a few moments. At least she couldn't see him, if only for a few moments.

When the audience sat he was still on the stage, not a vision out of her nightmares, but a handsome man in impeccable, conservative tailoring. Black was definitely his color. In fact, she couldn't recall ever having seen him in any-thing but black, except for the frequent times when she'd seen him in nothing at all.

Sherrie forced these inane thoughts out of her head and concentrated on the moment. When she glanced around, Lady Anne caught her gaze for a moment. Lady Anne smiled and nod-ded toward Jack—showing smug pride in the public acknowledgment of the paragon she was trying to foist off on Sherrie.

"I've been foisted by him," Sherrie muttered, half-hysterical. "No, that's not the right word, is it? It's that other word that begins with F."

"What?" Aunt Dora asked.

"Nothing."

Dora leaned over and whispered. "Sherrie, honey, you look like you're about ready to pull a gun. What's the matter with you? Why aren't you happy for the man? I thought you were in love with him."

In love? with *him*? Where the devil had Dora Comstock gotten that impression? Sherrie con-centrated on the stage rather than trying to make any effort to answer her aunt's foolish ac-cusation.

On the stage, Lady Julia was saying, "Her Majesty the Queen-Empress wishes to express her gratitude for your efforts on behalf of her-self and those of her less fortunate subjects. It is my honor and pleasure to announce that, as part of her Jubilee celebration, Her Majesty has made a surprise addition of Lord St. John PenMartyn, Earl of PenMartyn's name to the

Honors List of 1887." Another ripple of applause went through the audience. Lady Julia went on enthusiastically, "So our own dear Jack will be joining those other admirable men at the ceremony to receive the Prince Albert Medal at the Buckingham Palace Monday next."

Jack felt Sherrie's accusing gaze on him. He felt nothing else except the shame. He had never felt it more acutely than at this moment, as the audience once more rose to its feet to applaud for the honor being shown him. If he had any true courage he would take this opportunity to explain to the gathering, to all those people who thought him kind and generous and good, that once upon a time he had let selfishness and passion overrun sense, had indulged in every vice he could find, he had reveled in degradation—his own and others'. And it had been glorious.

He could not speak the truth. Not now. For Sherrie's sake he could not speak. For Minerva's sake he could not speak. For MacQuarrie's sake he could not speak. Revealing his past, accepting the condemnation he deserved might free his soul, but it would not help the people who needed him. Accepting the responsibility he bore them in the present kept him silent about the past. Duty helped him to smile and bow, to kiss Lady Julia's hand. To say, "Thank you. And God bless our beloved Queen-Empress."

I think he's going to be sick. Fear and concern stabbed through Sherrie at the sight of Jack PenMartyn's pale, stricken face. Her reaction was as unexpected as it was unwanted. Sympathy flooded her. Around her everyone was applauding and wishing Jack well. She wanted to shout angrily at them to leave the man alone. Didn't they see their love hurt him?

He looked just like Minnie when she was hurt and scared. Sherrie's arms ached from wanting to hold him.

"Damn him," she muttered. How dare he make her feel sorry for him! He didn't deserve any sympathy. She could tell from the stricken look in his eyes that he didn't think he deserved any, either.

Why did he think that, she wondered. She was as confused by his reaction to the adulation as she was by her reaction to him. The man ought to be smirking in triumph, hugging his secrets close, and laughing silently at all these people who thought he was some sort of hero. Nothing in this moment made sense to her.

All Sherrie knew when he exited the stage was that she had to get to him. She didn't think about why, she just went.

Summers didn't mind sharing the audience's adulation with Jack PenMartyn. Not at all. He stood beside PenMartyn's Scottish friend at the side of the stage and watched the earl haltingly make a short, falsely humble thank-you speech for the upcoming honor. The man's inclusion in the Honors List was going to prove very useful, so Lord Gordon wasn't at all perturbed that Jack was going to see the reclusive Queen. In fact, perhaps he'd had a hand in suggesting that

Lord PenMartyn should receive some small reward for his charitable acts. Perhaps he had been aware of Lady Julia's closely kept secret long before she'd revealed it on the stage.

No good deed goes unpunished, now, does it, Cullum?

Summers masked his amusement at all the secrets he knew, hugging them closely and carefully to himself. He was well aware that the tall Scotsman's attention was focused on him, so Summers kept his expression bland, his attitude one of pleased interest in the proceedings out front. MacQuarrie, Summers well knew, was with Scotland Yard. Scotland Yard was interested in his affairs. To night, MacQuarrie had used his relationship with PenMartyn to come see Lord Gordon Summers speak.

MacQuarrie suspected him of something—but by the time his suspicions were proved to be well founded it would be too late for the feckless, frivolous, thoughtless world order MacQuarrie represented.

But there was a bit of work to be done yet, before the reins of power would be completely in his hands. In the hands that deserved them.

Lord Gordon saw Mrs. Hamilton rise and make her way toward the small door at the front of the building that led to the backstage area. She was pale, her eyes burning, her expression set and unreadable to anyone but himself, Lord Gordon supposed. She really was a very simple soul, her whole being concentrated on one thing and one thing alone. The poor dear really was Cullum Rourke's complete and devoted slave. The wonder was that the Tiger had let her go.

Or perhaps she had run away. Lord Gordon's sources of information were rather unsure about how the pair had parted and why. It had happened the night Cullum Rourke's Russian rival had persuaded the Great Khan of Kuzay to have the White Tiger's home and ships burned, or so one story went. Another claimed that the girl had run away after Cullum had given her to Rhu Limpok's son in an effort to save his waning influence at the khan's court.

Why the Tiger and his woman had parted didn't truly matter now. Lord Gordon had seen how she still affected the man. He saw that she was doing her best to come back to her master, though it appeared that both the Tiger and his woman were fighting against the inevitable. Lord Gordon was enjoying watching the battle. The outcome was going to prove very useful.

Lord Gordon consulted his pocketwatch. The night was young enough. This entertainment was over. People in the audience would be heading off to parties, to suppers, to dances and romantic trysts. Many would be going to an evening service at his home. He would not be there to lead the prayers. He had just decided upon new plans for the evening. A meeting with Mrs. Hamilton and the Earl of PenMartyn, though neither of the pair were aware they were destined to spend the night with him. He hadn't yet issued the invitation.

Lord Gordon clicked his watch closed, nodded politely to the Scotsman, and went to make the necessary arrangements.

Jack was surrounded by a thick crowd in the narrow wings of the theater, and everyone was talking at once. Sherrie could only stand back and watch for now, and wonder, *Why am I doing this?*

She damned the impulse that had driven her to make her way to Jack's side in the back of the theater. She only knew she had to reach him.

She was amazed at the genuineness of the well-wishers' words as she made her way past them.

"Well, done, Jack," a man in a general's uniform proclaimed.

"It is about time," Lady Julia added.

"You've served the Empire well, my boy," the general went on.

"Hear, hear," the other men around him chimed in.

Sherrie felt very much the outsider, the stranger. These people had known him for years. They had more claim on his affections and attention. She could tell these people that she knew the true Jack PenMartyn—but did she?

Nine years was a long time.

People changed. People sinned, but sometimes they changed.

She told herself that she was furious at the blatant show of hypocrisy she'd just witnessed. She wanted to know how he'd pulled off this ruse of respectability. Or maybe she wanted to know if the respectability was the truth and the man she knew had been the mask. She deserved that much from him, surely. She moved closer, though she had to push aside a plump matron holding a violin to get to the front of the crush.

I want to know you, she thought in desperation, as she finally reached his side. *Who are you? What have you become? I don't know you. How can I hate you when you've become a stranger to me?*

She wanted to scream these questions at him, to pound her fists against his chest and demand answers, to demand—she wasn't sure what. Instead, she gently laid her hand on his arm. Whatever she did, it wouldn't be here, not while he was surrounded by his friends, maybe even his family. All she knew was that she desperately *wanted.*

Let me help, she thought, still acutely aware of his pain. She felt Jack flinch when a large bearded man wearing a chest full of medals effusively shook his hand. Sherrie was sure Jack's reaction wasn't to the strength of the older man's grip. No, the pain came from the inside. She ought to revel in the knowledge that he hurt, but that wasn't her response at all.

That was the worst reason of all the ones that drove her to confront him, the most frightening. Every other thought, every word she spoke, was a shield from the truth of why she was really here. She had promised a holy man that she would confront the truth. The truth stood before her, bigger than she remembered, more complex, more compelling, more attractive, more mysterious and elusive than the images out of her memory. More interesting, too. Certainly more annoying.

He finally turned to her. Their gazes locked. Was that fear in those cold blue eyes? Was that joy as well? At seeing her? Relief? Was there a tinge of pride in the smile that suddenly quirked up her lips?

"Hello," she said to the truth. "What am I supposed to do with you?"

"Get me out of here," Jack murmured, before he could catch the words and hold them back.

She understood. He didn't know how. She stepped close and slipped her arm through his. She stood beside him, tall and commanding, and spoke with good-humored authority, "Ladies and gentlemen, Lord PenMartyn already has an engagement for this evening." Her smile glittered with sensual, teasing promise. She let down her respectable guard, accepted the freedom offered by the night and the surroundings. She looked every inch the sophisticated widow as she purred, "I'm sure you don't want us to be late."

People laughed and moved aside. Several of the men murmured that the lady was a finer reward for Jack's work than any medal from the Queen. Several women shot jealous glances Sherrie's way as she led Jack hurriedly to the stage door at the back of the building. For some reason those dirty looks made her want to laugh in triumph rather than cringe in shame.

Chapter 22

"You shouldn't be alone with me."

"Don't be silly, my reputation's not that fragile." She waved all the fuss of propriety away. "Besides, everyone knows what Lady Anne has in mind for us. I'm a widow, and my virgin cousins are being safely guarded by their mother. I can be alone with you if I want."

Jack stopped her at the bottom of the theater steps, put his hands on her shoulders, and turned her to face him. "Did you just hear what you said?" The question was deadly serious, and full of worry. "This is you and me, Scheherazade, not—"

"Jack and Sherrie?" She felt like stomping her foot—not like shooting him, or throwing a punch. What was the world coming to when her normal outrage at the wickedness of this man had simmered down to just plain foot-stomping annoyance? "Why can't we be Jack and Sherrie this evening?" she demanded. "Why does it have to be so *complicated?*"

"Because it is."

It was even more annoying that he was right. Until and unless everything was settled between them, their relationship was going to stay a dark, tangled mess that consumed both their lives.

She sighed. "I'm tired of life being complicated."

He shook his head. "I won't let you pretend that it isn't. Not even for a few minutes."

He drew her closer, one hand on her shoulder. His other arm circled her waist and his palm rested flat at the base of her spine. The movement was slow, inexorable punctuation. Sherrie felt their bodies touch, the inevitable press of thigh to thigh, the contact of her breasts against his stiff, starched shirt front. His scent filled her nostrils, just as hers did his. Her perfume was a heady, spicy scent from India. He bore the scent of bay rum and almond soap, delicious and exciting. She felt him growing hard, and that was exciting, too. Flesh craved, and they both trembled, with emotion, and with wanting. Heat rippled through her from the places where they touched, and it served to fuel her temper.

"I'm not afraid of St. John," she said, with another proud lift of her head. "But I don't know St. John. I don't know Jack."

As her head came up, his came down. Bringing his lips close to hers, he whispered, "You will," and kissed her.

Her arms slid around his neck. Her lips parted to welcome his probing tongue. She breathed a long sigh into his mouth. It was a moment of ecstasy, and complete folly.

Broken by a nasal Cockney voice saying from behind her, "That's enough of that, you two."

"Hurry up," another voice spoke anxiously from the head of the alley. "Place is going to be swarmin' with toffs in a minute."

A third man, this one behind Jack, laughed. "The toffs are waitin' for their carriages out front. We got these two all to ourselves."

Jack lifted his head from the sweet drug of Scheherazade's kiss and cursed himself for not hearing the robbers approach. They shouldn't have left the theater this way. They shouldn't have lingered in the alley for a moment. They certainly shouldn't have left together. He couldn't think when he was with the woman. Once again, his thoughtlessness had put her in danger.

This time, though, the danger would last no more than a few seconds. He even managed to give her a reassuring smile as he loosed his hold on her. Then he wheeled around, swift and deadly.

The nearest man fell to a fast kick in the gut. When he doubled up, Jack's heel came down on the back of his neck, sending him sprawling, and out of the fray. Jack turned as the man behind Sherrie made a grab for her. She let her muscles go slack and collapsed to the ground before the villain could get a proper hold on her.

"Good girl," Jack commended, as he jumped over her. Jack's hand swept down in a hard arc. The man's arm snapped loudly from the force.

Jack's arm swept back up and outward, delivering a stiff-fingered blow to the other man's throat. When he turned again, to face the alley mouth, the third attacker was already gone. And Sherrie had rolled clear across the filthstrewn brick paving and gotten to her feet.

Their gazes met, and the excitement arcing between them was as palpable as the lust of a few moments before, and just as sweet. She grinned at him, her teeth flashed brilliant white in her dirtied face. Strands of gold hair hung loosely around her face. She threw back her head and laughed, as wild and wanton and in love with danger as ever.

She hadn't changed. She hadn't changed at all.

"Damn it, woman," he complained. "Why did I go to all the bother of letting you go if you won't stay out of trouble?"

He turned to her once they reached the edge of a grove of trees outside the palace grounds. The necklace he'd fastened around her throat just before they slipped back into the night had a faint, rich, mysterious glow in the full moonlight. They didn't have time for it, but he took her in his arms anyway. Her kiss was warm and sweet, her hands roamed frantically over his chest and back and inside the band of his trousers. She wrapped a leg around the back of his thighs and drew him closer. Damn, but the woman was wild! Wild for him, just as he was for her. He knew that she was a moment away from dragging him down to the ground and having him. He desperately wanted that moment, but they didn't have time. He could hear the alarm being raised back at the palace. Rhu Limpok's guards would be rushing out the gates within moments. The time bought by his bribe money had run out.

He pushed her away, rougher than he intended. "We have to get back to the house. Now." He grabbed her hand and they ran. Through the woods on the edge of the city, down to the sea, along the docks and across a bobbing row of small junks lined up side by side in the water. Angry voices and shaking fists followed them as their passage woke the sleeping families who lived on the little boats.

They ran on, laughing through the narrow, stinking streets of the port, past the brothels and warehouses. They hurried as fast as they could up the hill overlooking the bay, back to the safety of the walled compound he'd made his home on Kuzay. He knew as they ran that it wasn't a home or a haven anymore. The private meeting with the khan had gone badly after Rhu Limpok had Scheherazade taken to his harem. He should have been more amenable, he should have dissembled. He should have put his own survival first. All he could think of was getting his woman back, and that was what he had done. And now he was going to have to abandon everything he'd worked for, load his two ships with his people, and escape the island tonight. He had to get some papers from his office first.

They stopped briefly by the gate of the compound where some of his men waited. "Prepare the boats, we're going," he told them. "Wait here," he told Scheherazade as the men ran off. He pushed her into the shadows just inside the protection of the wall. "I'll be right back."

"What about the servants?" she asked, following

despite his orders. "What about May?"

"They're not my problem. Will you stay put?" he demanded, and pushed her onto a bench next to the garden fountain.

"But—"

He ran off with her shouted questions in his ears. Her concern for others was touching, and it rubbed his conscience raw. It reminded him of the soft-hearted fool he'd once been. "I don't care about any-one but me," he reminded himself, as he reached his office. In the distance he could hear shouting, and shots. He could smell smoke. Damn. "I don't have time to care."

The house was a roaring blaze by the time he gath-ered what he'd come for and dashed back outside. The crackle and roar of flames was loud in his ears as he headed back through the garden, the fountain pool reflected the growing wall of flames as the house went up behind him.

Scheherazade was not where he'd left her.

"Why am I not surprised?"

He heard the crunch of stones underfoot, and whirled around. "Schehera—"

The man holding the gun on him smiled. "You aren't happy to see me, I can tell."

"What are you doing here, Grigori?"

The big Russian shrugged, but the pistol didn't waver. "I don't trust the khan's men to finish you off. So I came to kill you myself." He gestured with the gun. "But first I want what you have. Our games are over, my friend. There is a list of names you've been collecting. You can give it to me now, or I can take it from your body."

He swore to himself. He owned several pistols.

There was one in his office, another in the bedroom of the burning house. The only weapon he had on him was a knife in his belt. He'd be shot by the Russian as soon as he made a move toward the knife. His sense of futility was almost overwhelming. He should have suspected Grigori would move against him at the first opportunity. If he died, what would happen to Scheherazade? Who would protect her in this ugly, dangerous world he'd dragged her into? Losing the documents to the Russian would cause even more deaths. Damn, but he was an irresponsible, thoughtless fool!

And there was nothing he could do. "I can't give you the papers, Grigori." He smiled slowly as a desperate idea came to him. "But I will play your game with you for them." He put his hands up, and took a step closer to the crazy Russian. "What do you say? Leave one bullet in your pistol and we'll pass it back and forth between us."

Grigori looked tempted, but only for a moment. "No time, my friend," he said. "I have a boat waiting for me. I must go." He grinned, and fired.

A second shot sounded a split second before Grigori's gun went off. The impact from the bullet in the back threw off Grigori's aim.

When the Russian fell, he saw Scheherazade standing a few feet behind where Grigori had been. She had a pistol clutched tightly in her fist. Smoke from the shot wreathed her head, or maybe it was a stray tendril of smoke from the burning house. She looked stunned.

He quickly stepped forward over the Russian's body. He pried the gun out of her hand. "Where the devil'd you get that? What did you think you were doing?"

"From the house. From the bedroom. I went to get some clothes before I realized the house was on fire. When I heard the shooting outside, I saw the gun and thought it might come in handy."

He glanced at the body. Dead. Definitely dead.

She looked down at Grigori's body, then slowly up at him. What he saw in her eyes frightened him more than anything else he'd seen in the last few hours. There was no fear in her, no regret. The excitement that glowed in her expression was as fiery hot as any glow of passion he'd ever seen on her face. He knew how addicting excitement was, worse than opium. He'd done this to her, too. Taken a girl who traveled with gentle missionaries and made her into a wanton hellion capable of killing a man.

He stuck the gun in his belt and took her arm, just as a faint scream from the house reached his ears. "We're going."

She shook him off, and pointed back at the burning house. "May's in there! She can't get out on her own! We have to go back."

He glanced over his shoulder. Flames licked out the windows, through the doors. A portion of roof was already collapsed. It was impossible. Another scream sounded through the night, followed by a desperate call for help.

"Damn!" He pushed her toward the garden gate. "Meet me at the boat!" he ordered, and ran back into the house.

This time Scheherazade actually listened to him. She was waiting on the landing as he came out of the smoke-filled night carrying the Chinese girl in his arms. He set May on the dock, carefully out of the way of the men who rushed back and forth getting the boats ready. Scheherazade ran up to him and threw her arms around his neck. He'd had to kill a man who'd come at him with a spear in the garden. He had the man's blood on his hands as well as burns from the housefire.

He kissed her once, hard, then pushed her away. He'd done a lot of thinking in the last few minutes. "Listen to me," he said as she gazed worshipfully up at him. "You're going home, back to America."

She blinked in confusion. "We're going to America?"

"No. You are going to America."

"What?" She took a stumbling step backward, beginning to understand what he meant. She shook her head. "No. I'm not."

He kept his voice cold, his expression indifferent. "Our bargain is ended. I've had you as long, longer, than we agreed."

"I don't care about any bargain. I've stopped counting the days. I'm going with you," she declared.

He grabbed her by the shoulders. "You'll do as I say, and you'll do it now." The boats were nearly ready. They had to sail. "We're going on different boats. I'm sending you to Hong Kong. You can make your passage home from there."

"I want to be with you. Wherever you go. Cullum, I lo—"

He shook her hard. "Don't you say it." His voice was a vicious growl. "Don't you dare say it. It isn't true, and you know it. I've had enough of you," he went on coldly, cruelly. "You're more trouble than

*you're worth. I took you back from the khan only
because no one takes what's mine.''*

*He saw the anger begin to grow in her, and the
pain, and was thankful for it. He couldn't let her
believe she loved him, or that he loved her. He'd done
enough damage to the woman already. He had to do
what he could to salvage her battered soul in the few
moments they had left.*

*"I see,'' she said. Her breath came in hard, sharp
pants as she fought through her emotions. "I see.
You can throw me away if you want, but no one
takes what is yours?''*

*He answered with an indifferent shrug. "Of
course.''*

"Son of a bitch!''

*Her blue eyes flashed with fury as she snatched
off the pearls and held the necklace out to him. Behind her the fire that had lit the night was finally
burning out. Her face was covered in soot and shadows, making her eyes seem even brighter.*

*"Keep them,'' he told her. His hands and arms
and face stung like hellfire, but he kept the pain from
his voice. Holding her hurt. Letting her go hurt even
worse. "Please.''*

"Why? Because I earned them?''

"As a memento.'' Please keep them, *he thought.
He forced himself to smile, cynical, heartless. "To
remember me.''* Please forgive me, *he thought, but
didn't have the courage to say it aloud. He barely
had the courage to do what must be done.*

*"Fine.'' She pulled away and looked around at the
chaos as the boats were loaded. "May's coming with
me.''*

"All right. Fine. Just take May and the necklace, and go."

She didn't bother arguing with him anymore.

She was more than ready to argue with him now. She stood in the middle of an alley littered with the bodies of their recent attackers, put her hands defiantly on her hips, and demanded, "Damn it, Jack, is that why you sent me away? To keep me out of trouble?"

He swept an arm around her waist and hurried her out of the alley without answering. This was no place for arguing. He did say, "This is no place for a lady."

"I'm no lady," she growled back.

"I know. I'm sorry."

Sherrie's feet barely touched the ground as he hastened her along. Glancing at his profile, she became aware of the set, pained look on his face. His apology rankled. Revelation made an effort to make its way through her seething emotions. The understanding that dawned did nothing for her already seething temper. It occurred to her that May had always been right about his seeking some kind of redemption that night.

"Don't tell me you think you're responsible for everything that's ever happened to me?"

A long parade of carriages and hansom cabs lined the street outside the theater, the alert drivers observing the street from their perches above the horses. Buskers in button-adorned costumes sang and danced for the laughing, well-dressed crowd leaving the theater, flower girls plied their wares under the lamplight, whores lingered in the shadows. This busy circus was no place for a confrontation, either. Jack spotted his own carriage waiting far down the street and hurried her toward it. He took her into the anonymous darkness where the mud and tears on her emerald gown would not be noticed and commented on, before anyone saw her grime-covered, furious face.

"I'm not going to ruin your reputation twice," he whispered to her as they moved along. "Keep still and I'll have you safe away in a few moments."

"I don't want to keep still," she answered, and not in a whisper.

"Please."

"Say it again."

"Why?"

"You need the practice."

"You've always had a vicious tongue on you, you know that?"

"And I'm proud of it. And another thing, Jack PenMartyn, I was having adventures long before I met you, and I've had plenty since. What do you think I was doing when we met?"

"Visiting your cousins. Your missionary cousins."

"But I wasn't studying to be a missionary, you fool!"

"You were a lady when I met you. A prim, proper, innocent child."

She snorted. Loudly. "I've never been proper in my life. I grew up in the gold and silver mining camps, in the West, when it was *really* wild."

"You grew up a rich man's daughter."

"Who got his money digging in the dirt, with my mother and me beside him. What kind of pedestal do you have me on, Lord PenMartyn?"

"A very high one," he answered breathlessly. "And you're going to stay on it."

He pulled her back into the shadows of a doorway and kissed her hard. A whore fled from the spot, squawking at being dislodged from her customary space, but no one would take notice of an angry prostitute. They would of an angry lady of quality. He was determined to protect Sherrie whether she wanted it or not. To the whore he threw two guineas and suggested she go home.

The streetwalker thanked him and disappeared into the night. Sherrie wiped the back of her hand across her mouth and didn't look in the least thankful. Her cheeks were flushed, her lips swollen from the kiss he hadn't meant to be so rough—and satisfying. He couldn't help smiling his old dangerous, knife-edged smile at her.

She wasn't intimidated by it. The tiger in him stirred and stretched its claws at her show of spirit. He fought the beast down, or at least he tried. "I'm taking you home," he told her. "Don't argue with me about it."

Her angry eyes glittered and burned. "Your home or mine?"

"Yours," he responded.

Tears appeared in the corners of her eyes, but the fury didn't lessen any. "Really?" she asked, voice tight with emotion. "My home?"

He gestured toward his carriage. "Yes. Of course. Where else?"

"I don't have a home."

"Primrose House. I'll take you to—" He felt helpless all of a sudden, floundering. He looked at her and her pain shot through him like a knife, skinned him alive, cut out his heart.

Tears spilled down her cheeks. She gasped in agony, her arms crossed tightly across her waist. "I haven't had a home," she told him, throat tight from trying to hold back the sobs, "since the day you sent me away."

Jack couldn't breathe, and he didn't care. To die right now would be a blessing. He couldn't think from the shock. From the sorrow. From the loss. Once again his world crumbled and spun around him. He was so damned sick of living in a kaleidoscope.

All he could do was take a step toward Sherrie, though that step was none too steady. Only to stop and turn when the door to his carriage opened and Jhou Xa stepped down, his saffron and red robes whirling around him. Several other Asians stepped out of the shadows as Jhou Xa came forward. These men were dressed in black, and moved with familiar, deadly silence. They efficiently blocked any chance of escape. Jack would fight them if he must, but he turned to the Shaolin monk first.

"I would not interrupt if it was not important," Jhou Xa said. He gestured toward the carriage. "There is not much time. Rhu Limpok must see you. Now."

Chapter 23

"You kept the necklace," Rhu Limpok said. "How nice." The Great Khan of Kuzay smiled, showing broken, stained teeth. "Sit, my friends. Have tea." He waved a servant forward, and the guards who'd brought them from the carriage took up posts in the back of the room. The Khan sat back on a pile of peacock silk cushions as Jack, Sherrie and Jhou Xa took seats on the opposite side of the low table. He had been speaking Mandarin. Now he switched to the dialect spoken on Kuzay. "And you kept the girl." He raked his gaze over Sherrie, and sighed. "I suppose it was a mistake to try to take her from you. I'm an old man now," he said earnestly to Jack. "I regret many things."

"Like trying to have me killed?" Jack questioned. He was calm now, his mind focused on the moment. The ride to the estate where the delegation from Kuzay was staying had been brief, but it had given him time to get his emotions under control. He had to stay calm. Not for his own sake, but to keep Sherrie safe.

He picked up the teacup that had been placed before him, and ran his thumb along the smooth porcelain rim. He took a drink to acknowledge the Khan's hospitality. "Am I supposed to forget that night and be your friend now?"

Rhu Limpok made a fluttering motion with his hand. "That is long in the past. I have long ago forgotten your offenses. Forgotten and forgiven. We are different people now."

There was a flower-draped statue of a seated Buddha in the room, its bronze skin gleamed warmly in the lamplight. Incense burned in front of the serenely smiling statue, sending up fragrant curls of smoke behind Rhu Limpok's head.

"Jhou Xa told me you are now a religious man," Jack commented.

The old man shrugged. "Perhaps." He flashed his broken teeth again, and cackled. "My Great Wife's become a nun. Did he tell you? I bless Buddha daily for that."

From the corner of his eye, Jack saw Sherrie try to hide a smile. Rhu Limpok noticed, too, and turned his attention on her. "My son sends his greetings, Golden One. And my Great Wife as well. She prays that you have given your husband many sons in the years since the two of you left our land."

Sherrie looked at her hands rather than answer Rhu Limpok. Jack studied her profile as she remained humble and silent—like a proper wife—for once, waiting for him to respond. Damn her.

Rhu Limpok looked at him expectantly.

Jack cleared his throat. "The Golden One has given me the blessing of a girl-child."

Rhu Limpok looked sympathetic. Sherrie shot Jack a swift look, but held her tongue. A rush of pleasure went through Jack as he realized just how much he meant his words. Pleasure wasn't something he was used to, he hated having to fight it off to retain his calm, alert attitude.

"They are young," Jhou Xa chimed in. He was seated between them, and put a hand on each of their arms as he went on. "There is plenty of time for them to have sons."

It sound like a blessing, and a prayer of hope. The holy man's gentle, sure, touch very nearly set off a spark of hope in Jack. He wondered if Sherrie felt it as well.

Rhu Limpok took a sip of tea. When he set the cup back on the table, his expression solemn and worried. "There may be little time left for any of us."

Jack was glad to have the polite preliminaries over with so quickly. It was time to get down to business. "What do you want of me?"

"There is a plot against me and my people," Rhu Limpok answered bluntly. "You must stop it."

Jack laughed. "Why? Why would I help you?"

"Because this plot will destroy your people

as well. You serve your people, old friend, that much truth I know about you."

It's nice that somebody knows some truth about the man, Sherrie thought bitterly as she did her best to sit quietly and unobtrusively through the men's conversation. All she wanted was to go home to her baby, and her empty bed, and to try to forget the truth she'd revealed to Jack PenMartyn, and to herself.

She looked at the Buddha rather than give in to the urge to focus her attention on Jack PenMartyn. She had promised a holy man, the holiest man in Asia, that she would face the truth. The truth May had been trying to get her to own up to for years. Nine. Long. Years. Well, damn it, she didn't want to face it!

Jack said, "I served my country by trying to stop Kuzay becoming a base for Russian financed piracy of British shipping."

"And you succeeded, my friend," Rhu Limpok replied. "Though our last conversation didn't go particularly well, I did take your advice about ridding myself of the Malay pirates I had thought were my allies. You were right in telling me they couldn't be trusted."

"You didn't have to show your gratitude by trying to have me killed and burning down my house."

"You and your friend Grigori used my country to play out your Great Game," Rhu Limpok countered. "I wanted to be rid of both of you."

"You knew who I was? And Grigori?" Jack gave a faint, self-deprecating, bitter laugh. "We thought our disguises as renegades and criminals were quite good. Sometimes we even fooled ourselves, if never each other."

"I was fooled, for a while," Rhu Limpok told him. "But you weren't excessive enough in your bad habits, my friend. You never seemed to enjoy all the wicked things you did."

"I enjoyed them." Jack's tone was clipped and cool.

Rhu Limpok waved his hand dismissively. "But I always saw the underlying hint of guilt, of worry. I thought you wanted to be decadent but didn't know how. I put it down to your youth and being a foreign devil. Eventually I guessed the truth, though I never had any real proof. I am a man who trusts his instincts," the Khan went on. "That is how I have survived. My instincts tell me that your land and mine are on the verge of a terrible war. I need your help to stop this war."

Jack very nearly laughed again at the notion of Kuzay and the British Empire at war. But having the old man reveal his very accurate reading of Cullum Rourke's twisted soul in front of Sherrie was making him bleed internally. He couldn't laugh, not even at the expense of that foolish boy Rhu Limpok so unerringly described.

"Why?" he asked the ruler of Kuzay. "Why would the British Empire go to war with one tiny island nation that long ago stopped being a threat to it?"

"And was never much of a threat to begin with," Rhu Limpok added. "Thanks to you."

"I'm flattered," Jack growled. "Now, what do you really want?"

The Khan of Kuzay shrugged eloquently. "Gordon Summers' head in a basket would be nice."

Jack was taken aback by such bluntness. "I—see." He looked at the Khan with narrow-eyed suspicion. "Why?"

"Because Gordon Summers is going to start this war."

"How do you know about Lord Gordon? What do you know about him?" Not that anything Rhu Limpok said could be trusted, of course.

"He visited Kuzay once. I greeted him as a friend."

"Just as you did me," Jack added sarcastically.

"And, as I did with you, I set my people to watching him. It is a wise precaution."

"True," Jack admitted.

"He bribed my watchers, but that is only to be expected. He learned much from them. In the last year he has been in contact with them again, and they have supplied him with information about Kuzay's defenses."

"Seems like an odd thing for a religious leader to want to know about," Jack agreed. "Perhaps he was doing a favor for one of his converts in military intelligence. Spies get their information from any source they can."

"You would know, White Tiger."

Jack winced at the name, and slid a sideways glance at Sherrie. Her hands gripped her teacup tightly, her eyes were lowered, her expression blank and bland. "Go on," Jack said to Rhu Limpok.

"I believe he wanted the information for himself. I know that he seeks to rule your country through those he influences. I know he is close to achieving this goal."

"The Prince of Wales," Sherrie spoke for the first time. She couldn't stop herself.

He believed her implicitly. "What do you know?"

"I saw the prince at Lord Gordon's yesterday. He wasn't there with any advisors or staff. He was alone. He was—" She blushed. "Forward."

"I see." He didn't, but he wasn't going to discuss anything involving the Prince of Wales in front of Rhu Limpok. Jack rubbed his jaw thoughtfully. That there was more involvement between Summers and the prince than he'd thought was not good news. Tonight he'd seen firsthand Summers' ability to sway crowds. He feared that he'd sharply underestimated the man. He'd let his personal concerns cloud his judgment. It didn't feel cloudy now, even with Sherrie's involvement in the matter.

"Thank you," he said to her, though her gaze slid away from his when he spoke. Just like old times. He concentrated on Rhu Limpok. "I still don't understand what you think Lord Gordon has to do with your country."

"We are a small country with a bad reputation and no friends. No one would come to our aid if we were attacked. No one would come to our aid if those who attacked us claimed they did so in a just and righteous cause. Those who attacked us would profit from the war."

"War always brings profit to those who make the weapons and supply the warriors, never mind the cost in lives," Jhou Xa added. "Lord Gordon has friends who profit from war. They will share their good fortune with him if he can bring about the conflict."

That the Shaolin monk was a warrior himself didn't temper his loathing of warfare. Jack knew that Jhou Xa's order trained hard, but fought only when they must, and never in a petty cause. That Jhou Xa gave credence to Rhu Limpok's claims disturbed Jack. He didn't want any proof that the tricky old ruler was telling the truth. About anything.

He said, "I'll look into the matter." It was the most he was willing to give. He would make no promise, trust not a scrap of whatever, probably forged and faked, proof Rhu Limpok offered.

Rhu Limpok banged a fist on the low table. "I do not need you to look into anything!"

Jack rose. He took Sherrie's arm and helped her up. "Then what do you want from me?"

"I need to speak to the Queen, to the Prime Minister, but no one will see me. I am told that Kuzay is an outlaw country, that I'm not important enough to deal with. I send emissaries, write letters, speak to underlings. My way is constantly being blocked."

Jack laughed. "You want me to get you in to see Queen Victoria?"

"Yes. Open the way for me, White Tiger, and I will defend myself."

It wasn't possible, Jack knew that. Kuzay was an unimportant outlaw kingdom, no longer strategically important. Policy and politics had passed the island by. No one would have any respect for the khan. No one would listen to him, even if his wild claims against Lord Gordon proved to somehow be true. Jack was certain that neither Queen nor Prime Minister nor anyone at Cabinet level would deign to speak with the old rogue.

However, he wanted to leave, to get Sherrie safely away. There were armed guards in the room and around the house, and Rhu Limpok's temper was up. With all that in mind, Jack made the only promise he could, and would try to keep. "Very well," he told his old adversary. "I will see what I can do about getting you an interview with Her Majesty." *For all the good my efforts will do you,* he added to himself. "Come, Great Wife," he said to Sherrie, with no irony at all. "It's time for us to go home."

Chapter 24

~~~~~~

Sherrie resented Jack PenMartyn greatly, and not for all the usual reasons. Not even for his temerity at claiming her as his Great Wife, though that gesture was going to take some thinking about. She resented the fact that she looked, felt, and smelled like she'd been rolling around in a filthy back alley, while the Earl of PenMartyn sat on the opposite side of the carriage looking only faintly mussed and none the worse for wear. She'd seen the man quickly and efficiently polish off two attackers, then calmly face down the Great Khan of Kuzay, all without breaking a sweat or wrinkling his beautifully tailored coat.

She ached, too, physically and mentally, and she also stank. The pain from a few scraps and bruises was easier to deal with than the other wounds that had been opened this evening, so she concentrated on them for a while, trying to imagine herself in a hot, fragrant, soothing bath. But the ride went on, and the silent man so carefully ignoring and being ignored in the shadows across from her finally got on Sherrie's nerves to the point where she had to say something. Besides, thinking of hot baths made her think of being naked, and being naked made her think of—

"Where are we going?"

He continued to look out the window. "To Primrose House."

The carriage swayed slightly, and the wheels made a rumbling, rushing sound against the brick paving of London's streets. Sherrie was not soothed by the motion or the noise.

Being so close to Sherrie was agony—being so close and thinking about what might have been was even worse than remembering what had actually taken place.

Sherrie didn't like the tense silence from the other side of the carriage. He was so subdued, as if all the fire had gone out of him. She was used to his arguing with her, used to his possessive touch. Now he seemed to be making an effort to ignore her studiously. She should have been grateful, or at least annoyed that he would dare to try to blot out her presence. Instead, she found his mood worrisome. She felt like she ought to say or do something to make it better.

Just because he was guilty of a few specific, very personal wrongs concerning her didn't mean he deserved to be condemned for every sin mankind had ever thought up to commit. A great many people saw Jack PenMartyn as a hero. Maybe he was. She'd learned tonight that he'd faithfully served his country's interests even while he'd deceived her. He deserved some—small—credit for doing his patriotic duty. Was it her job to be the man's judge, jury and executioner? It looked as if he was doing a pretty good job of carrying out those tasks himself.

Sherrie strongly considered offering Jack a penny for his thoughts, but then decided on something better to talk about while she had him alone and not in his usual arrogantly annoyed mood. "Can I ask you a question?"

After a long silence his answer came back, a tautly spoken, hoarse, "Yes."

She knew what he expected. She didn't give it to him. "What happened to you?"

"Happened?"

"After you sent me away? After you left Kuzay. Did you go right back to England?"

"Why would you want to know?"

He sounded tired, defeated. She should have enjoyed the sound of weakness from him, but she hated it. Every fiber of her being abhorred the thought of him broken and bleeding inside. Of all the emotions she'd nursed about the man over the years, the yearning for vengeance had never been one of them. Justice, yes, but she wasn't sure what she meant by the concept, not at the moment anyway.

Sherrie leaned forward, closer to him. Almost touching but not quite. She could make out his face better this way. "Call it curiosity. I've always been curious."

"That will get you in trouble someday, Mrs. Hamilton."

"Curiosity kills cats," she answered. "We're

dog people in my family. Always have been."

"I see."

"Tell me," she urged. "Please."

He couldn't refuse her any request. He would
rather she asked him to tie a weight around his
neck and jump in the Thames, but since she
hadn't, he did as she asked. "I didn't return to
England," he told her. "Not immediately."

"How come?"

"I was in prison."

She didn't look repulsed. She didn't show
any surprise. She said quite calmly, "I can see
why that might put a crimp in your traveling
plans."

"You should like this part," he said. He even
sounded slightly amused when he went on.
"Cullum Rourke was a wanted man, a dangerous brigand and pirate. Before I arrived at the
British compound in Canton, a Chinese official
who recognized Cullum the pirate had me arrested."

"But the British government got you out, I
suppose."

"No."

"What happened then?"

She really was a curious creature. She looked
like a child listening to a bedtime story. She reminded him of Minnie. He couldn't help but
smile at that, and continue. "I ended up in a
prison somewhere in the interior of the country."

"A foreign devil in a Chinese prison? That
must have been unpleasant."

She reached out and touched his knee. He didn't think she noticed the gesture, but he did. It sent a shock wave through him, that was composed more at wonder at her sympathy than lust, though lust was involved, too.

"It was actually the best thing that ever happened to me," he admitted. He shrugged. "And the worst, but let's gloss over the bad parts. Unless you would like a catalogue of the tortures. Lord knows you deserve to get some entertainment out of this evening."

"How gentlemanly of you to think of my entertainment."

"I try."

"Why don't I just use my imagination on the bad parts, and you tell me about the part you enjoyed?"

He noticed that they were both speaking with the sort of bright, brittle, ironic humor people used to mask terror and despair in the midst of dangerous, hopeless situations. In fact they were very much in dangerous territory, walking together into the depths of his past. Surprisingly, not being in it alone, it didn't seem quite as bad as he remembered. No, it was as bad, just more bearable.

"I met a man in prison," he went on. "A holy man."

She laughed, but he realized as he looked at her face that it wasn't at him. "Not you too!"

He reached out and flicked a finger teasingly against her cheek. "What?"

"Remind me to tell you about the Dalai Lama sometime."

"I just read your book about that journey."

He wondered just how much he'd revealed about how much he still cared for her with that revelation. And why shouldn't he let her know he cared? That thought had never occurred to him before. It was like suddenly finding the door to a room he'd never explored in a well-known house. He pushed it down before he could act on it. What he felt didn't matter, that he lived in solitary confinement didn't matter. Protecting her from what he felt was what mattered.

She didn't seem to notice that he'd made a confession of sorts. "I didn't put everything about Tibet in my memoirs," she went on. "Was the monk who took us to Rhu Limpok the one you met in prison?"

"Jhou Xa? No."

"How did you meet a holy man in prison?"

"The Shaolin monks took part in a rebellion against the Manchu Dynasty. Their order has been outlawed and living underground for years. Chan got caught preaching and teaching. He kept preaching and teaching in prison."

"And he converted you?" she asked skeptically.

"No, he helped me escape. Then he took me to one of the Shaolins' secret monasteries where I was hidden until I could get back to the British enclave in Peking. It was all very dramatic."

Jack didn't try to explain how much he had learned from the monks. The fighting and meditation skills he still practiced were only a small part of the knowledge he'd brought away from the experience. While it might not be possible to save his black and bloody soul, at least he had learned how to keep the beast inside him from doing any more damage. He'd learned how to give compassion rather than pain to those around him. Except where Scheherazade was concerned, of course. She would never be safe from the lusting animal he could keep caged around others.

Of course, he hadn't raped her yet this evening. Truth be told, he was too tired to make the effort, though the occasional touch and look that passed between them sent pleasant shocks of desire through him, but not enough to rouse the beast. Odd. He didn't recall desire as ever being pleasant before, or undeniable, adding to his senses rather than stripping them down to pure carnal need. He must be much more exhausted than he thought.

Before he could add any more about his journey back from the East, from Cullum Rourke to St. John PenMartyn, the carriage came to a halt before the door of Primrose House. It was just as well. He got down from the carriage and helped her alight.

He didn't offer to escort her to the door. He didn't kiss her, not even to brush his lips across the back of her hand, though the temptation to take her in his arms reared up as strong as ever. She looked at him as though she expected some such gesture, and why shouldn't she? He'd never been civilized with her before.

He did say, "I didn't tell you because if I had I couldn't keep you. Jack wouldn't have been able to make love to you, and I desperately needed to make love to you from the first moment I saw you. Cullum Rourke was no gentleman, so I let him have his way. I was wrong, and I am sorry."

He couldn't look at her, and he couldn't say anymore. All he could do was get back in the carriage and signal the coachman to drive away.

He needed a better class of minion, Lord Gordon decided, for dealing with ruffians like PenMartyn. He gazed with weary annoyance on one of the men he'd sent to fetch PenMartyn. The man shifted nervously under his stare. The unshaven Cockney looked as anxious as a schoolboy called on the carpet by the headmaster. It was partially the setting that gave this impression, Summers supposed, since they were meeting within his large, book-lined library. Summers sat behind his desk, the ruffian actually was standing on the carpet in front of him, head down, dirty hands clasped behind his back.

Summers assumed the only reason the fool had showed up without his quarry was out of greed. He hoped for a reward of some sort for trying, and found himself under Summers' disapproving stare. The poor man jumped and looked ready to bolt when Summers' butler opened the door and brought in the brandy Summers had requested.

The butler set the snifter down before Lord Gordon and would have retired, but Summers gestured for him to stay. He valued the servant's opinion.

Summer lifted the brandy, and took a deep, appreciative breath of the smoky aroma. "Go on. What happened then?"

The Cockney swallowed hard. "Don't know, guv'nor. With Pace and Farrin laid out, I wasn't waitin' to be next."

Yes, he definitely needed more efficient thugs where PenMartyn was concerned. It had been foolish to engage the services of men who were not also followers. Summers blamed himself for being impatient. He had wanted to threaten PenMartyn as well as speak to him, so had engaged toughs loitering on the street outside the theater rather than send any of the well-armed, well-trained men he employed.

The rub now was that PenMartyn had been warned. He would be likely to expect another attack. He might mention the incident in the alley to MacQuarrie. Once alerted, the man from the Yard would be likely to put a guard on PenMartyn. Summers thought another incident might lead MacQuarrie to him. He wasn't ready for that. He had to be subtle, careful. He needed another means to get PenMartyn to his home, and sincerely doubted a dinner invitation would work.

He sighed, and tossed a fold of pound notes to the tough. "Get out." When the butler moved to show the man out, Summers said, "He can find the door on his own."

"Yes, my lord."

Summers knew very well that a footman

waited in the hallway, not to show the Cockney out of the house, but to send the man on to his next incarnation on the wheel of life. The body would never be discovered, of course.

Once the Cockney was gone, Summers turned his attention on the butler who waited faithfully by his side. "I really wish you hadn't gotten yourself dismissed from PenMartyn's service, Moss," Summers complained mildly to his butler. "Having your eyes and ears in his household right now might prove useful."

"I'm sorry, my lord," Moss answered contritely.

Summers waved away the man's apology. "Couldn't be helped. Besides, I'm glad to have you back. Your service was greatly missed. I need your pointed reminders of the superiority of all things British to keep from getting lost in all this Oriental nonsense I spout to the masses."

Moss gave him a grateful look. Then his hangdog expression lightened with an idea. "What about the urchin, my lord?"

Summers sat forward in his chair. "Urchin?"

"The one who came to see PenMartyn the night I was sacked. I heard more about the brat when I saw my aunt who cooks for PenMartyn yesterday. Seems the earl took the brat to Mrs. Hamilton's house." The butler looked at him hopefully. "He's fond of brats, my lord."

Brat? Mrs. Hamilton's brat, perhaps? Her lovely, dark-haired, pale-skinned Minerva? The child who was just the right age to be the White

Tiger's bastard? Scheherazade Hamilton had gone to a great deal of trouble to conceal the evidence of her sins, but when you thought about it, the connection between PenMartyn and the child was obvious.

Oh, this was going to be good.

A sly smile lifted Summers lips. He very nearly laughed in triumph, but hugged the pleasure selfishly to himself instead. He nodded graciously. "Yes," he said to his devoted butler. "This could be most helpful. Thank you, Moss."

Chapter 25

"**H**e apologized! I can't believe it!"

"Perhaps he wanted to."

Sherrie turned and paced back the few steps across the floor to where May sat at the breakfast room table.

"I wish he hadn't."

"Be happy he did. Men aren't very good at it. Of course, neither are you."

"I don't have anything to apologize for."

"I suppose, but men still like for women to apologize. It makes them feel better."

Sherrie paced back and forth a few times. She didn't want to talk about it. Yes, she did. She turned to May. "For not telling me who he was."

"Good. You've been too angry about that."

"What do you mean, too angry?"

"It has blinded you to the man he is now."

Sherrie walked from the table to the windows and then turned to the sideboard. She stared at the food piled on blue china and silver serving dishes but didn't see any of it. "I asked him the wrong question," she muttered. "I don't know what I was thinking."

"You probably asked the wrong question," May answered, "because you don't want to hear the answer you already know. Hating is so much easier."

"Yes, it is," Sherrie agreed, and made one more circle of the room.

She'd been doing a lot of pacing since she'd come home. First in her room after getting cleaned up from the night's adventures. Then in Minnie's bedroom, watching her daughter sleep until her own restlessness wound down enough for her to lie down next her child on the narrow nursery bed.

She hadn't slept much, but she had cried a little. She didn't cry often, and didn't like doing it when she did. She was glad Minnie hadn't awakened and asked what was wrong.

Even now, after joining May in the airy breakfast room that looked out on the garden from a half dozen stained-glass windows, she couldn't curb her restlessness. The morning sun shone gloriously through the jewel-toned windows, throwing pastel patterns against the walls.

"Sit down," May said. She poured them each a cup of coffee from a tall silver pot. "You look terrible, by the way. You should get more sleep."

"Thank you very much for that suggestion, Mrs. Gartner."

"You're welcome. Sit."

Sherrie sat, and accepted the coffee from her

friend. "I hate the way you're always so damn calm. And don't tell me not to swear. Minnie's nowhere within hearing distance."

As if to deliberately give the lie to this statement, Minnie came running into the room just as Sherrie spoke. "Mama, mama, it's almost time! When do we leave?"

Sherrie pretended not to notice May's laughter. She put down her cup without having taken a sip and concentrated her attention on the excited child. "Go where?"

"Sherrie, honey, you have to do something about this fool child," Aunt Dora announced loudly, as she came marching into the room, followed closely by her two daughters and Ira.

"To the picnic!" Minnie clasped both of Sherrie's hands eagerly. "Please say we can go. *Please*."

Sherrie looked helplessly at Ira. He was looking out the windows. "It's a perfect day for a picnic," he said.

She had no idea what her daughter and Ira were talking about. She was underslept and distracted. It didn't help that Faith and Daisy were arguing over Lord Gordon Summers, or that Aunt Dora was staring at her with an irritated expression.

"I am not wasting my time going next door to services!" Daisy declared angrily.

"Unbeliever!" Faith shot back just as angrily. "What do you want to do? Go husband-hunting? Lord Gordon will be happy to find you a husband."

"What?" Sherrie asked.

Faith was happy to have their attention; at least she smiled. Her expression had a disturbing, glazed look that worried Sherrie. "Oh, yes. He arranges marriages all the time. He says it's our duty for those who follow the Way to marry within the faith." She held her hand out to her sister. "Come with me, Daisy, and Lord Gordon will find you a wealthy, powerful husband, just as he promised me."

Jack needs to know about this, Sherrie thought.

"The hell some faith healer is finding you a husband," Aunt Dora declared, stepping between her daughters. "If anyone finds my girls a wealthy, powerful husband, it's going to be me!" She looked back at Sherrie. "You tell 'em, honey."

Minnie tugged on her hands. "Please, Mama! The picnic. Can we go?"

Picnic. Sherrie suddenly remembered the invitation. And she suddenly remembered the things Rhu Limpok had said about Lord Gordon Summers. Not that she believed the old rogue, of course, but she did believe the evidence of her eyes. She believed her own instincts. Lord Gordon Summers was up to no good. No member of her family was getting involved with him. They weren't even going to stay in a house next door to his cult headquarters. She'd move them all into an hotel if she had to. Right now, she was going to get the Hamilton, Comstock, Gartner menagerie out of Primrose House, at least for the day. And kill a few birds with one stone while she was at it.

She stood, with Minnie clinging to her hands.

She swept her gaze commandingly around the breakfast room. "We're leaving," she told them all. "Immediately. I want the carriage brought around and everyone in it in fifteen minutes. Ira, make sure that Faith is in the carriage with us, even if you have to tie her up and throw her in."

Ira gave his slow, laconic smile. "Yes'm."

A howl went up from Faith as Dora asked, "Where are we going?"

Sherrie smiled reassuringly down at her excited daughter. "We're going on a picnic, of course."

"This is a mistake. What am I doing here?"

"Having a good time?" May suggested.

Sherrie stretched her legs out on the blanket beside May. "Yes," she agreed grudgingly.

But why did I come? she asked herself. May would say the answer was obvious. Sherrie wasn't sure anything was obvious or straightforward or guileless or what it seemed. The reasons people did things were too complex, and frequently hidden even from themselves. Maybe hidden from themselves most of all. Sherrie was very, very confused.

"But I am having a good time." This time the words didn't come out sounding quite so hostile.

"So am I." May laughed with delight. "Will you look at Ira and those boys?"

"He always was good at improvising."

"And with children. He'll be a good father. Speaking of which . . ." May pointed.

Sherrie forced herself to smile as Jack picked up a delightedly squealing Minnie and swung her around.

"Look at me, Mama!" Minnie called

Sherrie waved. "I *am* looking, sweetheart!" After a moment her smile became less forced. The pair really were having too good a time. She was jealous and worried, but she said, "I'm really happy to see them getting along."

"Very good," May replied. "That hardly sounded forced and stiff at all."

"I miss the days when you were meek and submissive, May Gartner."

"So do I, sometimes," May agreed. "It's such an easy way to live." She took a deep breath. "Doesn't the air smell wonderful?"

It was indeed a beautiful day, and it was good to be away from the city. They were seated on a beautifully tended lawn that stretched from a manor house in the distance down to the river. There were children everywhere, racing each other through the flowers and trees.

Most of the children at the picnic were from an orphanage the Earl of PenMartyn supported. Others were the children of the earl's servants, men of business and the staffs of his charities. The parents were at the outing along with their children. There were a modest number of "People of Quality" mingling on the sunlit grounds of the estate with all these working folk and deserving poor. Jack's true friends, Sherrie supposed, seemed to share the same loose definition of class barriers Jack did, at least on properly orchestrated occasions such as this.

Sherrie noticed that there were also some shy, modestly dressed young women who kept to themselves at one of the tables. She'd been told they were from a school where they were being "trained for a better life." Sherrie suspected just what sort of lives they'd led before they started training for better ones.

Their presence didn't offend her, but reminded her of Jack's reaction to the prostitute they'd encountered the night before. Sherrie had been too angry to take much notice at the time, but now she recalled Jack giving money to the woman, and kindly asking her to go home. She wanted to deride the man's gesture as hypocritical, but couldn't quite work up the nerve to. His kindness had seemed too natural, too much a part of who he was.

"You're looking thoughtful," May said.

"I am thoughtful."

"Well, at least you don't look angry. Pass me a slice of jam cake, please."

Many adults were seated on blankets and at laden picnic tables. There were games of croquet in progress, and lawn tennis. Ira, with his shirtsleeves rolled up, was attempting to teach baseball to a group of youngsters used to playing cricket. It was idyllic and lovely, and the peace and normalcy of the day scared Sherrie to death.

Minnie, with Lhasi on her heels, was on her feet once more, and following the gathering's host as he went from one group to the next. An insanely happy grin lit her face whenever Jack

PenMartyn paid the least little bit of attention to her, and he was paying quite a bit of attention to her. He seemed to be as happy to be with the child as she was to be with him. Sherrie was annoyed that the big Tibetan Mastiff was just as worshipful of the man as Minnie was. Lhasi was supposed to be a guard dog! The animal obviously didn't see anything that needed guarding against in Jack PenMartyn.

Neither did anyone else, apparently. She saw that the man was certainly popular. Even more than that, he gave every appearance of being genuinely admirable. She was the only one with any suspicions, and even she was fighting against herself to keep those suspicions alive. She had to be cautious, to be wary. She had the evidence of the past. And she had Minnie to worry about.

Minnie, who was having a wonderful time. In fact, after a while Sherrie's gaze stopped following Jack PenMartyn warily for Minnie's sake. She continued to watch him, but more for the pleasure of looking at such a fine-looking male animal than for any other reason. Doubts and anger dissipated beneath the summer sunlight, the lulling sounds of the river, and the laughter of children.

Temptation to get up and go to him began to grow in her. The constant itch of longing that hadn't disappeared in nine years began to be felt just under her skin. *I'm addicted to the man*, she admitted. For once she didn't curse him, or cast around hopelessly for a cure. She just had another piece of chicken.

Sherrie didn't give in to temptation. She let Minnie have her time with her father. Other than greeting her when they arrived, and making some introductions, Jack hadn't spoken to her. It looked as if he was carefully keeping his distance from where she sat. She told herself it was a good thing he was ignoring her, and that she wasn't in the least upset about it. They would have to talk before she left, about Minnie, about Lord Gordon. It could wait, she told herself.

She deliberately stayed with May on the blanket under the shade of a gigantic oak tree. They shared the contents of the basket and chatted about babies, and Sherrie pretended she didn't have a care in the world while her daughter ran around like a happy puppy and scarcely looked her way at all.

Sherrie even kept her place and held her peace while Faith sulked and simply stood with her arms crossed, staring at the river. She didn't do a thing to intervene despite Aunt Dora's appalled looks as Daisy happily played croquet with a tall Scotsman who was obviously not a Lord or a Sir or even wealthy but seemed quite intelligent and nice just the same. She let the day happen and stayed out of its way, and, except for her fits and starts of nerves, this approach was surprisingly restful.

After a while she even relaxed enough to lean back against the tree trunk. "I think I'm going to have a little nap now.'' She needed to discuss Summers with Jack, but it could wait for a few minutes.

When she dozed off it wasn't Cullum who filled her half-waking dreams, but Jack Pen-Martyn.

Chapter 26

It started quite innocently. "You have to meet my Aunt Dora," Minnie announced. "When she isn't worried about Faith and Daisy getting married, she's really nice."

Unable to deny the child anything, he dutifully sat down in a lawn chair next to Mrs. Comstock when Minnie led him to the woman. The next thing he knew, Minnie was securely ensconced on his lap, the dog was sitting on his feet, and Aunt Dora was telling him all about Sherrie, when she wasn't darting concerned glances at her unmarried daughters.

It was probably improper for Minnie to be on his lap, but it felt very nice and natural to cradle the child. Her warm weight gave him a kind of comfort and peace he'd never known before. Dora Comstock didn't object. Sherrie didn't come marching over and snatch her child away, either. He was grateful for that. Grateful for the time Sherrie was allowing him to have with Minnie.

He had hesitated to send the invitation and

had been certain it would not be accepted. His heart had very nearly broken out of his breast in reaction to the sight of Sherrie and Minnie coming across the lawn in the morning sunlight. It had taken all his self-control not to take Sherrie Hamilton in his arms and kiss her senseless with joy and thankfulness. He didn't understand it, but he found the sight of Sherrie laughing and smiling at their daughter as compellingly sensual as everything else about her.

"Minnie insisted we come," she told him when he greeted the family.

Of course she had come because of Minerva, and not because she wanted to see him. "How kind," he said, without showing the unreasonable disappointment he felt.

Once he was engaged in conversation with Aunt Dora, he almost forgot that Sherrie was at the picnic, though his attention was totally taken up with learning about her. He learned how Sherrie had come dragging home with a Chinese girl months after everyone thought she was dead. How she'd been widowed after only a few months of marriage and bravely raised a daughter alone while overseeing the mining, logging and ranching empire her father left her. How she oversaw her family as well—everyone turned to decisive, responsible Sherrie for every little and large thing. How she restlessly traveled the world, looking for something—Aunt Dora had no idea what.

Dora Comstock's stories gave a more complex picture of Sherrie Hamilton's life than the memoirs he'd read. Taken together, and from his own impressions when he wasn't lost in a fit of rut, he saw that Sherrie Hamilton was no longer the girl he'd loved. The knowledge broke his heart, but not because he loved her any less.

When Aunt Dora put a hand on his arm he nearly jumped out of his skin. "If you ask me, it's time that girl settled down," she told him. Casting a significant glance toward where Sherrie sat, she said, "You could do worse than marry my niece, Lord PenMartyn."

He couldn't do any better. He'd always known that. But Sherrie couldn't do any worse than him. He'd proven that long ago.

"You should talk to Ira now," his daughter announced, before he could find some excuse to get away from Sherrie's expectant aunt.

Minnie hopped off his lap, took his hand, and led him to where Ira Gartner was taking a rest from the attempt to instruct a group of boys in an American game.

Gartner smiled a greeting and said, "Minerva May, isn't it time you had something to eat?" Gartner was looking at Jack when he went on, "Go to your mama, now, honey."

To Jack's surprise, Minnie didn't argue. "You do that very well," he told the tall American when Minnie ran off to join Sherrie and May under the oak tree.

"She's on her best behavior today," he was informed. "Trying to impress you."

"Me?"

Ira Gartner put an arm around Jack's shoulder and turned him in the direction of the river.

"Let's have a little walk and talk, shall we?"

Jack wasn't used to this sort of familiarity. "Very well," he said stiffly. "I have been wanting to discuss your relationship with my—with the child."

"You've been wanting to fire me, you mean," Gartner said as they came to a spot beyond anyone else's hearing. "You don't think it's right and proper. You loathe the way Sherrie's let me help her raise her little girl."

"I—" Jack moved away from the other man's circling arm. They stared out across the width of the river in silence for a few moments. Sun sparked off the water. "Yes," Jack finally answered Ira, turning to face him. "You know exactly what I think. I heartily disapprove of your presence in Mrs. Hamilton's household."

"Well," Ira replied after another short, tense silence. "All I can say to that, *your lordship*, is, where the *hell* have you been?"

The American's words might have struck a harder blow if Jack hadn't been thinking them himself since he'd found out about Minnie's existence. Not that the words didn't burn like hellfire. The pain was enough to make his throat too tight to speak.

This gave Gartner the chance to go on. "If you'd care to call me out for my insolence, I'd be happy to oblige, but May wouldn't like it if I killed you."

Jack found himself looking toward the women under the tree. Sherrie seemed to be asleep. May saw him, smiled, and waved. Almost without any volition, he found himself waving back. "May," he croaked. He swallowed hard, and looked back at May's husband. Why would she be upset if he died? "If you wanted a duel, Mr. Gartner, perhaps it should be over her honor."

Ira looked surprised for a moment, then he laughed. "Why?"

"Because—" Jack made a helpless gesture.

"It's not your fault her father gave her to you as a bribe. That's her father's fault. May and I are both glad you didn't send her packing back to the old man. Who knows who he'd have given her to next?"

"Yes, but . . ."

"But what? You didn't send her home in disgrace. You could have. And I know how you risked your life to save hers." Ira reached out and snagged Jack by the shoulder again. Drawing closer, Ira said quietly. "I married a virgin, PenMartyn, not some ill-used concubine. That alone tells me that you're not quite as debauched as you think you are."

"She was a child!" Jack replied indignantly. "Of course I didn't . . . besides, I—"

"Had Sherrie," Ira finished for him. "And you sent her home when you came to your senses."

"I should never have lost my senses."

"No, you shouldn't have," Ira agreed. "But you're a man. She's a desirable woman. It happened." Gartner stepped back and shrugged. "And if Sherrie didn't tell you she was carrying a child, I guess it's not your fault you haven't helped raise Minerva." The man's look turned steely. "Sherrie didn't tell you, now, did she?"

Jack wasn't used to anyone knowing his past, let alone discussing it with him. It wasn't possible to remain reticent under Ira Gartner's stern gaze. "As God is my witness," Jack told him. "I had no idea."

"Well, it's not too late to be a father now."

Yes it was. Of course it was. How could this man, this man who knew what he was, say such a thing to him? Most likely because Ira had absorbed the wrong woman's view of life in the White Tiger's household. Sherrie knew better. No matter what anyone said, he didn't have a hope in hell for any future with Sherrie and Minerva in it.

Ira gestured toward where the women sat. "Shall we join the ladies?"

Jack glanced that way again. Sherrie napped on the blanket with Minerva leaning against her. The dog was lying across the blanket as well. Daisy Comstock and David MacQuarrie were also seated under the oak. May waved again. The scene was all very charming, very domestic. It called to him like nothing ever had before.

He had never felt more empty, more tainted, in his life. He couldn't bear it.

Rather than taking Ira Gartner up on his invitation. Rather than going about his duties as host. Rather than throwing himself in the Thames to drown, Jack said, "I can't."

He shook his head, and backed away. He had to get away. He didn't run, but it felt like all the hounds of hell were on his heels as he left the sight of the life he could never, ever have.

"My lord?"

Jack frowned at the butler's worried tone. "What?"

Hawton closed the door, and looked over the tattered state of Jack's clothing. Then he glanced significantly at the grandfather clock on the other side of the hallway. He said not a word.

"Yes, I am late in returning from an event I was responsible for managing. And I also don't give a damn how many of my friends have called at the door or sent notes expressing their concern for my untimely disappearance this afternoon. I don't care. And yes, I have been in a fight," Jack informed the man irritably, brushing dirt off his jacket. He noticed a spot of blood on his shirt collar, but knew the blood was not his own. "With a gang of toughs down in Whitechapel. I won. It was most satisfying."

"Yes," Hawton responded, calm and collected as those in his profession were trained to be. "You do not care. That is why you are bothering to explain your absence to a hired servant. I was worried, Jack," he added. "We all were."

"I felt the need for a long walk."

"It's miles back to London from Dawes, my lord."

"I flagged down a ride."

"And ended up in the worst slum in the city. How inconvenient, my lord."

"It was rather entertaining, actually," Jack replied.

Taking on a half-dozen ruffians intent on robbing him had proved a decent outlet for all the emotion he hadn't been able to vent in any other way. He was tired, his heart and soul were shredded, but he wasn't going to follow the reckless impulse to run all the way to Primrose House that he'd been fighting for hours.

"As you say, my lord. Do you wish dinner, my lord?" He sniffed. "A bath?"

Jack headed for the stairs. "A bath, yes." He longed to call for a bottle or two of wine as well, and to perhaps add some single malt whisky and a flask of brandy on top of the wine. Oblivion would be so very nice and so very easy. Instead he said, "And tea, Hawton. I would dearly love a good, hot cup of tea."

He went straight through his bedroom and dressing room, dropping clothes as he went, intent on getting to the deep tub in the bathroom. Jack was glad that his valet was not up waiting for him, but expected Dabney at any moment.

He managed to give himself a quick bath and was just putting on a dressing gown, his back turned to the door, when he heard someone come into the bathroom. "Go to bed," he said to the valet. "I don't need any help, Dabney."

"I'm not ready to go to bed yet," a richly amused woman's voice replied. "As for needing help, I think you do."

Jack whirled around, his robe swinging open, the ends of the sash clutched in his hands. "Sherrie! What the devil are you doing here?"

Her arms were folded, and her gaze swept boldly over him from head to foot. A slow smile lit her features. "Well, at least you're clean," she said.

He wasn't in the least amused, nor did he like the reminder. "I bathe quite frequently these days, madam," he told her, as he drew his robe around him and firmly tied the sash at his waist.

Her smile was teasing as she answered, "I'm glad to know you've developed a few good habits, my lord."

She leaned a shoulder against the door frame. Her gown was the color of ripe peaches. Her hair was worn loose, falling in a golden veil around her face and shoulders. She looked irresistibly beautiful and provocative. As usual the very sight of her went to his head, his heart, and his damned betraying body.

"Get out of here!" he shouted at her. "Right now."

Sherrie retreated, but only as far as through the dressing room and into Jack's bedroom. She planted herself there, arms still crossed, and waited for him to come out of the bathroom. She wasn't sure if what she was feeling was defiance, or determination, but for the first time in years she felt free. How odd, she thought. She'd always given the appearance of being the freest woman in the world, but had never actually felt that way inside. Something had always held her back, held her spirit down. Tonight she was ready to fly. Ready to shout from the rooftops. To risk it all. To come face to face with all her demons and wrestle them into submission at last.

Several moments later he stuck his head out the dressing room door. His icy-blue eyes flashed angrily. "Didn't I tell you to go?"

The strength of his emotions were almost enough to force her back, but she stood her ground. "This is as far as I'm going," she told him.

"You can't be alone with me."

The intensity of his gaze burned into her, but she forced her tone to be light. "Because it isn't proper?"

"It isn't safe. You know what I'm like."

"I know what you were like," she answered solemnly.

He emerged from the dressing room slowly, and closed the door behind him. His attention remained intently focused on her. She knew that look. Possessive. Hungry. It made her feel utterly female. This time it didn't make her feel vulnerable, though. She also admitted, at last, to how much she'd missed it. She never wanted him to stop looking at her like that.

He came closer, a big, stalking black-and-white cat. "I haven't changed."

Jack just barely managed to stop the impulse to take hold of her before he reached where she stood. An hour ago he had been physically and emotionally exhausted. That was all changed now. Having her alone, alone in the privacy of his room, where he could do anything and everything he wanted, set his mind reeling with the possibilities. Fresh energy surged through him, along with growing, demanding need.

It was only with great effort that he managed

to keep his senses, keep control, to ask, "What are you doing here? How did you get in? Why?" *For God's sake, why?*

Sherrie was glad he hadn't come any closer. She wasn't yet ready to be touched by him, to touch him. Fire was inevitable when they touched, and it was impossible to hold a conversation when the world was burning up around you. She left Jack where he stood and moved backward toward the center of his room.

From a safer distance she answered, "I decided it was about time for you to find me lurking in your bedroom for a change."

The faintest of smiles played on his lips. There was a glint of amusement in his eyes. "Turnabout's fair play. Is that it?"

Sherrie nodded. "Your butler didn't object when I said I would wait here."

Jack crossed his arms. The faint signs of amusement were replaced by a frown. "I shall have a talk with Hawton. How long have you been waiting?"

"I'm told I arrived just after you got home. I decided to let you get cleaned up before we talked. But not being very patient, I got tired of waiting and spoiled the surprise."

He arched an eyebrow. A very British, aristocratic sort of gesture, in Sherrie's opinion. "I see." He gestured toward the bed. "Were you planning on waiting there, naked and panting with need?"

Sherrie put her hands on her hips. "Oh, don't you wish!"

"Yes. I do, as a matter of fact."

She shook her head. "Now there's a typical male fantasy—finding a willing body in your bed without having to work for it."

"I'm a male." He walked toward her again, and stopped again as a wide smile tilted up her lips. His eyes narrowed suspiciously. "Why do I have the feeling I just stepped into some kind of trap, Scheherazade?"

She held her hands out. Despite her determination to keep away from him, she couldn't stop from taking his hands in hers. "A trap," she agreed. "Not a tiger trap, my love, but a man trap."

He had no idea what she meant, but her touch was warm and welcoming, and strong. When he tried to pull away she wouldn't let him go. "Sherrie—"

"How old are you?"

He could tell by the look on her face that the question surprised her as much as it did him. "How old?"

She drew closer, and looked him over carefully. Her hands still held his, she drew them down to their sides while she stood toe to toe with him. "I never did find out how old you were when we met."

There was but an inch between them, and he was sharply aware of her proximity. He ached to close the gap, and he dared not move. "When we met." He let out a long breath. "What a mundane way of saying it."

She tilted her head a bit. "Cut out the melodrama, Jack, and just tell me how old you are."

"Impertinent woman."

"Age."

"Thirty-three."

Her eyes widened. "That's all? Thirty-three? That means you were—"

"Twenty-four," he provided with a pained nod.

"How long were you in the Orient? When did you go there? Why? Were you always a spy?"

There was a surprising lack of hostility in her curiosity. She was looking at him with eagerness, with interest. Every question stung, and the stings bled, but not from the way Sherrie asked them. "I do not discuss my past with anyone," he told her.

Her fingers tightened around his wrists. Her expression hardened. "With me you do."

He sighed. She was right. She was the one person in the world he owed explanations to. He was still reluctant to give them. He turned from her steady gaze, and looked at a framed print of a sailing ship over the bedroom mantel rather than face her.

"I know exactly how you feel," she said, after silence stretched out for a bit. "You've held it in for too long, so long that protecting your secrets becomes more important than the secrets themselves. You come to think that the secrets are all you have, so you hug them close and hide them, even from yourself."

"I don't know what you mean."

"At least I've had May to talk to," she went on. "But there were things I kept, even from her."

He looked back at her. "Such as?"

Her eyes held an expression he couldn't understand. She said, "We're talking about you right now, Jack PenMartyn. You are going to talk to me, aren't you?"

"I don't want to talk to you." He broke her hold with a twist of his wrists and put his arms around her. "Talking never was what I was good at with you."

"I know." She put her hands on his shoulders. "But talk to me. For once. For now. Before I push you down and have my way with you."

He was utterly shocked. "Have your way with me!"

"You heard me. Later. Talk first." She pushed the sides of the robe aside and laid her palms flat on his chest.

He closed his eyes. "I can't think when you do that."

She leaned close, her breath brushing his ear. "Try."

The husky timbre of her voice did nothing to help his concentration. Why was she behaving like this? Didn't she know what was likely to happen at any moment? His control was only so strong . . . growing weaker by the moment.

Jack forced himself to concentrate. He made himself talk rather than do what he wanted. "I was the youngest of four sons," he told her. "Luckily, I had a gift for languages. A cousin who worked in the Foreign Office offered to take me on as a clerk. I ended up in China when I was seventeen. I got into a few scrapes, ended up running with a wild crowd, and discovered

I also had a knack for picking up information.
Eventually, my employers in the Foreign Office
approached me about going underground—to
establish myself as one of the renegades that
preyed on shipping in the China Sea. The point
of the operation was to gather information, and
to thin the ranks of those pirates whenever possible." He laughed softly, without any humor.
"It was the most freedom I'd ever known. The
most fun I'd had. I ended up enjoying the role
a little too much—as you well know." He
stroked her hair. "I—uh—"

"It's all right," she told him. "Open your
eyes, Jack, please."

"Are they closed?"

"Yes. Look at me, not at the past." She slid
her hands slowly up his chest, sending a shiver
through him. She cupped his face in her hands,
caught and held his gaze. There was a room
somewhere beyond her eyes, a house, a sleeping city, a country, but all there was in his universe were Scheherazade's eyes. Eyes that were
full of questions, but held no tears, and absolutely no fear. Anger, yes, there was anger in
her, simmering deep down, as well there
should be.

He made himself speak. "Have I answered all
your questions?"

"Not quite."

She looked away. She let him go. She stepped
away. She grew tense, and silent, and all the
light slowly left her eyes. Eventually she slowly
turned her back on him. He watched the play
of her muscles as her shoulders hunched and

she wrapped her arms protectively around her waist. Watching the change in her as her bravery drove a knife through his heart.

He took a step toward her, his hand out to touch her shoulder. She sensed the movement and drew even further away. "What?" he asked, voice a low rasp. He knew that he would do anything to stop her pain. "What more do you want to know?"

She whirled around suddenly, hands out as if to ward off a blow, eyes wild, her hair swinging around her face. There were tears on her cheeks.

"Oh, Scheherazade—"

"Why?" she demanded, somehow making the sound a hiss of fury. "Why did you send me away? Was it something I did? Were you ashamed of me?"

He stared at her, utterly dumbfounded. His universe wheeled slowly, darkly, around him, crashed, burned and blew away.

Chapter 27

❦

"**B**ut . . . how—?"
"Just tell me!"
She shrieked the words at the top of her
lungs. She was well beyond caring who heard
them. Well beyond making any sense. She'd
come here to make peace, but right now, seeing
the stricken look and confusion on the man's
face, all she could feel was the burn of hate that
had been smoldering in her blood since that
long ago night when he'd given her the world
in a prince's bedroom and taken it away a few
hours later.

"One glimpse of paradise was all I got?" she
asked, her voice a ragged snarl. "What made
you change your mind? Wasn't I good enough
for the earl to bring home? Even as a mistress?
I loved you. You said you'd give up your life
for me—and then you threw me away." She
snapped her fingers. "Like that. Easier than
that."

"It wasn't easy."

"I hated you. Do you know how much I

hated you? Sometimes the hate was the only thing that kept me alive." She turned her back to him once more. What she said next was a thin, anguished whisper, pitched so low he could barely make out the words. "I love you so much, but the hate was easier."

And that, he knew, was the secret she'd kept even from May. The secret that ate at her. One more burden he'd given her.

"You loved me?" he asked helplessly. His heart raced, his head spun. Hope and heartbreak warred inside him, and the desolation of all his sins won out over both. "How could you possibly have loved me?"

She faced him with the same speed and suddenness of a few moments before. "Love," Sherrie snapped out. "Not past tense. Love. Then, now, forever."

He shook his head. He knew what he'd done to her. He had to make her understand. Maybe the knowledge would bring her some peace. "It wasn't love, Sherrie. I made you want me, but what you felt wasn't love. Wasn't and isn't. It's not possible."

Her glare very nearly burned holes in him. "Don't you tell me what's not possible, Jack PenMartyn. I know what I feel, even if I haven't wanted to admit to it. I promised the Tibetan holy man I'd face my fears and get on with my life." She pointed at him, at herself, and at the floor. "And we're staying right here until we get this worked out."

He couldn't help the fleeting moment of frustrated amusement. "You are so, so—American.

Forthright. Plainspoken. Impossible."

"I told you not to use that word. I'm *difficult*, not impossible." She wiped away the last of the tears from her momentary weakness, and took a steadying breath. "Now," she went on determinedly. "Answer my question." She made herself look him in the face, her chin lifted proudly, her shoulders bravely squared. "I can take it, Lord PenMartyn. Did you think you were too good for me back then? Had you just gotten word that you'd inherited the title and needed to rush home to find a proper English virgin to marry?"

"You may have noticed that I have never married."

"And why is that?" she demanded.

"Because I love you!" he shouted at her, as loudly as she'd shouted at him before. "I love you!" He turned around and slammed a fist into the nearest piece of furniture, a tall clothes cabinet. He had to have some outlet or knew he would simply explode. "Always and forever. From the first moment I saw you. Until my last breath." It was his turn to turn angrily on her. "Is that what you want to hear? Damn you, is it? Do you want to know how much loving you and losing you and knowing it was my own damn fault hurts me?"

"Yes!" she snarled back. "And you didn't lose me, you forced me to leave, and I want to know why!"

He grabbed her by the shoulders. "For your own good, that's why!"

"What?"

"I saw the look on your face when you saved me from Grigori. And the excitement, the joy you took in the adventure when we escaped from the palace. I saw what living with me was doing to you. I recognized the cravings in you."

"I was having fun that night."

"Fun? That wasn't fun. We were in deathly peril!"

She grinned. "We got out of it, didn't we?"

He shook her shoulders. "That is no way for a lady to think."

"I am no lady." She said each word slowly and distinctly. "Haven't you figured that out by now?"

"I don't have to figure anything out. It's my fault." He forced his hands to drop from her shoulders, forced himself to take a step back. He had no right to touch her. "I made you what you are."

She crossed her arms again. Her brows lowered over her big, china-blue eyes. "No, you didn't. And I fell in love with you of my own accord," she went on.

"I raped you," he reminded her. "Repeatedly."

"No, you didn't."

How could she sound so calm, so certain? "I was there," he recalled, sounding as calm as she did when he was screaming inside. "I know what I did."

"I was there, too," she reminded him. "And you never forced me. Never hurt me. You gave me unimaginable pleasure."

"I coerced you. Threatened you. Forced your

compliance. That is rape. And if I thought falling down on my knees and begging your forgiveness would do any good, I wouldn't hesitate for a moment."

Sherrie considered his words for a moment, before shaking her head. "I don't want you begging my forgiveness. I just want you to forgive yourself."

"What I did to you was unforgivable."

"It was also nine years ago."

"What difference does that make."

She almost sputtered with frustration as she answered. "We're grown ups now. Adults. We have a child to think of. And the rest of our lives before us." She picked up a statue off a nearby table and threw it at him. He ducked and it crashed against the dressing room door. "Can't we just get past all this guilt and remorse and vindictiveness and get on with our lives?" She threw another statue, an ugly one of a hunting dog with a pheasant in its mouth. "Let's try for a little acceptance and compassion and forgiveness, why don't we?"

Jack looked at the remains on the floor behind him, then back at Sherrie. "You have an interesting way of showing forgiveness and compassion, my dear."

"If I wasn't feeling forgiving and compassionate, my aim wouldn't be off, my lord."

"You tried to shoot me two nights ago."

"That was foreplay."

He came toward her. Had it been only two nights since he'd forced his way into her bedroom? Perhaps three? And perhaps it hadn't been all that forceful. He had given her plea-sure, he did remember that. It hadn't been at all one-sided, despite her justifiable anger. She was telling him now that what he recalled as rape had been no such thing. Of course he wanted to believe her. It was easier on his conscience to let himself believe that of course she had wanted it.

"I want it now," she said, as if reading his mind. "I want you." She held her arms open as he came to her. "I want you to make love to me, Jack. Jack and Sherrie, not Cullum and Scheherazade. Let them go. Let the past go. Live in the moment. Don't worry about the future." She pointed at the bed. "Let's start over, you and me. I've seen how good you are," she went on, before he could object. She took him into her embrace and held him close. "I think you've always been good, that's why having been bad hurts so much."

He wrapped his arms around her. Her words, the warmth of her, were an anchor, and maybe a lifeline. He could almost feel her pulling him back toward some peaceful shore he'd been lost from far too long. How could she love him? He didn't know. But he began to believe it was true.

"It was more than a little bad."

She chuckled, the sound low and sexual, and a blessing. "I like you bad. In bed."

"Maybe you never were a lady."

"Not in bed." She put her fingers over his lips. "Come to bed with me, Jack." Her words were spoken in a soft, sultry voice, but he recognized the implacable will behind them.

"Jack," he said. He closed his eyes for a moment as a shiver of dread went through him. When he opened them, her gaze trapped his. "What if I can't—?"

"Can't what? Can't be Jack PenMartyn? Why don't you believe that that's who you are? Jack the good, Jack the caring, Jack the responsible. Jack the doting father. Jack—the lover. Come be my lover."

His voice was a pained rasp as he replied, "Jack the liar? The sham? What if—?"

Her hand caressed his cheek. He felt the rough scratch of his beard stubble against her soft skin. Her body shifted subtly closer to him. Another shiver went through him, one of need this time.

"What if you learn to believe what everyone else knows. Love me, Jack."

She took his hand and led him toward the bed. He came with her, without volition, drawn by the look in her eyes. It was the tender, loving expression she poured into her gaze that was keeping him alive. He couldn't bear to be away from that look. Her belief and trust in him was the most frightening thing he'd ever faced.

He was already close to naked, wearing nothing but the black brocade robe. Sherrie's deft hands loosened the sash as they reached the bed. She pushed the robe open and off. The heavy material made a soft sighing sound as it settled onto the floor. Sherrie's hands, then her mouth, moved slowly and surely over his bare sensitized flesh. Her touch brought both arousal and comfort so pure it was agonizing. He stood beside the bed, eyes closed, trembling with need, accepting, reveling as her lips, tongue, and fingers kissed and stroked and tasted him. She moved slowly, with deliberate hesitation, down to his hard, aroused shaft. When she finally reached that one, neediest spot, she knelt before him and flicked her tongue swiftly, teasingly, across the sensitive tip. Jack let out a sharp gasp, his knees began to buckle. His hands clutched at her hair, but she pulled her head away. At the same time her palms shoved against his thighs.

Jack fell back onto the bed. Pillows scattered, and he rose up on his elbows to look at her. She stood before him, fingers working on the numerous fastenings of her clothing, a look that mixed arousal and triumph lit her face. God, but she was beautiful!

"What are you looking at?" she teased, and stepped out of her skirt. She posed in her undergarments. "What do you think of the corset?"

It was covered in lace and satin roses. She began to undo the lacings that held it closed. It couldn't come off fast enough for him. "I think that I have a knife around here somewhere," he answered. "Maybe I should fetch it and just cut it off."

She laughed. "Don't you dare! This came from Paris."

He held out his hand to her. "I'll get you another. Come here."

Sherrie reveled in the possessiveness in his

eyes. She loved the imperious tone in his voice. When it came to sex, the man always knew what he wanted, and she was always happy to give it to him. "How I've missed making love to you," she told him.

A flicker of surprise crossed his face, and a shadow of all his deep, lingering guilt. Sherrie wouldn't have it. She finished tearing off her clothes and threw herself onto him. He caught her by the waist and rolled her onto her back. She gasped as his mouth closed around her breast, then purred with pleasure as he nursed sweet arousal out of her with all the skilled passion she could possibly desire. His hands moved over her, his mouth worshipped her. He gave her his complete attention, and she arched—writhed—opened herself to his every delicate or demanding touch.

To think that he'd sent her away from this heaven they created together because he loved her! It had been a selfless and noble gesture—and someday, if he made love to her two or three times a day for the next thirty or forty years—she might actually forgive him for it.

He was all she'd desired, ever. Even from her first sight of the filthy, cruel pirate who'd demanded a devil's bargain from her, the connection had been there. Maybe they should have started out better, differently, but she knew that even if their first meeting had been in a ballroom, even if their courtship had been tame and proper, they would have still ended up here, in bed, making passionate, possessive love. They were meant to be, mated, dark and light halves combined to make a whole. Each held the completing part of the other's soul. *Karma.* Fate. Destiny.

"Do that again."

He laughed against her navel, and kissed her in the same sensitive spot he'd found a moment before. She loved the sound of his laughter, the feel of it on her skin, as much as she did his kisses. Laughter would heal them both. Laughter and lots of practice—practice at talking to each other, at being together, at being a family, being lovers, and becoming friends. All they needed was time. She was determined that they would have all the time in the world.

"And babies," she said. "I want to have more babies."

Jack's head came up sharply, his eyes full of shock and terror. Sherrie threw her head back against the pillows and howled with laughter. "Minnie couldn't have scared you that badly."

Jack moved up to come face to face with her. He stroked her cheek, ran his fingers through her hair. His look of surprise had turned to one of wonder. "You want to give me children? Me?"

She rested her hands on his broad, hard-muscled shoulders, and looked at him as earnestly as he looked at her. "Yes. You." She moved, shifting beneath him, opened her legs, felt the hard length of him pressed in the valley between her thighs. She kissed him gently. "Come into me," she whispered against his lips. "Come and make a home."

Come home. Jack heard the words and could

wait no longer. She had said that she had had no home since he'd sent her away. He had had no home, no peace, without her. Perhaps he didn't deserve peace, but Sherrie didn't care. She was determined to give it to him anyway.

He could deny her nothing she wanted. Even if it was to save his wretched soul.

He flexed his hips, drove into her. She pulled his mouth down to hers, wrapped her legs around his waist and rose to meet his surging strokes, her soft, yielding heat fitted perfectly to his pulsing, driving hardness. They drove each other mad with their shared passion, they brought each other to the edge of heaven, then over that edge into long-drawn-out ecstasy. It was a place they went together, the place where they belonged. Home.

Chapter 28

$\sim\!\!\!\bigcirc\!\!\!\bigcirc\!\!\!\sim$

"**Y**ou make me look bad. You know that, don't you?"

Jack was more than half asleep when Sherrie suddenly spoke. They'd been lying together on the rumpled bed for a long time now. He supposed it must be near dawn. He was too comfortable with her warm, soft body wrapped around him to care. He could just lie here like this forever. He thought she might have said several things to him in the last few minutes, but these were the first words that actually penetrated his satisfied, lethargic euphoria.

Her head was resting on his shoulder, her hair fanned out across his face. A few strands rested on his cheek. He brushed her hair aside and turned his head, to find her looking alert despite the lateness and the hours of lovemaking. "You don't look bad," he told her, then kissed her forehead. "Considering . . ."

She laughed, and they shifted position to lie face to face. "I know what I look like."

"Decadent at best. What would Lady Anne

say?" He pretended shock. "What about Aunt Dora?"

"They'd say 'Well done, my dear,' and tell me that I'm a lucky woman." She kissed him. "I am."

"You're mad."

"Probably."

"And I still have no idea what you are talking about, my beloved madwoman. How can I possibly make you look bad?"

She trailed her fingers slowly through the thick black hair that covered his chest. "Just by being you, philanthropist, supporter of widows and orphans, good friend to those in need."

His skin flushed deep red in embarrassment at her praise. "I have a great deal," he told her. "It just makes sense to share it."

"You're a good man," she told him. "You've made a difference in a lot of lives. All I've ever done is indulge my urge to travel." She made a disgusted face before he had a chance to argue that of course she made a difference. "I'm going to have to reform my selfish ways, Jack Pen-Martyn," she complained. "And it's all your fault."

He laughed, and pulled her close. "You are absolutely correct," he told you. "I suppose I have my work cut out making a decent woman out of you."

She threw her leg over his hip and wiggled closer. "Why don't you make an indecent one out of me first?"

He would have, but a knock came on the bedroom door before they could get started, loud, insistent and continuous. Jack rolled out of the bed, grabbed his robe up from the floor, and marched angrily across the room.

"Damn it, Hawton, what is it?" he demanded as he flung the door open.

Hawton was there in the hallway, but a much larger man stood in front of the butler. His height and width filled the door. His worried expression riveted Jack's attention. Tension and fear flooded through Jack.

Sherrie came up behind Jack before he could speak, a blanket wrapped around her, sarong fashion. She put a hand on Jack's rigid arm. She said, "Ira, what is it? What's happened.?"

Ira ran a hand worriedly through his dark curls. "She's not here, is she? The butler said she wasn't, but I hoped—" He shook his head, and visibly got himself under control. "Minnie," he answered their questioning, frightened looks. "Minnie's missing."

Sherrie made a small, terrified sound. She clutched hard at Jack's arm as his kaleidoscope reality shifted and shattered again. He had known fear and desolation in his life, but nothing to match this sudden helpless panic. His child. His beautiful, perfect child was missing.

His heart raced. He wanted to run out into the streets and start blindly searching. He took Sherrie into a comforting embrace instead. He couldn't feel his arms around her, though.

"Get dressed," he heard himself say. It was like he watched himself from the depths of a particularly dark circle of hell. "Don't worry," he went on, voice adamant with certainty he didn't feel. "We'll find her."

It was his fault. Whatever had happened to his child was his fault. All he could think was that Minerva had decided to make the trip from Primrose House to his townhouse by herself again and not been so lucky in crossing the city alone this time.

It was his fault, but he turned his anger on Ira Gartner. "I thought you were supposed to protect her."

Ira threw Jack's fears right back in his face. "If she wasn't so desperate for you to love her, she wouldn't be missing."

"If you'd kept a closer watch on her—"

Ira took an angry step forward. Both Sherrie and May moved between the men. The nursery was crowded with too many people and a large dog. "This is no place for a brawl," Sherrie announced. "So don't even think about it."

Sherrie had felt the hostile tension growing between the two men on the way back to her house. She wasn't going to put up with them getting into a cockfight now. It was an hour past dawn, they had no idea how long Minnie had been missing. Sherrie was done with her initial panicked reaction. She had to get a search for her missing child organized. She didn't think this gathering in Minnie's room to rehash what little they knew was going to do any good, but both Jack and Ira had insisted. They wanted facts, to investigate. Sherrie was being eaten up inside with worry, and not famous for her patience at the best of times. She wanted to *do something!*

While Jack and Ira continued to glare at each other, Aunt Dora touched Sherrie on the arm. "Honey," she said quietly, with a significant glance toward Jack. "I can appreciate Lord PenMartyn's concern, but why's he so—?"

"Because I'm Minerva's father," Jack interrupted the woman.

There were gasps from where Daisy and Faith stood on the other side of the room. Aunt Dora's brows rose, but she didn't bother with asking any more questions just now. "Then I suppose you have every right to be concerned about my great-niece's welfare," she told him. To Sherrie, she said, "What do we do now, honey? Where do you think she went?"

"When did you discover she was missing?" Jack asked Ira. "How many hours?"

"I came to wake her at five o'clock," Ira said. "We wanted to get to Hyde Park for her early riding lesson. I found that her bed had been slept in, but she was gone. My first thought was that she'd gone looking for you again."

"Perhaps she was abducted." The suggestion came from Daisy.

Ira turned to her. "Lhasi would have made some noise if a stranger came into the room. I checked the stables first," Ira said before Jack could ask. "Her horse is still there."

"But—" A knock on the nursery door interrupted whatever objection Daisy was about to make. She turned and answered the door, spoke to the person who'd knocked, then turned back. She held an envelope in her hand. She crossed the room. "Todd said this was sent for you, Lord PenMartyn."

Jack took the heavy vellum envelope from the young woman's hand. In the ominous, fearful silence that suddenly descended on the nursery, with every gaze turned on him, he looked at the writing done in a strong, decisive hand on the front of the envelope.

It was addressed to the White Tiger of Kuzay. He tore the envelope open with trembling fingers and read the short message from Lord Gordon Summers inside. Sherrie moved to read over his shoulder.

After a few horrible moments they looked at each other.

"I was right," he whispered. "This is all my fault. Our child is in danger, and it is all my fault."

"You told me to come alone. I'm here. Where's Minerva?"

Lord Gordon smiled, but remained seated behind the desk in his library. The width of it gave him a certain reassuring distance from the angry White Tiger and lent him an air of authority. Not that he needed any symbol of authority; he was the one in control here. Besides, there were enough guards posted around the room and within calling distance, should PenMartyn decide to make any violent move.

All this open show of power felt wonderful. Summers was ready to make his move at last.

He didn't mind taking the time to gloat, just a little.

"Have a seat," he directed with an expansive gesture. "Shall I call for tea? Or perhaps a brandy might be appropriate under the circumstances. No, that's right, you prefer opium. I can provide that as well, of course."

"What do you want?" PenMartyn demanded. His voice was an angry, low rasp. Rather the way Cullum Rourke had sounded, Summers thought.

The man's eyes were bloodshot and puffy. *From weeping?* Summers wondered. *Or just lack of sleep?* Looking over PenMartyn's disheveled appearance, he commented snidely, "Your whore certainly knows how to wear a man out. Good. That will come in handy." He couldn't keep from adding, just to see PenMartyn's reaction. "I shall raise Minerva to be just as skilled as her mother. If I let her live, that is."

A moment later, Gordon Summers saw his death looking him in the face. From about an inch away. Summers was on his back, on the floor. One of PenMartyn's hands was at his throat, the other was poised, like a giant claw, just over his racing heart, ready to rip it out. How the man had gotten over the desk, Summers didn't know. All he knew for a moment was that he looked into ice-colored eyes and saw the deepest, coldest circle of hell.

Out of the corner of his eye, Summers noticed the barrel of one of his henchmen's revolvers resting against PenMartyn's temple. The sight gave Summers the courage to speak.

"If I die, you'll never find the brat. She'll be sold to a brothel," he went on, relishing every disgusting, debased image that must be conjured in the White Tiger's mind. "I've already arranged it." PenMartyn's eyes narrowed; the hand on Summers' throat tightened. "She's safe for now," Summers croaked.

"Let him go," one of his men said. "Release Lord Gordon or I'll blow your head off."

There was a promise of retribution in PenMartyn's cold eyes, but his grip relaxed. Summers knew it wasn't the threat of death that made PenMartyn relent for now. Summers also knew he would have to be careful to make sure PenMartyn got no chance to carry out his silent threat. PenMartyn stood and moved back. Summers let one of his men help him to his feet while another escorted PenMartyn to the other side of the desk. Summers resumed his seat. He folded his hands on the desktop, rather proud that he hadn't made the gesture because they were shaking.

"Now that we've had the mandatory demonstration of your prowess," he said, with amused disdain, "shall we continue?"

"What do you want from me?"

"Something very simple and easy to accomplish," Summers replied. He leaned forward a bit in his chair. "I want you to kill Queen Victoria. A simple, straightforward assassination," he went on, as he watched PenMartyn's already pale face drain of even more color. "My plans require Bertie on the throne. It's well past time the old bird gave up the ghost, and the Crown.

Our dear Albert Edward isn't getting any younger."

"Why?"

Summers relished the chance to explain his plan in full at last. There were those who knew bits and pieces of what he intended, but until this moment he had kept the full extent, the enormity, the brilliance of his ambitions to himself. It was good to have someone to share his most closely guarded secrets with. Especially since that someone would be dead very, very soon. Besides, PenMartyn needed to know what part his loved ones would play in the new order Summers was creating, as punishment for daring to lay hands on the man who was going to rule the world.

"It's really quite simple," Lord Gordon told PenMartyn. "A few years ago I discovered this knack for manipulating the masses."

"I noticed."

"I considered using it for the good of mankind. Then I thought, why not use it for the good of me instead? The good of myself and a few chosen friends, actually. I'm not a selfish man."

"No, of course not."

Summers ignored the other man's dry sarcasm. "I began using some of the philosophy I'd studied in the Orient to gather followers. To form a fanatically loyal core of influential people who obey my every whim. And for those who aren't fanatically loyal of their own free will, I've managed to gather an astounding amount of blackmail material. I'm very good at learning secrets. Yours, for example."

He gestured, and PenMartyn was forced to sit in the chair opposite Lord Gordon. Summers began toying with a silver letter opener from the desk. The handle of the opener was shaped like a tiger. "I know that you were employed as a privateer for the Khan of Kuzay. I know you've met with your old friend since he came to London. Proof of that meeting will be quite useful for me, by the way."

"Why?"

"I'm getting to that." He wagged a finger at PenMartyn. "Patience. It is not one of your virtues."

"I'm patiently waiting to kill you at the moment." PenMartyn flashed a slow, dangerous smile. "Haven't you noticed?"

Summers nodded. "I also find your training in Chinese fighting techniques quite useful. Those who have tried to kill the Queen in the past have always used guns. Three attempts in fifty years," he added derisively. "In two the guns misfired, and in the third, John Brown wrestled the gunman's weapon away. I'm not making the mistake of having my assassin use a gun. Just break the old woman's neck," he ordered. "You'll be close enough, and you're certainly quick enough."

"I see," PenMartyn said. "You expect me to kill her at the awards ceremony." He laughed. "I'm to murder the woman who is giving me a medal for my humanitarian services."

Summers joined in the earl's laughter. "Delightfully ironic, isn't it? You will, of course, be captured."

"I'll be murdered. I'm sure you've already arranged it."

"Actually, yes. I do have that detail taken care of."

"Wise of you. After I kill the queen, and am killed myself—what then? Why bother? What good will it do you to have Bertie on the throne? How do you plan to control him? How do you plan to control the government? And does the Prince of Wales know about your scheme? Is he complicit in his mother and sovereign's death?"

The questions were shot at Lord Gordon with almost overwhelming speed and tenacity. The Earl of PenMartyn, Peer of the Realm, expected to be answered when he spoke. Summers understood the other man's attitude, and shared it. They were very much alike. Men whose right it was to have everything they wanted. Men who recognized that there didn't have to be any limits on what they wanted.

Though PenMartyn seemed to have put limits on himself since his return from Asia. The poor man had been trying to fit in to the strictures of British society. Lord Gordon, on the other hand, had returned from the East with a determination to spread his wings and fly, to take that same society and remake it rather than try to be a part of it.

In that they were opposites, Summers supposed, dark and light. PenMartyn was lost in the darkness of convention, while he grew in the light of complete freedom. Summers enjoyed being able to explain himself to his dark, doomed, twin.

"It will be useful to have Bertie on the throne because the poor man burns with ambition to control world affairs. And I will let him think that every move he makes, every decision, is completely his own. I will be nothing more than his humble advisor and spiritual guide. I have no claim on the throne, it's the power behind it that interests me. Bertie wants your American whore as his mistress. Did you know that? I intend to give her to him. She'll do whatever is required to keep her daughter alive. Such a highly trained courtesan will be useful in helping me control her royal lover. She's only a small part of my scheme, but every little bit helps."

PenMartyn ignored the references to his lover and child. "But even as king, Bertie won't control the government."

"He will, eventually. The first step will be my manipulating the country's reaction to Her Majesty's horrible murder. The press will be quite useful in rousing the people's justifiable outrage. The Khan of Kuzay will be blamed through his association with you, among other proof. Of course it will be discovered that Kuzay is merely a pawn of China, and China of Russia. The world will soon be at war. I and my friends will become immensely rich and powerful from this war. The King will be granted more and more power as this war drags on. I will rule the King. Eventually, I'll rule the world. It's really a very simple, elegant plan," he finished. "Don't you think?"

"It's—" Whatever PenMartyn meant to say, he changed his mind. "I see," he said calmly.

"I knew you would."

"And all you need in order to set this conspiracy in motion is for me to kill Queen Victoria."

"Yes." Lord Gordon waved a hand toward the door. "And I think it's about time you got to it. You're surprised that I'm releasing you, aren't you, PenMartyn?"

His pawn nodded.

Summers chuckled. "You can't just disappear, man. You have engagements, appointments—one at the Foreign Office, I believe."

PenMartyn acquiesced, his expression wary.

Impressed at last, I see, Summers thought. *He begins to understand my power.* "I know what you do. Everything. You're my prisoner, Jack. I own London and you." He smiled. "Now, don't I?"

PenMartyn hesitated a moment, then agreed. Summers waved toward the door again. "You may now inform your bitch that she belongs to me as well. Good day!"

Chapter 29

"**H**ow could you?"
      "I didn't! I swear!"
"Your cousin. Your flesh and blood. A help-less child—and you turned her over to that monster." Why hadn't she told Jack her suspi-cions of Summers yesterday? Why hadn't she moved her family before Summers could take her baby?

Sherrie shook Faith again. The girl half-heartedly tried to fend Sherrie off, so Sherrie pushed her back against the parlor wall. They'd all gathered in the large downstairs room after Jack left to meet with Summers. Neither Faith's mother nor sister objected to this treatment. Daisy, in fact, stood in front of the door, just in case Faith tried to bolt.

Faith looked around wildly, but there was nothing for her to see but hostile, accusing faces. "No! I swear."

"No one broke into the house," Ira said.

"But it wasn't me who took Minnie. I wouldn't do anything to hurt my family."

341

Faith looked sincere, but Sherrie didn't believe her for a moment. She let the girl go for now, and turned to Ira. "Why don't we just go get her?"

"Because she's not at the house next door," Jack said as Daisy moved aside to let him in the room.

Sherrie ran to him, and as she did, Faith took the opportunity to dash past through the parlor and out the door. Sherrie would have run after her fleeing cousin, but Jack took her in his arms. She saw the look on his face, and forgot about everything else. Her heart tried to stop from the terror, but she didn't have time to let it.

"What?" she demanded.

Jack just held Sherrie for a few moments. The feel of her in his arms was the only anchor he had. One that he would have to let go soon enough. How could he speak? How could he tell her that because of his ugly, irresponsible past he was being forced to make the choice between a precious child's life and the ultimate act of treason? Only there was no choice. He knew what his decision must be.

"I'm sorry," he said at last. "I am so desperately sorry."

There was something dark in his voice that was even worse than the bleak expression on his face. Sherrie stepped back, shivering with a sudden premonition. They looked at each other in anguished silence until she couldn't take the growing screams of denial in her head. She had to know. "What are you going to do?"

Jack would have told her, but David Mac-

Quarrie's entrance to the room drew everyone's attention.

"I sent for him," Daisy explained as MacQuarrie came toward Jack and Sherrie. "I know he's a police inspector. I thought he could help."

Jack cast a quick look of thanks at the young woman. "You did well. David," he said to the puzzled MacQuarrie. "We most definitely can use your help."

MacQuarrie spoke to Sherrie. "Your daughter is missing, Mrs. Hamilton?"

"Our daughter has been abducted by Summers," Jack answered. He didn't hesitate to make the news official by informing the Scotland Yard man. If he hesitated he might yield to temptation. The devil with Summers' supposed spies. He *would* tell the truth and act on it.

He could tell by Sherrie's anxious glance at him that she suspected his motives. She'd guessed that something terrible was about to unfold. He would have reassured her if he could. He knew that it might seal his child's fate to bring the authorities into the matter, but it had to be done.

"Your child, Jack?" MacQuarrie questioned.

"It's a long story. One we don't have time for now."

"Aye. Well, I did notice a resemblance when you were playing with the lass yesterday."

The inspector was an observant one. Jack allowed himself a moment of memory of yesterday, knowing full well he might never see

Minerva again. Guilt gnawing at him, he prepared to go on.

But before he could speak, three other men crowded into the room. Jack's butler, his valet, and his teacher came in, their expressions anxious.

"We came as soon as we could, my lord," Hawton announced. Both the butler and Dabney were ex-military men. They both stood so straight they might as well have been at attention. Jack almost expected them to salute.

"What are you doing here?" he asked the trio.

"After we gave your townhouse a thorough searching without finding any trace of the missing child, we decided that perhaps we could help find the little girl by starting at Primrose House and fanning out around the neighborhood," Hawton responded.

"Form a proper search pattern, my lord," Dabney added. "Thought you could use all the help you could get."

"Thank you," Sherrie told the newcomers. She quickly wiped away a tear, one she told herself was from gratitude at the men's eagerness to help. "We appreciate your concern."

"Or we could simply take apart Summers' residence brick by brick until we find the girl," Jhou Xa said, looking at Jack levelly. "It would save the bother of any other search, would it not?"

"It would," Jack answered. "If Minerva was there. Summers says she's hidden outside the city."

Ira Gartner spoke up. "It wouldn't hurt to start with Summers' house, though. He could be lying."

"I doubt it," Jack answered. "He's had plenty of time to spirit Minnie away, he's not that stupid. Don't blame yourself," he added to the worried man. "You could not have anticipated Minnie was in danger because of me, or that someone inside the house would be capable of something as unthinkable as kidnapping."

"I'll blame myself as much as I want," Ira answered.

"As will I."

"Neither of you is at fault," May spoke up for the first time.

"Gordon Summers is." Sherrie agreed with her friend. "So is Faith for helping him." She looked from Ira to Jack. "I think we can all agree that Summers is a dead man, right?" When both men nodded, she added, "We will now do whatever we must to get Minnie back."

Jack noted that MacQuarrie looked uncomfortable with Sherrie's adamant words, and his and Ira's agreement that Summers was going to die. MacQuarrie might agree with the sentiment, and look the other way when Summers met his deserved fate. What shocked the Scotsman, Jack thought, was hearing the kidnapper's death sentence spoken so coolly and calmly by a lady.

But then, MacQuarrie didn't know Scheherazade. Neither did Summers, come to think of it. Jack smiled at that.

"What's so amusing?" Sherrie demanded, her voice shrill with nerves.

He put a calming hand on her shoulder. "I was just thinking how lucky I am in my friends. And in the woman I love," he added, gazing deeply into her eyes. He turned from her and explained, "Summers doesn't know as much as he thinks. In fact, the man's not only mad, he's a rank amateur when it comes to conspiracies. Rhu Limpok's warning about Summers was right, though," Jack told Jhou Xa. "Summers plans to implicate the Khan in the death of Queen Victoria."

"What?"

Jack didn't believe he had ever heard David MacQuarrie shout before. It was quite impressive. The inspector's face was bright red with fury when Jack turned his attention on him. "I was getting to that," he told his friend. "There is so much going on that it is hard to know where to start."

"Summers doesn't really know about me. He thinks I made my fortune out East as a pirate. He doesn't know about the rest."

"Pirate?" MacQuarrie asked.

"It's a long story," Jack answered. "I'll leave it until later." He took a deep breath and quickly went on to explain what Summers planned to the roomful of eager listeners.

When Jack was finished, MacQuarrie scratched his jaw and said, "The man's quite mad. I think I had best march next door and arrest him immediately."

"No!" Sherrie said.

The word came from her as no more than a faint, rasped whisper. Jack was the only one who heard her, but the word was shouted to his heart. She looked at him then, her eyes full of pleading and hope. And with utter faith and trust. She whispered his name.

Jack moved to block the Scotland Yard man's way. "Not yet."

Jack knew that if he had any sense he would let MacQuarrie do what the law demanded, go after the man who threatened the safety of the monarch. He had deliberately informed the Scotland Yard inspector of the madman's scheme, knowing that doing so put Minerva even more at risk. Summers had told Jack in vivid detail what would happen to the child were Jack to betray him to the authorities. Jack had returned to Primrose House with his mind made up to ignore Summers' threats to the child. He thought he could do it. Do his duty for Queen and country.

Then Sherrie spoke his name.

The hell with duty! To hell with Queen and country. He'd given enough of his life and soul for the sake of duty. He wasn't going to live in hell any longer. Not one he'd made for himself, or one that a madman and duty were busy preparing for him. Sherrie and Minnie held out the promise of a new life for him. Sherrie had forgiven him his sins. She wanted a future with him. Yesterday he had run from the image of a peaceful, contented life with Sherrie and Minerva. He'd been a frightened fool to run. He wasn't frightened now, he was angry.

"Summers will pay," Jack promised her. He stroked her cheek. "Never fear, my love. He will pay." He turned his attention back to MacQuarrie. "We aren't touching Summers yet. We can't. We do nothing to endanger the child. The man's life is sacred until we've got our daughter back."

"But we have to find out where he's keeping her first," Sherrie pointed out.

"I can help with that," Faith said from the doorway, and pushed Todd before her into the room. Both the girl and the maid were disheveled and breathing hard. Todd cowered, however, while Faith's eyes shone triumphantly. "Ask her." She pointed at the woman. "She's the one who took Minnie. She knows where she is."

Sherrie looked at her maid in horror, but saw by the look on Todd's face that what Faith had said was true. Sherrie saw hatred there, and fanatical loyalty. MacQuarrie started toward the maid, but Sherrie moved past him. "Get out of my way. This is women's work." She pushed the maid into an empty chair. Aunt Dora, Faith, and Daisy came to stand around the chair. "May," Sherrie said, and held out her hand.

Jack knew that Todd was going to tell them everything from the look of terror on the maid's face when May silently took a very long, very sharp pin out of her elaborately arranged hair.

Jack and Ira exchanged a glance as Todd hurriedly began to give directions to the house where Minnie was being held. Good Lord, their shared look said, what a pair of tigresses we love!

"If my papa doesn't kill you, my mama will. So will Ira."

"Incorrigible brat!"

Moss called her that whenever she spoke to him. Minnie knew he wanted to hit her, but she'd also overheard the butler being given instructions before taking her away from London. She'd pretended to still be asleep, but wasn't. She thought somebody had put a sleeping powder in her bedtime glass of warm cocoa.

She had *told* Ira it had tasted funny.

"You are not to allow any harm at all come to the child," Lord Gordon had said. He'd been very firm about that. That was one of the reasons Minnie wasn't scared—at least, not *too* scared. She wished Lhasi was here with her, though.

She looked at the tray Moss set down on the table in the little room where she was being kept. The room was tiny, with a window high up in the old stone wall. The room was in a tower, at the very top. The whole house was like a castle in a fairy story. She'd gotten a good look at it as they'd driven up the long drive off the main road. There were even gargoyles, and funny, twisting brick chimneys. She would have loved exploring the castle, if she wasn't locked in. Since she couldn't poke her nose through the castle, she poked her finger into the dry bread Moss had brought her instead.

"I'm not eating this."

"Suit yourself."

Moss smiled when he said it. He'd be happy to see her starve, not that she'd give him the satisfaction. There was a bowl of porridge besides the bread. She actually liked oatmeal. She'd eat that, but not until Moss left. Eating in front of her captors would be like showing some kind of weakness. Her mama wouldn't approve of that. And Papa would want her to be brave. After all, she was a pirate's daughter.

"Go away," Minnie told the man. He shrugged, made a face at her, and left.

Minnie waited until the key turned in the heavy door's lock before she did anything else. First she ate the porridge. Then she looked around her prison. She had to get out of here. She thought she knew how. The window was high and narrow, but she thought she could squeeze through it. She'd have to pile a chair on top of the table to reach it. There were sheets on the bed, and she found clothes in a tall old chest. She was a long way up, but she would only need to make a rope long enough to reach a window on one of the floors below. She should be able to sneak right out the front door.

She could do it. It wouldn't be *that* difficult. She just wished it wasn't raining so hard outside. It was going to be wet and the wall might be a little slippery, but Minnie knew she couldn't let that stop her.

Chapter 30

✦◞◝◞◟◜✦

There had been some loud discussion between the two of them about Sherrie's accompanying the rescue party. He had not been in favor of it. It might be dangerous. He did not want to encourage her penchant for adventure. She had countered that Minnie would be frightened, and that having her mother with her as soon as possible would do the child worlds of good. He hadn't liked it, but he had conceded the sense of her argument.

"Fine," she said with a decisive nod, before she went to fetch herself a gun. "I'll get back up on the pedestal for you after I've got my baby home."

"See that you do," he demanded.

Now here they were: himself, Sherrie, Ira, and MacQuarrie. Hawton and Dabney had been set to watch Summers' property and monitor the madman's movements. Jhou Xa had gone off to call upon the aid of Rhu Limpok. For now Jack had persuaded MacQuarrie not to call in any help from the police or the govern-

351

ment. Summers did have an unknown number of followers in high places, perhaps even at the highest levels. Word could filter back to him from agents he had planted in the bureaucracy.

Now here they were in the rain, hidden on the edge of woods that surrounded Colbey Castle. Jack wanted to make sure it was full dark before approaching it. They had left Jack's carriage back on the main road, slipped over a low wall and through a narrow band of trees to this spot on the Colbey estate.

The small castle was a great neo-gothic mess that sprouted gargoyles and towers, turrets and crenellations. Colbey's owner was out of the country. His wife and daughters were well-known devotees of Summers.

The castle loomed menacingly in the gloom, an ugly, tasteless blot upon the countryside. The only light showing from where they stood was a faint glow high up in a tower window about five stories above the ground.

"I don't like the looks of it," Sherrie said worriedly, as she paced in front of him. "The house is so dark and sinister."

"And very nearly empty, by the looks of it," Jack answered, trying not to be distracted by her nervous pacing. "That isn't sinister, it's useful."

Jack watched in wonder at her control. He'd been aware of the tension and fear growing in her as they got closer to their goal. He had feared an explosion, or hysterics that would hamper the rescue, seeing how tightly she controlled her emotions.

He put his hands on her shoulders. "You are a wonder and a marvel," he told her. "Now, let's get to work, shall we?"

"Right," Ira agreed. "Come on, MacQuarrie," the American said, "you and I can go around to the back, while Sherrie and his lordship take the front."

Jack and Sherrie waited a few moments, then cut straight across the wet lawn toward the front of Colbey Castle. They hurried, but were carefully alert to the possibility that Summers had some of his followers patrolling the grounds. They saw no one on the lawn, or the gravel drive when they crossed it, but there were two men standing guard at the front door.

"Wait here," Jack said, after he and Sherrie slipped behind a statue of a pair of battling knights. He meant it. Much to his surprise, she nodded and stayed put. It took him but a few moments and several quick, skilled blows to render the men before the door unconscious.

"Don't worry, they won't be going anywhere for a few hours. We'll be long gone by then." He started toward the door. "Come on."

She followed, but a shout for help from the side of the house halted them before they reached it.

"Minnie!" Sherrie's answered her daughter's call and ran in the direction the shout had come from. Jack ran after her toward the base of the tower that hulked over the side of the house.

"Minnie, where are you?" Sherrie called, after she followed her child's voice as far as a heavily carved door at the base of the tower.

"Here!"

The wall around the door was of rough stone that rose windowless to an overhanging ledge dominated by statues of fierce winged monsters.

Sherrie looked around frantically. "Where?" Jack tugged on her sleeve and pointed up. "Minerva May!" she called, once she caught sight of her dangling daughter in the illumination of a bolt of far-off lighting. "Come down off that gargoyle right now. Do you hear me?"

Jack turned on her angrily. "Wouldn't it be more appropriate to ask if she's all right?" he demanded in a fierce whisper. Thunder punctuated his annoyance.

"She wouldn't be yelling like that if she wasn't fine," Sherrie explained to the concerned father. Her heart was racing with terror, but she took a moment to explain patiently to Jack, "If I act angry, she won't be quite so scared. If I seem to be annoyed, she'll think that she can't be in too much danger. Understand?"

Jack nodded, then looked appalled. "You've done this before?"

She nodded. "Just before she fell out the window of the raja's palace. It wasn't the fall I was worried about that time, but I was scared she'd annoy the raja's pet tigers when she landed in their enclosure. And then—"

"Stop! I can't bear to hear any more." He looked up and called to Minnie. "Don't move."

"I can't. My foot's stuck."

"Well, just hold on, then. I'll be right up to get you."

"The tower door's locked," Sherrie said. "I already tried it. I don't think the spot where she landed can be reached from anywhere else in the house. See the rope dangling from the window?"

"I see it. She must have climbed down as far as she could and then gotten stuck." Jack spoke as he ran his hands across the big blocks of stone that formed the wall. "This will work. I can climb this." He took off his shoes and handed them to Sherrie. He pointed a finger sternly at her. "Don't move. And after this is over with," he added, "there will be no more adventures in this family. Do you hear me?"

She ignored his admonition and took his shoes. "*Hurry.*"

The wall was wet, it was still raining, and the wind was brisk, but Jack didn't have much trouble climbing the rough stonework. He did bless every day of disciplined training he'd put in in the last nine years as he made the climb, however.

Once he reached the narrow ledge, a bolt of lightning helped him see that Minnie's foot was indeed wedged into a space between the back of the statue and the wall. She was hugging the gargoyle much the way he'd seen her holding her big dog the day before. Minnie looked at him with wide, trusting eyes as he edged nearer her.

Taking a lesson from Sherrie, Jack fought down any urge to show his worry. "Child of mine," he said to Minnie. "We really must do something about this tendency of yours to use windows rather than doors."

"Hello, Papa."

He was warmed by the utter trust in her voice. He reached her and gave her a quick kiss on the forehead. "Stay still," he directed, as he went to work on loosening her foot. "We'll have you out of the rain in a few moments."

Once her foot was free, it took a bit of careful maneuvering, but eventually Minnie was riding his back, holding on as tight as any monkey-child. Jack said a few prayers, but kept calm and focused as they made the slow trip down.

Once they reached the ground, Sherrie snatched Minnie off his back and into her arms. He put his arms around Sherrie. They held their daughter between them, the embrace fierce and tight, the connection unbreakable. Jack had no compunction about standing out in the rain and letting it wash away his tears of relief and joy.

"She's safe," he whispered over and over. "You're safe. Everything is fine now. We're here. We're safe."

After a long while he let them go, Sherrie put Minnie down, though Minnie still clung to her mother's waist, and Sherrie solemnly handed back Jack's shoes.

"Let's go home now, please," Sherrie suggested.

The loving look she gave him struck deep into his heart. Everything truly was going to be all right.

He nodded. They headed back toward the front of the house. They were met at the front

door by Ira and MacQuarrie. Their fellow res-
cuers held a prisoner by the arms between
them.

"Look who we found," MacQuarrie said to
Jack.

"That's Moss," Minnie told her mother.
"He's not nice. You can kill him if you want,
Papa."

Jack wasn't surprised at finding his former
butler in the service of Gordon Summers, not
after learning that Sherrie's maid was also a
minion of the cult leader. He did wonder how
many followers Summers had secreted in other
households. The man had to be stopped before
he became as powerful as he claimed he was.

"I have to kill someone else first, sweetheart,"
he answered Minnie. "And your mama has to
get you home to bed," he added, making it
clear with a look that Sherrie was not coming
along on the next phase of the operation.

Sherrie smiled and nodded. She had her child
back. Jack was now free to bring Summers to
justice. "Have fun, dear," she told him, and
kissed his cheek. "I'll wait up."

"She's—different—your lady," MacQuarrie
said to Jack, as they approached Summers
house from the garden of Primrose House.

"Yes," Jack agreed. His lady. Quite impossible to tame. He smiled. Who would even want
to try?

They came to where Hawton waited, just on
the Hamilton edge of the adjacent properties.
Dabney was stationed across the street, and sev-

eral of MacQuarrie's men had been called in to inconspicuously surround the other sides of the house. Ira Gartner remained at Primrose House, on guard in case Summers attempted to make some other move against Sherrie's family.

"Lord Gordon is still at home, my lord," Hawton reported.

MacQuarrie rubbed his hands together in anticipation. "Good." He put his hand on the garden gate.

Before he could open it, Hawton cleared his throat. "Excuse me, sir, but I do not believe that would be wise."

MacQuarrie looked impatiently at the butler. Jack heeded Hawton's tone. "What's going on in there?"

"Lord Gordon is entertaining this evening, my lord. Several attractive young Asian women arrived after the last group of worshippers left. Those young women were soon followed by the arrival of a group of rather well-known gentlemen."

"Powerful, influential gentlemen," Jack guessed.

"Come to spend the evening dallying with the women, most likely," Dabney said. "We counted at least three barons, an earl, two dukes . . ."

"And the Prince of Wales," Hawton added.

"My God!" MacQuarrie gasped. He went rigid with shock, and sputtered, "Don't tell me the Prince of Wales is in there right now having a—having—!"

Jack pitied his friend, knowing that the man's

stern Presbyterian soul was seizing up. He put his hand on MacQuarrie's shoulder. "An orgy," he said, just to get on with it.

"What are we going to do? We can't arrest Summers with the prince in there."

Jack had to admire the way Summers had surrounded himself with a layer of people the authorities would not dare to disturb. Men he'd corrupted, but who thought of him as their friend. Men who would protect him politically.

"What do we do?" MacQuarrie asked.

Jack smiled. The answer was obvious.

"It would be better if Scotland Yard stayed out of the matter," Jack told his friend. "I'm going in there alone."

"You can't get in by yourself," MacQuarrie protested. "Summers has men posted inside the house and out."

"Yes," Jack answered. "He does. They'll make good practice."

He didn't wait for MacQuarrie to reply, but jumped over the fence and disappeared into the darkness beyond Sherrie's garden.

Summers smiled and nodded and paid little heed to what the prince said when he got Bertie settled in the library with all the proper amenities to hand. He looked attentive, and that was what was important. Bertie's arrival was not unwelcome, but it was unexpected. The important thing was to keep him out of the way and suitably diverted.

The Prince of Wales had not been included in the invitations to spend an evening learning the joys of the *Kama Sutra*. In fact, Bertie was completely oblivious to what was going on in the large, lavishly decorated room upstairs. He was curious, of course, having glimpsed some of the arrivals and overheard a snickering comment or two before Lord Gordon had politely ushered him into the library. Bertie probably expected that there was going to be some sort of lecture on Oriental sexual habits rather than hands-on demonstrations of the sensual arts.

Lord Gordon didn't think the prince was quite ready yet for decadent pleasures he'd been introducing other members of the peerage to. He wanted to lead the prince gradually into a great, inescapable quagmire of hedonistic pleasure and perversion. Lord Gordon didn't plan to use Asian prostitutes, old school camaraderie, and exotic titillation to corrupt his future king. It wouldn't be at all politic for the King of England to dally with an Oriental mistress. His people wouldn't put up with it.

No, Summers needed Sherrie Hamilton for what he planned for Bertie. Sherrie was tall, blond, beautiful in an acceptable, seemingly safe Western way. As an American, she might be considered a foreigner, but she wasn't a damned dirty yellow-skinned one. She'd do. And she'd do anything to keep her daughter safe. Fortunately for Summers, Bertie was playing unwittingly into his plans.

Bertie sat back in his chair by the library fire and said. "There's talk of Mrs. Hamilton marrying PenMartyn." He took a puff on a cigar, followed by a sip of brandy, and went on, "I quite approve, actually. That will keep the roving American lady in the country. I would very much like that."

"Give her a title. Make her acceptable at court," Summers supplied helpfully. He'd already thought this all through. She'd marry soon, of course, but she'd be Lady Summers, not Lady PenMartyn.

The words came out easily, though his mind was in two or three other places. He knew his house was being watched by PenMartyn servants, something he found more annoying than disturbing. The only truly disturbing thing was that none of the men he had set to watch and follow PenMartyn had reported back.

And of course, there was the small matter of the Prince of Wales putting in an unexpected appearance at an awkward time. There wasn't a thing Summers could do about anything until the prince chose to leave. For now he had to sit and listen to the fool yammer on like a love-struck schoolboy over a whore Summers knew he was going to have to beat and break into submission before the prince could get on with the affair he so eagerly anticipated.

"I'm sure Mrs. Hamilton will be most amenable to spending time in your company," Summers went on with a lascivious smirk.

The prince nodded. "Precisely." He took another puff. "Married women make more discreet lovers," he went on. "I like discretion in my women. Think you can help the courtship between PenMartyn and the lady along, Summers?"

"I'll see what I can do, Highness."

"I'd appreciate it."

Lord Gordon was relishing his secret knowledge that Jack PenMartyn would soon be dead when a knock on the door disturbed this pleasant reverie.

"My lord, there's a man who insists on seeing you," the servant who opened the door said in a rushed and hurried voice. "A convert, my lord. Very distraught. He says if he doesn't receive the wisdom of your counseling right now he's going to kill himself. In the meditation room!"

Summers sprang to his feet. He glared angrily at the cowering messenger. "Now? I don't have time for—"

He was about to order that the intruder be tossed out. Then he saw Bertie rise from his chair. The prince looked at him intently. Damn. Summers knew that this was no time for a show of temper. Bertie needed to believe implicitly in his wisdom, his love for mankind, or this scheme would never work.

Summers took a deep breath and calmed his temper. "I shouldn't have raised my voice to you, Simon," he said contritely to the servant. "I grow impatient at times, and tired." He went to the door. "Of course I will counsel this poor lost soul. Excuse me, Your Highness," he said. Bertie waved his hand in dismissal, sending a curl of smoke into the air.

Lord Gordon barely managed not to slam the door behind him as he left. The only pleasure he had at the moment was knowing that counseling the desperate soul that waited in the meeting room was doomed to failure. Of course the stranger's death would be reported as a suicide, and the body found many miles away.

Jack hadn't resorted to threats to get the servant to disturb Summers when bribery had been so much easier. Loyal minions, he had learned long ago, were a shilling a dozen for whoever had the coin to offer. Jack had had to dispose of four or five guards on his way in, but the footman he bribed was perfectly happy to cooperate, given the choice between a quick death and a tidy profit.

"You just have to know how to approach people," Jack murmured, as he waited in the shadows behind the room's largest Buddha. The house was equipped with electricity, but the room was lit with hundreds of votive candles. The air was full of some cloying, smoking incense. All very theatrical.

"Melodrama," Jack said quietly, as Summers entered the large room and closed the door behind him. "I'm sick to death of melodrama."

Summers' yellow hair glinted like a bright halo in the candlelight. He stood in the center of the room, glancing around impatiently. "Show yourself," he demanded, hands resting on his hips. Summers was tall, handsome, commanding. If not for the viciously furious expression on his face, he could have been mistaken for an archangel.

"You're a pathetic madman," Jack told him, as he moved forward.

"You!"

Summers whirled toward the door, but Jack already blocked the way. Summers rushed toward him. He opened his mouth to shout for help.

Jack barely registered the surprised indignation on Summers' face. He was too intent on keeping Summers quiet. One quick blow to the madman's chest, and a chopping strike across the throat, ensured that Jack could kill Summers in silence.

Summers fell to his knees, hands at his throat, gasping for breath. He wasn't badly hurt—yet. Jack moved forward to change Summers' condition. The Tiger was loose and looking forward to playing with its prey for a while.

Summers looked at Jack pleadingly, then scrambled back toward the podium in front of the Buddha.

"I already disposed of the gun hidden there," Jack told him.

Summers, gasping and panting, used the lectern to pull himself to his feet. When Jack saw the pleading terror in the other man's eyes, his own anger died. He sighed and faced what he had to do with calm determination. The Tiger didn't need to play anymore. Time to end it. It was time for justice.

He would simply break the man's neck and let it be explained as a tragic accident, death from a simple fall. *Fall from grace?* Jack wondered with grim amusement, as he reached for the Summers' head.

It would have been a quick death, but for the

man who came out of the shadows just as Jack had a few minutes before. Jack spotted the newcomer out of the corner of his eyes, but knew as he turned to defend himself from attack that he wouldn't have seen this man if the intruder hadn't wanted him to.

"Jhou Xa," Jack said, relaxing from his defensive stance. He bowed to his teacher. "What are you doing here?"

The Sholin monk acknowledged Jack with a nod, then moved to stand before Summers. Lord Gordon was on his feet, but swaying badly. Jack watched Jhou Xa take the cult leader by the shoulders. "So, you are the false teacher?" The monk shook his head. "You have seen your death in the Tiger's eyes tonight. Accept the lesson from the fear you feel."

Jack moved to stand beside Jhou Xa. He suspected the reason for the monk's presence. "Lesson? A lesson to take to his next life, I trust?"

Jhou Xa continued to concentrate on Summers. "Fortunately, Buddha teaches us to be compassionate." He patted Summers on the cheek. "You are not going to die. Not tonight."

Jack stared at his teacher. "What?"

"Rhu Limpok says it is wiser to let Summers live."

"What does Rhu—"

"The khan has much to lose if this man succeeds in any way," Jhou Xa interrupted sternly.

He helped Summers to a chair and stood behind it after the other man was seated. Summers doubled up in pain while the two men stood face to face with him between him.

"We do not know how his followers would react to the false prophet's death. We do not know how much influence he truly exerts. We do not know what other plans he may have in place in case you failed in the mission he set you."

Jack listened. "We can't let him go," he answered. "And we can't expose him. Too many important people will be embarrassed, politically ruined, if their involvement with him is known."

Jhou Xa nodded. "You are trying to protect your prince. I am trying to protect the khan. We work for the same thing."

Jack pointed at Summers. "He needs to die."

"But are you the one who must kill him?"

Jack was glad the monk didn't make any arguments about forgiveness, compassion, or not casting the first stone. He wouldn't have listened to them. He did see Jhou Xa's point about who acted as Summers' executioner. "Rhu Limpok wants that privilege, I take it?"

"Perhaps." Jhou Xa clasped Summers by the shoulder. It was a gentle, protective gesture. "If a few years studying the path to Enlightenment in a monastery on Kuzay prove insufficient to cleanse this man's dark heart, then we will kill him."

Jack laughed. "Of course. It's a wonderful plan. Truly devious. Rhu Limpok is a genius."

"Yes," Jhou Xa agreed. "Lord Gordon will write a letter in his own hand to his followers. He will explain his sudden, uncontrollable need to return to Kuzay to study, fast, and pray. He goes to seek true Enlightenment for the sake of all those who have come to him. He does it for them. They should wait for his return."

"And do nothing until he returns," Jack added. He nodded. "Elegant." Jack tilted Lord Gordon's chin up. He saw that Summers clearly comprehended that Jhou Xa's plan was his only chance for survival. "I think we had better get you a pen and some paper," Jack told him. "And we'll tell you exactly what to say."

"Ah, you're home," Sherrie said, as the door to Primrose House closed behind him. She came toward Jack with her hands held out toward him. He paused for a moment, to gaze on her calm, assured beauty. Her smile lit the world for him.

He took her hands in his. "I missed you."

"You were only gone an hour or two."

"You know what I mean."

Sherrie basked in the love she saw in his eyes. "Tell me everything," she said. "I'm dying to know what happened." She looked around as though fearing to be overheard. Coming close to him, she whispered, "Is Summers . . . ?"

"No," he whispered in her ear. "He's something even better than dead." She looked at him with boundless curiosity. He continued to whisper. Todd might not have been the only one of Summers' followers in Primrose House. "Later. You'll enjoy the story, but let's wait until we're alone."

"Inspector MacQuarrie is waiting for news in

the parlor. With Daisy," Sherrie added with a smile. "Your men are having supper downstairs."

"All's right and well with the world, then," Jack said. "And Minnie?"

"She's asleep," Sherrie told him, as she dropped his hands and came into his embrace. "You can look in on her if you like."

"I'd like that." He would most definitely stop by his sleeping child's room, on his way to taking Sherrie to hers. For the moment he was content right where he was. It felt so good to hold her. She was warm, solid, real, no longer just the fantasy woman of his fever dreams, but the very real woman he loved.

And she loved him. Imagine that.

Jack stroked Sherrie's hair as she rested her head against his shoulder. They walked into the parlor together. She fitted so perfectly against him, her warmth and solidity as reassuring as it was enticing. "Minnie is a brave child of a brave mother."

"A tired mother."

He gently rubbed the tense muscles at the back of her neck. "Poor baby." MacQuarrie looked his way, but subsided when Jack gave him a thumbs-up, and mouthed "Later" at his canny Scots friend. MacQuarrie went back to talking to Sherrie's cousin. Jack continued rubbing Sherrie's neck, feeling the muscles relax under his loving touch.

"Oh, that feels good."

She sighed with contentment. The sweet sound penetrated all the way through Jack's soul. "Don't worry," he promised her. "I won't ever stop."

His reply from her was a small, relaxed purr that somehow managed to convey all the hope and trust in that world. That, and a sensual promise which managed to be arousing and comforting to him at once. It left Jack thinking that maybe purrs and growls were all two tigers like them needed to communicate.

Sherrie was all too aware of the people around them. Of Aunt Dora, seated by the fireplace, with her attention anxiously focused on Daisy and MacQuarrie. Of Faith, seated on the settee, her nose studiously in a book in an attempt to be inconspicuous. Faith would get over her chagrin soon enough, Sherrie supposed, and would be her old shopping-addicted self in no time. Ira rose and took May in his arms. The couple looked happy to retire to their own room for the night and paused only long enough to say good night.

As for herself, Sherrie wanted nothing better than to emulate her happily married friends and be alone with Jack. Her Jack. To make some new memories. She needed to hold him, to wrap her body around his, to have the comfort of contact, flesh to flesh. Their time for dreaming and looking back was over. Besides, Minnie wasn't the only one who was exhausted after this long, anxious day. Sherrie wanted to make love to the man she loved, and then go to sleep safe in his arms.

She sighed and lifted her head, then turned so that they were side by side, arms around each other's waists. Glancing at Daisy and Inspector MacQuarrie, who were standing by the bay window, gazing deep into each other's eyes, she said, "It looks like Aunt Dora is going to have to settle for a divisional inspector rather than a duke for one of her little girls."

"If David MacQuarrie can be convinced that he's worthy of someone so high above him on the social ladder."

She chuckled. "I think Daisy's up to the task."

He gave her waist an affectionate squeeze. "I think the women in your family are up to any task."

"That's the women in *your* family now. Daisy will be your cousin-in-law very soon."

"Oh, really?"

Sherrie nodded. She noted there wasn't the slightest hint of fear or reluctance in the man's voice, just good-humored teasing. "Yes," she told him firmly. "You're going to be making an honest woman of me quite soon. Then I'm whisking you away on a long honeymoon. How do you feel about the south of Italy?"

"Sounds wonderful. I suppose I had better marry you, if only for the travel opportunities. Shall we make the wedding the social event of the Season?"

"Why not? Lady Anne wouldn't have it any other way."

"You're quite correct about that. As you are about most things," he added, turning her to face him because he had plans to kiss her quite senseless in the next few seconds. "Do you think we should invite the Queen?"

"Oh, yes—and the Prince of Wales," she replied, and pulled his mouth down to meet hers.

Dear Reader,

It's so difficult to finish a book you love—you've had the chance to live in their world, and to fall in love with the hero…just as the heroine does! If you were swept away by the Avon romance you've just read, I invite you to be just as enraptured by some of these other upcoming love stories—only from Avon.

Readers of historical romance won't want to miss Linda Needham's *The Wedding Night*, a powerful and sensuous love story from an author who's a rising star of romance. Jackson Villard, a rich, ruthless lord has sealed off his heart from life—and love…until he meets vibrantly beautiful Mairey Faelyn. But he doesn't know that Mairey is out to betray him…

Scotland conjures up images of misty highlands, men of honor…and the women who love them. Lois Greiman's latest in her *Highland Brides* series, *Highland Enchantment*, is an unforgettable love story between a daughter of a laird and a man of honor. Don't miss this page-turner from an award-winning writer.

What if you're an attractive widow, respectable, above reproach, attending a London ball with the height of English society. Then, across the room, your eyes lock with those of a tall, mysterious stranger…only he's not a stranger to you—and he's capable of exposing your wildest secrets. This is just the beginning of Susan Sizemore's lushly sensuous *The Price of Innocence*.

And for readers of contemporary romance…everyone once fell in love with Peter Pan, the boy who wouldn't grow up. Now, talented newcomer Mary Alice Kreusi creates a wonderful spin on this story in *Second Star to the Right*. It's a richly delightful story, all about the power of love and the belief that dreams really can come true.

Be swept away—all over again! Enjoy,

Lucia Macro
Lucia Macro
Senior Editor

AEL 0499a

Avon Romances—
the best in exceptional authors and unforgettable novels!

THE MACKENZIES: PETER   by Ana Leigh
79338-5/ $5.99 US/ $7.99 Can

KISSING A STRANGER   by Margaret Evans Porter
79559-0/ $5.99 US/ $7.99 Can

THE DARKEST KNIGHT   by Gayle Callen
80493-X/ $5.99 US/ $7.99 Can

ONCE A MISTRESS   by Debra Mullins
80444-1/ $5.99 US/ $7.99 Can

THE FORBIDDEN LORD   by Sabrina Jeffries
79748-8/ $5.99 US/ $7.99 Can

UNTAMED HEART   by Maureen McKade
80284-8/ $5.99 US/ $7.99 Can

MY LORD STRANGER   by Eve Byron
80364-X/ $5.99 US/ $7.99 Can

A SCOUNDREL'S KISS   by Margaret Moore
80266-X/ $5.99 US/ $7.99 Can

THE RENEGADES: COLE   by Genell Dellin
80352-6/ $5.99 US/ $7.99 Can

TAMING RAFE   by Suzanne Enoch
79886-7/ $5.99 US/ $7.99 Can

America Loves Lindsey!
The Timeless Romances of #1 Bestselling Author

Johanna Lindsey

KEEPER OF THE HEART	77493-3/$6.99 US/$8.99 Can
THE MAGIC OF YOU	75629-3/$6.99 US/$8.99 Can
ANGEL	75628-5/$6.99 US/$8.99 Can
PRISONER OF MY DESIRE	75627-7/$6.99 US/$8.99 Can
ONCE A PRINCESS	75625-0/$6.99 US/$8.99 Can
WARRIOR'S WOMAN	75301-4/$6.99 US/$8.99 Can
MAN OF MY DREAMS	75626-9/$6.99 US/$8.99 Can
SURRENDER MY LOVE	76256-0/$6.50 US/$7.50 Can
YOU BELONG TO ME	76258-7/$6.99 US/$8.99 Can
UNTIL FOREVER	76259-5/$6.50 US/$8.50 Can
LOVE ME FOREVER	72570-3/$6.99 US/$8.99 Can
SAY YOU LOVE ME	72571-1/$6.99 US/$8.99 Can
ALL I NEED IS YOU	76260-9/$6.99 US/$8.99 Can

And Now in Hardcover
THE PRESENT: A MALORY HOLIDAY NOVEL
97725-7/$16.00 US/21.00 CAN